Garment bag in hand, I headed for the bedroom at the end of the hallway. That's when they got me.

Two of them, nailing me as I walked through the bedroom door. They must have worked it out when they heard me arrive, for one grabbed me from behind and twisted me toward the second man. He drove a fist into my gut. It doubled me over. I heard my own cry of surprise and pain. Inside my head, it sounded like a car backfiring. I braced for a punch in the face, but the second blow was an uppercut to my shoulder, the one wounded at Lovers Crossing.

I tried to raise my head. No good. Goon One had bent over to punch my upper body down. Goon Two drove his knee up into my wounded hip. It turned my legs to spaghetti. He kicked them out from under me and I hit the floor face-first.

Get a look at them, I thought.

But it was too late for that. I could see the shadow of Goon Two lunging down toward me. A sharp pain tore the back of my head, and a bright, billowing flash—like an old movie of an atom bomb test—blew out my vision.

"Readers will value this taut tale of illegal border dealings...that showcases a new talent."

—Harriet Klausner

LOVERS CROSSING

JAMES C. MITCHELL

TORONTO • NEW YORK • LONDON
AMSTERDAM • PARIS • SYDNEY • HAMBURG
STOCKHOLM • ATHENS • TOKYO • MILAN
MADRID • WARSAW • BUDAPEST • AUCKLAND

For Marianne

LOVERS CROSSING

A Worldwide Mystery/June 2006

First published by St. Martin's Press LLC.

ISBN 0-373-26566-2

Printed in U.S.A.

Acknowledgments

Thanks to Pete Hautman, Mary Logue, Robert Irvine, and Angela Irvine for sharing their gifts with me. Esmond Harmsworth, my agent, offered invaluable insight and encouragement. Marianne Mitchell provided the Spanish and the faith.

ONE

"SILENT NIGHT," crackling from a loudspeaker across the border, drifted north through the cold, brittle air. Al Avila and I stood on the edge of Nogales Wash, looking along the tunnel toward Mexico. It was our second Christmas Eve on the Border Patrol. *Noche de paz.*

"Flak jackets would be good," I said.

Crime was so bad in the tunnels that the Santa Cruz County sheriff sometimes sent his SWAT team down there. Guys in body armor, packing high-powered rifles and nightscopes, chasing eleven-year-olds through a sewer.

Al and I, low-seniority agents, drew the holiday duty. It made a double shift. Most of the agents worked one tour for free on that Christmas Eve, volunteering to canvass neighborhoods and businesses, collecting clothing and toys for poor children on both sides of the border.

Just an hour before the long tour ended, we were checking out a report that young gangs had robbed other kids on the Arizona side, then run toward Mexico through the sewer tunnel.

Al said, "Let's get this over with, Brink." We scrambled down the side of the wash and walked south to the tunnel entrance.

Untreated Mexican waste flowed into the United States through the tunnel. Gangs congregated and homeless kids slept there. They sniffed spray paint, giggled with their friends, and fell upon anyone unwise or unfortunate enough to come by. Usually, that was some other homeless child who sought shelter underground.

The stench hit us fifty yards north of the tunnel opening. Human waste and decayed food, dead animals, and God knows what kind of chemicals seeping in from Mexico. Sometimes we carried little jars of pungent Vicks ointment, like coroners and homicide cops use at death scenes, to rub under our noses. We didn't have any that night, so we caught the full sensory assault.

"You hear that?" Al said.

We stopped to listen. The sound was familiar to anyone who works the border. Scrambling, scuffling, body blows, cries of pain. The underground echo chamber effect amplified the noise. It wasn't far away and was likely on our side of the border. We ran into the tunnel.

About twenty yards down, a cluster of small figures gathered around someone. Hands rising and falling fast, howls coming from the victim. The muggers heard Al and me sloshing through the muck. They stopped the attack and ran toward Mexico.

The object of their attention was a boy, maybe twelve years old. When he saw us running toward him, he pulled himself up and ran, too, following his tormentors into the gloom.

"Glad to help!" Al yelled after him.

I heard a cough from the other side of the tunnel. A tiny figure sat just above the shallow, fetid stream, propped against the graffiti-covered concrete wall. Her black hair was long and dirty. She wore jeans, ripped at the knee, and a filthy T-shirt with a Hard Rock Cafe logo barely showing through. No shoes, just socks of unknown color. There was dried blood on her upper lip, below her nose. Big, dark eyes watched us warily.

Al knelt, not getting too close. He said in Spanish, "Don't be afraid of us. We won't hurt you."

This must have sounded absurd to a Mexican child: don't be afraid of two big strangers wearing the green uniform of *la migra*. She drew herself closer to the wall.

"Cómo te llamas?" I asked.

"Alicia," she said. Her voice was little louder than a whisper, with no inflection.

"Where do you live, Alicia?"

"Aquí." Here.

"Jesus," Al said.

"Where are your parents?" I asked her.

She looked down and said, *"No sé."* I don't know.

"Do they live in Nogales?" Al asked.

Again, without looking up, *"No sé."*

"What happened to your shoes?" I asked. "Your coat?"

She pointed down the tunnel toward Mexico. *"Ladrones,"* she said. Thieves.

"Can you stand?" I asked.

She said nothing, but stood slowly. She kept her back against the wall, arms at her sides, as if awaiting execution.

There is a word in Spanish that described her: *desesperada*. To the English speaker's ear, it sounds like "desperate." But the native tongue carries a meaning far more powerful, a poignancy that tears the heart. A *niña desesperada* is a girl beyond mere desperation; she is utterly without hope, without a chance, without anything.

"How old are you, Alicia?" Al asked.

"Seis," she said. Six years old.

"We'll help you," I said. "We'll get you home."

She did not resist when I picked her up. She was almost

weightless and smelled terrible. I felt a skinny, shivering frame through her thin shirt. She put an arm around my neck and tentatively rested her cheek on the wool collar of my uniform jacket.

"What do we do?" I asked Al.

"Which side are we on here?" he said.

"Ours, I'm pretty sure," I said. "The line is halfway through the tunnel. We're probably fifty, sixty feet inside the States."

"Only one thing to do, then," he said. "She's on the U.S. side. Procedure says we take her to the station, call Mexico child services, hand her over to them at the Port of Entry."

"Yeah," I said. "That sounds right."

"Right," he said.

"Christmas Eve, this late, we'll probably get the *policía* instead of child services."

"Probably," Al said. He took off his jacket and draped it over the girl's back. I tucked the lapels between her belly and my chest. She clung a little tighter to hold the jacket fast.

"Let's get out of this toilet," I said.

The child's shivering eased a bit as we walked north, toward the wash and the fresh air on the American side. We scrambled up the bank of the wash to our Bronco. When the engine warmed up and the heater kicked in, I poured some drinking water from a plastic bottle onto my handkerchief and washed the girl's face and hands. We used Al's handkerchief to dry her. She took it without complaint, her expression unchanging. Her eyes seemed too big for her gaunt face.

"Kid could use a couple of Big Macs," I said.

The little girl smiled.

"They're closed," Al said. "Nobody stays open this late on Christmas Eve."

"I think I got her hopes up, though," I said. "This kid *habla* Big Mac."

She smiled again.

"Alicia," Al said. *"Quieres una hamburguesa?"*

"Sí," she said in her tiny voice. And after a pause, *"Por favor."*

"Now you've done it," I said.

"Yeah," he said. "Where do we find a hamburger on the night before Christmas?"

I put the Bronco in gear but kept my foot on the brake. Al felt me watching the two of them.

"What's on your mind?" he said.

I have never thought much about destiny or karma or the inexplicable luck that lets a petty crook win the lottery while a hardworking farmer goes broke. Al and I once went to a Kurosawa festival at the Loft Theatre. One of the films began with a samurai, out of work in his increasingly irrelevant trade, wandering the countryside. At a fork in the road, he picked up a long stick and tossed it in the air. When it landed, he grunted and walked in the direction it pointed. Down the other road, I suppose, was a very different movie.

Once or twice in a lifetime, we come to a crossroads that could change everything for us and for people we love. We may not recognize the moment; we may be forced to choose too quickly. If we are lucky, some personal compass—implanted years ago and calibrated over time—will point out the right path.

"You know," I said, "there's a pay phone at the Texaco over on Morley. It was working this afternoon."

Al broke his gaze from the child and looked at me. I could see the wheels turning. If we have to make a call, why not make it for free back at the Border Patrol station?

"Anna waiting up for you?" I asked.

He kept his eyes on mine and said, "Sure. We're Santa's helpers when Anita falls asleep."

"I heard them talking a couple of weeks ago," I said. "Anna was saying something about a little brother or sister for Anita, maybe."

Al looked down for an instant.

"We must have read the instructions wrong," he said. "Not having much luck with that."

"Well, then," I said.

He thought for a while. I knew him as well as anyone alive knew him, except Anna, and even I couldn't always tell what he was thinking. I sometimes wonder if it's a deeply recessed Indian gene that drops a mask of serene mystery over his face, revealing nothing.

Al used a dry corner of his handkerchief to wipe the girl's runny nose.

"We'd have to stop at the office," he said at last. "Sign out. Can't leave her in the vehicle alone."

"You stay with her," I said. "I'll sign out for you, too. The brass won't be too particular tonight."

Al nodded. He took the girl in his lap. A clump of Alicia's matted hair had fallen over her eyes. Al brushed the hair away, then flicked some dirt from his fingers.

I eased the Bronco off the wash bank and drove to the gas station on Morley. The phone booth in the parking lot was empty.

"Good time for you to bail out, Brink." Al was looking out the window on his side. "No need to make it a conspiracy, too."

"Hell, we've been coconspirators since we were six years old," I said. "Wouldn't feel right to quit now."

Al thought for another moment, then went to call. It was an

actual booth, the old kind with a light that went on when he closed the door. He and Anna did not talk for long. He came back to the Bronco, walking fast, with a small smile on his face.

"The phone works," he said. *"Milagro."*

"No argument, then?" I said.

"None," he said. "Anna's a little worried about later. Immigration papers, custody, all that. But she said yes."

We headed back to the Port of Entry. The town lay deserted, dark except for the twinkle of Christmas lights in windows by the roadside. The Border Patrol radio frequency was dead quiet.

"I heard about a guy," I said. "A lawyer in Tucson. He does criminal defense, but the cops there like him because he handles personal stuff for them free. Wills and things. He makes friends and gets a lot of inside information that way. He's supposed to be pretty sharp."

"We'll see," Al said. "For sure, we have to check on missing kid reports from both sides. If she does have parents anywhere, we have to take her home."

I shook my head. "We'll check, but she doesn't," I said. "This is an abandoned child."

The Border Patrol station loomed on the right. Little Alicia looked up and saw the ugly steel fence, the customs kiosks, and Mexican cops looking across the line at our solitary headlights. She held tighter to Al, as if trying to keep his arm away from the door handle.

"Allejandro," I said. "That was the guy's name. The lawyer."

"Okay, good," Al said.

I went inside, signed us out, and made a note on the vehicle board that we had the Bronco, going to Tucson. I checked for missing child reports from Arizona and Sonora. Nothing matched our little girl. When I went out to the Bronco and slid behind the wheel, Al was speaking in Spanish to the girl.

"If you want to," he said, "we'll go to my family's house. My wife Anna is there. We have a little girl named Anita. She's asleep now. You can meet her tomorrow morning. Tonight we'll have some food and Anna will give you a bath, and then you can sleep in a warm bed. And I'll bet you can share Anita's Christmas presents tomorrow. Is that okay?"

Alicia said, *"Sí, señor."* Her tiny voice was tentative, accustomed to betrayal. But she put her head back on Al's shoulder. Her face had begun to soften with fatigue and the first signs of letting go.

"You can choose, though," Al said. "If you want, we can take you safely back to Mexico. People will help you there."

The child said nothing, but pursed her lips and shook her head, no.

"I don't think you sold that last choice quite as sincerely as the first one," I said.

"She was living in a sewer," he said. "Let's go."

I made a U-turn and eased through the lonely city streets. "O Holy Night" played on the radio.

"Feliz Navidad," I said.

And Al said, "*Feliz Navidad* to you, *hermano*."

The little girl labored to keep her big eyes open as we hit the freeway and drove parallel to the border fence. When the road curved north and over the first rolling hills, Alicia watched the fence fall away from view behind us. Then her eyelids fluttered and her breathing relaxed. Her blank expression gave way to something almost like a smile. She was asleep before we left the city limits. She still slept an hour later, when Al delivered her into Anna's arms.

TWO

IF AL HAD STAYED on the Patrol, maybe things would have gone better at Lovers Crossing. But he left just a few weeks after we brought Alicia up from the tunnel, finally giving in to pleas from the Tucson Police recruiter and from Anna. So I took the call with two other agents, one I barely knew and one I didn't trust.

We reached the mesa just after midnight, four-wheeling over rocks and ruts, kicking up sand. Several miles south of the county's nameless dirt road, I cut the engine. The three of us climbed out and shut the doors softly. We stood there, listening, hands close to holsters. Cirrus clouds filtered the pale glow of a crescent moon.

Just enough light to give someone a shot at us, I thought.

Marques said, "Not much cover up here." He was focused on the mesa, looking left to right and back again, like a pilot scanning his flight instruments. Sanchez had already moved a few yards to the west, keeping his eyes on the Mexican side of Lovers Crossing.

"If anyone's out here," Marques whispered to me, "they're in the canyon. And they're not moving. I can't hear a thing."

Sounds carry on cold, still nights in the desert: animal howls and human cries, pops of distant gunfire, people stumbling through the dense brush of the canyon that marks the border.

"Or they could be way back on the Mexican side," I said. "Not up to the high flats yet."

You won't find Lovers Crossing on the map. It's east of Nogales. The long, solid steel fence along the border near town has not been extended that far. Even the wars on drugs and illegal immigration have financial limits. Only chain link and barbed wire divide the countries at Lovers Crossing. The flimsy fence is not much more than a make-believe barrier. It served its purpose in the old days, before aggressive enforcement around Nogales pushed the illicit traffic deeper into the desert. By the time I joined the Patrol, it was no match for desperation and cheap bolt cutters.

I eased over to Sanchez. "Your guy was sure about tonight?" I asked.

Sanchez shrugged. "He's been wrong, but he's been right plenty of times. Those twenty kilos the Naco station caught last month? That was on his tip."

"I hope he's right tonight," I said. "Let's spread out from the vehicle, try to get some cover." Sanchez moved farther west. Marques was already hunkering down fifty yards to the east.

Along the U.S.-Mexico frontier, place names tell stories. Smugglers Gulch, where couriers haul drugs to the voracious North American market. Deadman Canyon, where vicious false guides known as coyotes rob their illegal immigrant customers and often leave them dead, a few yards into the promised land.

Lovers Crossing, too, was nicknamed for something that happened there. One night in the 1970s, before the frantic buildup at the border, agents caught eight Mexican nationals who had entered illegally. The five men and three women were walking toward the outskirts of Nogales, Arizona.

"Where did you cross?" the agents asked.

Apprehended aliens usually cooperated with their captors, just as my recruit manual promised. Some illegals were sullen and crestfallen, but others accepted their failed crossing with equanimity. Their attempt was like a baseball game with endless innings: picked off tonight, try again tomorrow. Maybe they thought the American authorities would take pity and let them in if they acted helpful. Many feared that the men of *la migra* would beat them if they didn't help. That was seldom true. I can't say that it never happened, but not often.

"Cañon Pequeño," the aliens answered.

The Mexican entrance to Little Canyon was about an hour's walk from the edge of Nogales, Sonora. The successful crossing there puzzled the officers, because they knew that at least one Border Patrol agent was assigned to that very spot. He should have seen anyone crawling up the American side of the shallow, narrow canyon. The last stretch was on a steep slope. Climbing it was almost like hauling yourself over a fence, so illegal entrants were more likely to struggle and stumble into the States than they were to burst in and run for cover.

"You were lucky," the agents said. "We have a man out there tonight."

All eight aliens laughed. The women blushed.

"What?" the agents asked. "What's funny about that?"

The man who appeared to be the aliens' leader spoke English. He said, "Your man had a girl out there. We could see the two of them sitting in the truck. We just waited until they dropped down out of sight, you know? Then we knew we had time."

In Spanish, one of the women said, "Maybe not long. Who can tell?"

The women giggled. The young men laughed, hoping to sound knowledgeable about such things.

"Anyway," the leader said, "it was long enough to get past them and out of the canyon on this side."

The agents drove their captives to town, laughing all the way. At the border station, the aliens climbed out of the van and crossed quietly from one Nogales into the other. The agents never reported their amorous colleague, but the story became part of Border Patrol lore. When I joined years later, hearing the tale was part of my welcome to the Southern Arizona sector. Little Canyon was known among agents, from that night on, as Lovers Crossing. After a reporter heard agents laughing about it, the name began turning up on television and in the papers. Self-styled family-friendly media never explained it.

These days, as the fence grows longer, the Patrol adds thousands of agents every year, and helicopters carry infrared cameras overhead, Lovers Crossing is not so popular. Much of the action has moved east, to Douglas and Naco, or west, to the merciless desert near Yuma. But in my time, illegals still favored it on moonless nights when *la migra* was occupied elsewhere. Or otherwise.

I have two terrible reasons to remember it. The first happened that night.

The agents with me were as different as men in the same service could be. Sanchez, the old hand with a bad attitude and a worse reputation, and Marques, a new guy recently assigned here from the academy. When the moonlight dimmed as denser clouds drifted by, I couldn't see either man. They were down, just as I was, taking cover behind bushes.

"We need night glasses," I said.

"I forgot to bring 'em," Sanchez said.

We had spotted three silhouettes of figures coming across the mesa in Mexico. They ran into the little canyon, out of sight. Sanchez, Marques, and I spread out farther, with me in the middle, to cover the path up to the U.S. side.

I heard shots and hit the ground.

Then it fell dead quiet. No one calling out, no one trampling through the desert brush. No more shots.

What would the other agents do? Henry Sanchez, somewhere on my right, would wait them out. He knew the drill, as I did, although he had already screwed up by forgetting the night glasses. If the people in Lovers Crossing were *pollos,* Mexicans or Central Americans coming up illegally for work, they would have scurried back into Mexico or blundered out on the U.S. side and surrendered. Shooters were a very different problem. They almost certainly would be drug smugglers. They might have night glasses, plenty of ammunition, and no inhibition. Sanchez would wait them out. He would let them commit first.

There was just one thing about Sanchez. Nobody trusted him. His car was a little too expensive and his house was a little too big for a Border Patrol agent's salary. He didn't care. His sneer made fellow agents, with their honesty and idealism, feel like chumps. He stared at them with the hard, watchful eyes of a desert predator. Sanchez had been shrewd enough to dodge complaints from citizens and even fellow agents, but few of us wanted to show him our backs on a dark night. This night, I had little choice.

Off to my left, Marques, from Puerto Rico. Marky Marques, the other agents called him. He didn't like it, but he played along to get along. He finished the academy in Georgia just the year before, I realized. He came to Nogales only a few weeks ago. Marky was a smart kid with fresh training, but no real experience yet. Until tonight. I couldn't be sure of what he would do.

We had bulletproof vests back in the Explorer, a hundred dark yards away. Stupid to venture onto this exposed ground without them. I wished that Al Avila had not quit the Patrol. Good cautious Al would never have let us out of the station without the right gear. I turned to crawl toward the Explorer, checking back over my shoulder to see if anyone came out of the canyon. I looked hard for Marques, because this was the kind of jam where kids got impatient and got hurt. There was no sign of movement on his side. Maybe the young man would stay cool, waiting for the other guys to show themselves.

I was halfway to the Explorer when a vehicle came over a little rise on the Mexican side. Its headlights swung around, their beams falling close to the spot where I thought Marques had flattened out on the sand. In the peripheral light at the edge of the beams, I saw Marques wiggle farther behind a clump of brush. Just then, across the canyon, a shadowy figure raised a rifle to his shoulder and leaned close to the left headlight.

It seemed too long for a good shot, but I had no choice now. I raised myself to my knees and shouted, "Marques! Gun!" Marky was already scrambling out of the light toward a boulder on darker ground. I heard a blast and saw the sand explode around him, but it looked as though Marques had made it behind the rock. The shot was too close to have come from the Mexican side. Someone with a gun must have climbed up from the canyon. Or perhaps someone was there already.

I tried to whirl around to look for Sanchez, but I heard another gunshot just as a bullet crashed into the back of my shoulder. In the great open expanse of desert, I couldn't tell where the shot came from. Even before I fell, another bullet caught me high on the leg. As I hit the ground, I saw the Mexican vehicle's headlights go out. The motor revved, then faded into the dark distance.

I looked up as Sanchez ran toward me. Half-formed thoughts ricocheted around in my mind, battling the pain for attention. Something seemed wrong about Sanchez as he approached, gun drawn. Then I heard Marques running to my side, shouting about a hospital. Sanchez slowed down.

They lifted me into the Explorer. The movement was excruciating. I remember screaming. I might have passed out; I didn't know. Marques stayed in back with me, yelling at Sanchez to drive faster.

In the Nogales emergency room, a doctor said, "Nasty, but I've seen worse," then stuck something into my arm. In my pain haze, he looked like Alan Alda.

"This is high-test painkiller, buddy," the doc said, "so don't worry if you feel like you're losing it. It's just nap time. You're going to live."

"Where's Hot Lips?" I asked, or so they told me later.

"She's not covered by your HMO," the doctor said. The pain eased quickly and the room floated away.

I stayed in the hospital for six days. Dolores Gonzales came before dawn, ignored the doctors' orders to stay briefly, and left only when I slept. Al and Anna and the Patrol agent in charge, a Detroit transplant named Golski, visited every day. So did Marques. Other agents dropped in. The chief Patrol agent, who ran our sector, rushed in the first afternoon. His boss, the INS regional commissioner, phoned. The Attorney General of the United States sent a handwritten note on thick bond paper with the Justice Department insignia embossed in gold.

Sanchez never showed up.

I never went back on patrol.

But I wasn't free of Lovers Crossing yet.

THREE

WHEN I LEFT the Border Patrol and started my investigations business, I expected to ask the questions. Mo Crain, as I would learn, enjoyed defying expectations. He wasn't my first client like that, but he was the most experienced at getting his way.

"Do you love your wife?" he asked.

He was talking to me, but looking at his own wife. There she was, eternally vibrant in the framed color photograph on his desk. The image had been famous briefly in the Tucson newspapers and on television. A woman with a *café con leche* complexion and short black hair, her face caught in sharp focus at the instant of a mischievous smile. The background was a blur of desert and sky, giving the sense that when Sandra Crain was in the picture, nothing else mattered to Mo.

He touched the picture softly with his fingertips. He still wore his wedding ring.

"I mean, profoundly love her," he said. "Think about her all day. Miss her, actually hurt from missing her? Do you love your wife like that, Mr. Brinker?"

Even if I were married, what could I say? But I was intrigued, not offended, as the great salesman set me up. Talking to Mo was like watching those expensive new commercials on Super Bowl Sunday. The customer enjoys being sold.

"You'd have to love her like that," Crain said, without waiting for an answer. "You'd have to, in order to understand how I felt when I lost Sandra. How I feel now, not knowing what happened."

We sat quietly in the edgy intimacy of exposed pain, watching each other across his mahogany desk. Crain broke the gaze, turning in his leather executive chair to stare out the picture window. I took the moment to glance around the office. The décor was autobiographical, like the workplaces of many successful business figures. Photographs of Mo Crain with presidents and senators. Mo at assembly lines in Detroit and Tokyo. Mo at the Masters golf tournament and the World Series. He had covered one wall with pictures of cars, from Model T's to modern racers.

"I want to know who killed her," Crain said, turning back to face me, "but right now I'd settle for why. It's all so inexplicable. You think, well, a crook sees a woman with a nice car, so he robs her. But it wasn't robbery. They didn't take her money. They didn't take an expensive car that was only a week old. It wasn't a sex crime. Thank God for that much. So why? It's this not knowing anything that's torturing me."

Even the wide tinted window behind him revealed a diorama of his wealth and clout in Tucson. The sprawling Crain Carplex was jammed with hundreds of vehicles. The Catalina Foothills rose from the desert beyond. Mo Crain sold all the cars and owned much of the foothills.

"Will you help me?" he asked.

There were calculations to be made. Taking Crain's case would mean serious money. I could probably name my fee. The long-term benefits would be even more valuable. In the tightly packed power cluster of Tucson, Mo Crain's endorsement was a career maker. But I asked myself: Is this the kind of work I want? Didn't I leave violence and death back at the border?

"Mr. Crain," I said, "this is murder. The cops are best for this. They have the resources, the experience. You should stick with them."

"Resources are no problem, Mr. Brinker," Crain said. "There's no point in my acting coy. I need help and I can afford it."

I waited, thinking of Dolores Gonzales. Wait and learn, she would say. Dolores was locally famous for enticing subjects to say astonishing things about themselves in television news interviews. Late one night, in front of our fireplace, she told me her simple interview strategy: just gaze at them as though they're the most fascinating people in the world. Eventually, they'll try to prove it.

"You're right about the police experience, of course," Crain conceded. "They are good. They've done everything humanly possible ever since...since it happened. I trust them. In fact, a police lieutenant recommended you."

That would be Al Avila, although he hadn't told me about this favor. It would explain why Mo Crain called me instead of a more established investigations firm.

"I don't blame the police at all," Crain said. "But just because they're stuck doesn't mean I have to give up."

"No case with your name on it will get cold," I said.

Crain did not contradict my kindly lie. We both understood that new murders make headlines and move to the top of the police agenda. When the media tire of a subject, bureaucrats' fatigue follows quickly. But Mo allowed himself a modest smile, the one he used for large charitable donations and luxury car commercials.

"I realize that," he said. "They'll keep at it for me. But I'm not the only citizen of Tucson. There are lots of other crime victims, God help us. I need more, Mr. Brinker. A fresh look at everything."

"I just don't know if I could advance it," I said. "And the last thing the police want is a private investigator mucking around in an open murder case. If they think I'm in the way, or if I just irritate them, they could have my license yanked."

"Perhaps," Crain said, nodding his understanding. "But I could probably persuade them to be tolerant. Not throwing weight around, you understand, but my relationships are excellent. And you do have a law enforcement background. Not to mention your 'in' with Lieutenant Avila."

"Maybe," I said.

"There's something else," he said. "In the last year, two of my friends' kids disappeared. You found them both, got them home. Those guys think you walk on water."

I shook my head. "Kids are amateurs, Mr. Crain. Half of them want to be found. They want to be dragged home. They resist just so they can bitch about it before they eat a good meal and fall into a clean bed. This is different. From what I've read, the police don't think this was an amateur crime."

Crain stood and walked around the desk. There was nothing extraordinary about his face, but his constant presence on television had created the local handsomeness standard—the way successful businessmen should present themselves. He looked youthful and energetic despite his prematurely white hair. Young executives and middle managers asked their barbers for a style like Mo's. Professional but outdoorsy, just long enough to flutter in the breeze when the convertible top was down. He was friendly and guileless, TV tan and tennis lean. On his feet, moving, doing something, he radiated easy confidence. But as he had sat in the chair next to mine, his body slumped. I had not met him before that day, yet he spoke to me with the voice of an old, good friend in anguished need.

"I grew up in Wisconsin," he said. "My parents fought all the time and my father used to whip me for reasons I could never figure out. We lived in a ratty little trailer that never had enough heat. So by the time I graduated high school, I knew what I wanted. I wanted to be warm, and have plenty of money, and a loving family."

He shook his head. "Talk about answered prayers," he said. "I got it all. I moved to Arizona, made good money, married a wonderful woman."

He turned from me and looked back at the photograph on his desk.

"I'd give up everything I own," he said. "She was a gentle, gracious woman, Mr. Brinker. She never harmed anyone. She brought happiness to people. She got up one morning, and went to perform acts of kindness, and somebody shot her in the face. She died in a pool of her own blood in a parking lot. She left two children who loved her. And me."

I thought, How do I get out of this?

"If you were in my position," he said, "wouldn't you try anything? Wouldn't you plead with anyone who had any chance of helping?"

The man of great wealth and power seemed ready to cry. Salesman or not, his grief looked and sounded like the real thing.

"Let me talk to some people," I said.

FOUR

ANNA AVILA SAID, "Of course he seems sincere. He's a car dealer. He's on television."

She looked warily at Dolores when she spoke, but her sister wouldn't resent the crack about TV. Dolores, her career prospects hot and her idealism undimmed, still believed that she had found a noble calling.

Anna had a sweet smile and patient schoolteacher's tone. She used them kindly with children and impatiently with grown-up fools. She was using them with me now.

"Seeming sincere is what he does," she said. "It's how he sells all those cars."

"Anna," I said, "it was your husband who gave him my name."

La Fuente bustled with the usual mix of tourists and locals. At the large tables, two or three generations of Mexican families enjoyed a long meal together. When the mariachis played "Jesusita en Chihuahua," even people who weren't listening tapped their toes. Al and Anna Avila were there, double-dating as usual with Dolores and me. Dolores, never as chatty as her sister, was even more quiet and distant on this night.

Al put down his Dos Equis. He looked so much the upright cop that a beer bottle in his big hand seemed like a breach of regulations. He wore light gray slacks and a cream guayabera shirt. Even the loose-fitting shirt showed what hours in the gym can do.

He said to me, "Oh, sure, blame me for getting Mo Crain to throw some serious bucks your way."

Anna turned her head to Al, then me, giving us the familiar, indulgent stare that said, I love you guys, but you're both idiots.

"Why did you steer him to me?" I asked.

"He called the chief and sounded him out about getting some private help," Al said. "The chief said okay. That's what people usually say to Mo Crain. The chief called me. He asked if I knew anybody who could nose around without getting in the way. I knew you."

"Thanks, I guess," I said. "Anyway, Anna, he's not trying to sell me a Yugo. He wants help. And I could use the job."

"Anna thinks Mo hired a hitman," Al said.

"You're kidding," I said, turning to Anna. "Even the paper said the cops ruled out Mo's being involved."

Anna said, "I just know that Al has come home a dozen times talking about murdered wives, and he says, 'It's the husband.' Now, first time ever, it's not the husband. And the only difference is, this husband can buy and sell half the town. I'm not saying don't take the case, Brink. I'm just saying don't take this guy's word at face value."

"What do you think, Dolores?" Al asked.

Dolores considered it. She didn't look like Dolores Gonzales from the news. She looked like Anna tonight, both of them with their long black hair pulled back to ponytails and no makeup at all. Dolores made cosmetic concessions for television, but neither sister needed anything to cover her complexion of light brown, glowing with a hint of reddish gold that I thought of as reflected sunset. Like everyone on television, Dolores appeared to be thinner in real life. Nobody walked by the table and did that double take of recognition, trying to be cool and keep going. That suited Dolores fine.

"Brink always claims he doesn't want any more danger, after the Border Patrol," she said to Al, without looking at me. "But now he's thinking about a murder case. If that isn't dangerous, I don't know what is. It doesn't make sense to me."

"It doesn't have to be risky," I said. "If I get close to a break, I can give it to the cops."

Dolores raised her eyebrows in an "oh, sure" expression.

Anna said, "Brink, the next time you're over at Mo's, search his trash. I'll bet he subscribes to *Soldier of Fortune*."

WE TOOK A FEW MOMENTS in the restaurant lobby, as we always do after a meal, admiring the grainy old photographs of Mexico's civil war. A man named Agustín Casasola had collected his own and other photographers' work, creating a visual history of the revolution. The pictures showed laughing generals, stern young soldiers, frightened faces of Mexicans crowding the chaotic train stations.

One shot captivated me. A young woman stood on the steps of a railway passenger car. She leaned out from the carriage, as far as her arm would extend from the vertical grip bar. Her gaze focused somewhere down the platform. She wore a wartime expression of anxiety and puzzlement, of pain and resolve.

Every time I saw the picture, I wondered. Was she fleeing the war or arriving in the midst of it? Perhaps someone met her, embraced her in welcome. Maybe she was alone in the tumult. Far down the platform, she might have seen a loved one left behind. Where had she come from? Where was she going? What had she done?

The photograph was famous, Anna said. It embodied the suffering and confusion in the civil war. Historians assumed that the woman was a revolutionary fighter, a *soldadera,* for they were often seen in the train stations. Her true name was a mystery, but all the women of the war—and that picture in particular—were known as Adelita.

Dolores, holding my hand, said, "She reminds me of myself, sometimes."

"Rough day?"

"Tell you later," she said.

Al and Anna came back from the rest rooms. The four of us stood quietly for a moment. With the sisters between us, Al and I could look at each other over their heads. When we started kindergarten, Al's mother began marking our heights on her kitchen doorframe. We were rarely more than a quarter inch apart.

Anna hugged Dolores, then me, and said, "Come over soon. The girls get lonely when they don't see you."

Dolores said, *"Nos vemos."* It's a nice way to say goodbye in Spanish, a promise that we will see each other again.

They left, with Al's arm around Anna's shoulder and her arm around his waist. Anna stood on tiptoes for a moment and whispered something into Al's ear. They both laughed and walked a little faster.

I said a silent *adiós* to the enigmatic Adelita. Dolores and I stepped into the heavy summer night, moving slowly with a little distance between us.

FIVE

AT HOME, a light northerly breeze cooled the night air down to the nineties. The low trees and brush moved gently with the wind. I took a small glass of Cuervo Gold, a bottle of Molson Ice, and a couple of ibuprofen out to the patio. Dolores called it my NAFTA cocktail: Mexican booze, Canadian beer, and American drugs. She brought only a glass of ice water. Working on television is like being a jockey, she often said. Every ounce of fat is an occupational hazard.

We often sat outdoors, quiet and close, on warm evenings. Tonight, a faint buzz of tension underlaid the silence. Something was happening with Dolores. She would tell me in her own time. So I was left to mull my own dilemma, Mo Crain's offer.

If Sandra Crain were merely missing, I thought, I would have jumped at the job. My success rate on missing persons cases was high. The work usually ended happily. But murder is different. Murder changes everything, somebody wrote, especially the lives of those it touches. It changed me, for sure. I had seen enough violent death along the border. I had come close to it myself at Lovers Crossing.

When the hospital discharged me after the shooting, Dolores had taken me home. The television station gave her emergency leave. She brought my medicine at the appointed time. She changed the dressings on my wounds and took me to my own doctor. A few years ago, she had done a story about a physical therapist. From her, Dolores learned a few basic skills of rehabilitation, then put me through my prescribed paces every day. She cooked good food and took on my housekeeping chores. When I watched sports on cable television, she sat beside me and tolerated the games.

One night, when it was finally clear that I was able, she came back to our bed. Our movement was slower and gentler than ever before, acknowledging my continued pain and the surprising sense of newness between two longtime lovers. Neither of us spoke a word or uttered a sound, even when we collapsed and held each other as tightly as my torn body would allow.

Afterward, we lay there for an hour, maybe more. Only our breathing broke the stillness. Her cheek was on my chest. I had lost track of time, but it must have been almost midnight. A time for drifting off to sleep, savoring the gentle protection of each other's arms.

Dolores said, "I heard from Kelly Lincoln today."

"The agent in L.A.," I said.

"Yes."

She had spoken vaguely of finding a talent agent to advance her career. For a local news reporter, that usually means moving to a bigger city, where pay and visibility are higher.

"What did he tell you?"

"He liked my tape," Dolores said. "He says I look like Jennifer Lopez. Do you think I look like Jennifer Lopez?"

"A little," I said. "You're thinner and sexier."

"That is the correct answer. Thank you for playing," she said, and she kissed me softly on the neck. "Anyway, Kelly says the market is still good for Hispanic women, even though there's a bunch of us out there. Lots of stations are looking right now. He's sure that he can get me some offers in the next few months."

"Where?" I asked.

"He thinks Top Ten," Dolores said.

One of the ten biggest media markets. New York was number one. More than two thousand miles away. Chicago or Boston, maybe. Even Los Angeles was a plane ride or an eight-hour drive.

"How about Phoenix?" I said. "It's almost in the Top Ten. You could make lots more money than you can here, and it's just up the road."

"Maybe," she said. "But Kelly thinks the other cities might have more openings. He says I shouldn't try to pick a town. I have to be prepared to go where the jobs are."

"What about your contract here?"

"I'm in the last year. It has an early out if I get an offer from a big market."

We lay there quietly. I wished that I smoked, or had a drink. Something to pass the time while I figured out what to say next.

Finally: "What about us, if you leave?"

"They're separate issues," she said, with the quick confidence of one who has already thought about the question. "I have to make the right career decision, then we'll decide how to handle it. It doesn't have to be now, thank heaven. Kelly needs time to send out my videotapes and to hear from stations. Weeks, at least. You'll be in lots better shape by then."

Eight days later, the first offer came in from Detroit. It would have tripled Dolores's salary. Featured reporting role, some substitute anchoring. But it was still wintry, and she came back from her interview shivering and shaking her head at the icy rain downtown. There was a big phone argument with the agent. You don't have to like the place, he said. You go where the opportunities are, then move again when you can. But in the end, Dolores said no.

Four months passed. As far as I knew, she had no other offers. To encourage her to stay, I had taken her advice and left the Border Patrol. At least, that was the reason I gave myself. But as it had with Al Avila, the bureaucracy and the burnout had gotten to me. I wasn't ready to get shot by some drug dealer who probably had another lawman somewhere on his payroll.

The state Department of Public Safety, with a prod from Al, gave me the requisite experience credit for my Patrol service and issued my private investigator's license. Al steered me to several lawyers for work. I wound up with an office in the Allejandro & Katz building, venturing out to snap candid pictures of insurance scammers and otherwise finding good news for the firm's clients.

Occasionally I saw Dolores carry packages of newscast videotapes to the post office. She didn't say much about career moves, though, until we came home after our night at La Fuente.

"I have to tell you something," she said.

It was her phrase for telegraphing bad news. This would be it.

"Kelly called the other day."

The other day. I wondered how long she had waited to tell me.

"An offer," I said.

"Yes," Dolores said. "Can you believe it? Nothing for months, then kind of a jackpot."

"Where?"

"New York." The biggest market. The career Olympus for media people. She would go.

High above, a plane made its eastward climbing turn after takeoff from Tucson International Airport. I imagined her on it. My eyes stung.

"Congratulations," I said softly.

She reached over and squeezed my hand. "This is why I feel like Adelita," she said. "I don't know if I should be coming or going."

"So," I said, "it's decision time."

"Do you want to come with me?" she asked.

"Do you want me to?"

"Listen to us," she said. "We sound like junior high."

"I want to be with you," I told her, "but it's hard to imagine leaving here. This is home. For my whole life. You know, I went to Georgia for twelve weeks at the Border Patrol academy, and I've taken some trips. But that's about it. My roots are pretty deep."

"Mine, too," she said. "And we share some. Anna and Al and the girls. But I went off to Missouri for college, and those first two jobs in Texas. Time away is an investment."

"You'll never come back," I said.

"What do you mean?"

"No way to keep you down on the farm after you've seen Manhattan, or however that goes. You think you won't get used to the big money and chic parties at *Vogue?* Helicopter out to the Hamptons for a weekend? Little old Tucson doesn't have much to compare with all that."

"Don't make me feel guilty," she said. "This could be the way to a network. I could cover some important stories instead of the local junk. Do something worthwhile, the way I hoped when I started out."

I got up and carried my glass into the kitchen. I poured another shot of Cuervo and grabbed two more ibuprofen. My shoulder still hurt and now I had a headache. When I went back outside, I caught Dolores sneaking a sip of my beer.

"What happens next?" I asked.

"I go back there for a few days," she said. "Meet the *jefes*. Do some auditions with the guys I'd be anchoring weekends with, just to see if the chemistry on the air is good. When I'm done, Kelly and I will talk and decide on the best deal."

"If it all clicks, when would they want you?" I asked.

"Right away," she said. "But I have to give four weeks' notice here."

"When are you leaving for the visit?"

"Next week. Kelly's setting up the appointments. Brink, if I don't try, I'll always wonder."

We watched a big cloud glide beneath the moon. Pulses of light glowed faintly along the northern horizon. A thunderstorm up near Phoenix, maybe, as the summer weather pattern fought to establish itself.

After a long time, Dolores said, "Are you going to take the job with Mo Crain?"

"Probably," I said. "Best offer I've got."

She looked away. I couldn't see her expression as another cloud blocked the moonlight.

SIX

TOMMY O'MARA was a widebody, red-faced and mostly redheaded. The hair was going a little gray. He joked about leaving Chicago to join a police force where being Irish didn't help. Like so many Tucsonans, he came west for a winter vacation and never went home. O'Mara had been a Tucson homicide detective for twelve years and resisted the department's occasional halfhearted attempts to move him into management.

"Yeah, I'll meet you," he told me on the phone.

Al had called O'Mara the night before. It never hurts to have an upward-bound lieutenant on your side, O'Mara must have figured. He suggested meeting at a pub on University Boulevard because the place had Harp Lager on tap. We took seats on the shaded streetside patio. O'Mara put a large manila envelope on the table. He ordered two Harps without asking me.

"You were with Avila in the Border Patrol, way back when?" O'Mara asked.

"We went in together, right after college," I said.

"Horrible job," O'Mara said. "Chasing around the desert all day, dragging those poor devils back to the other side."

"Those are the lucky ones," I said. "The worst thing is finding them dead out there."

"I was flipping around the cable the other night," O'Mara said. "Came to some Mexican network. They were running a warning, with pictures of bodies lying in the desert. Announcer saying in Spanish, it's too dangerous to cross the desert in the summer."

"They keep coming," I said. "Plenty of American farmers and meat packers and construction companies make it worth their while."

"Fourteen, fifteen of them dead out by Yuma last month," O'Mara said. "Coyote gets them over the border and tells them to walk a couple of miles to the road. Road's twenty miles away. You imagine that? Fuckin' Yuma in the summer. They were dead before noon."

People moved at summer speed along the sunny street. This block looked like campus neighborhoods everywhere, with bookstores, music and video shops, and cheap restaurants.

O'Mara leaned toward me and said, "Holy shit, check this out."

Two young women with long brown legs, dangerously short white shorts, and thin T-shirts walked by. O'Mara watched as they strode down the block toward the campus, laughing in the happy conspiratorial way of freshmen.

"I knew I should have gone back to school," O'Mara said.

I gave him a moment and said, "About Mrs. Crain."

He was in no hurry. He asked, "How come you didn't jump over to TPD when Avila did?"

"I'm not good with teams," I said. "Al is. He finished his master's in justice administration while we were on the Patrol, so TPD put a pretty big rush on him. And he had a wife and their first baby by then. Not a good time for him to go independent."

"He's a star with us," O'Mara said. "Half a brain and affirmative action, guy like that could go all the way."

I let it slide. Politics had something to do with Al Avila's rise, sure. Mainly, though, he was a bright guy who could handle any part of the modern police portfolio, from drug busts to public relations.

"You married to his sister, or what?" O'Mara asked.

"Sister-in-law," I said. "We're not married, but we've been together for a couple of years."

"Dolores Gonzales, right? She's some babe. Oughta be on the network." He held up his hand, palm outward, and grinned. "No offense with the 'babe' remark. I'm just saying she seems to have a lot of ability. She should go places."

Exactly what I was dreading, but I smiled to confirm his judgment and taste.

"So what can you tell me about the case?" I asked.

"Cop's worst nightmare," O'Mara said. "Our clearance rate in homicide right now is better than ninety percent. So wouldn't you know, the one we can't crack is Mrs. Crain's. The victim married to a guy who could really hurt us."

"Would he try?"

"Nah, not in a vindictive way. But campaign contributions are the language the mayor and council understand."

"So," I prodded, "she was at the mall?"

"Right. She was one of those rich lady volunteers, you know? Had about a dozen favorite causes, we found out. Went down to Nogales every week to help abandoned and battered kids."

"Into Mexico?" I asked.

"No. American side. And up here in Tucson, she did a lot of preventive medicine things. On Friday mornings, she did clinics at elementary schools. Every Thursday, she's down at the mall for the geezer walks, checking blood pressure, heart rate, passing out health leaflets."

"The geezer walks?"

"Sure," O'Mara said. "You know, every morning before the stores open, the mall lets people come in. Lot of old folks like it. Some of them just waddle around, window-shop. But they have organized walks, too. They all finish at the food court. Get their strength back with a couple of cinnamon buns."

"And Mrs. Crain was part of that?"

"Right. The Senior Health Society sets up tables on Thursdays. Mrs. Crain was a nurse when she married Mo. Kept her license up, I guess. So she puts on her little white lab coat and does those health checks for the oldsters."

I said, "She did this every Thursday? Somebody could have known she'd be there regularly?"

"No doubt about it," O'Mara said, "and that's what I think happened. This was no random thing. Somebody went there to kill her."

"Shopping mall parking lot seems like a weird place for premeditated murder," I said.

"Where you been, son?" he said. "The mall is the center of urban life. We used to have everything downtown. Shopping, movies, murders. Now they're all at the mall."

"Too many people, though," I said.

O'Mara finished his first pint and signaled the waitress for another.

"You're right," he said. "But this was one time when hardly anybody was around. The geezers start early, eight o'clock or so. Mrs. Crain finishes her work and comes out about nine. Stores don't open until ten, mostly. And it was a nice bright spring morning. Remember that early hot spell we had? So even the customers who came early tried to use that little bit of covered parking on the northwest lot. Mrs. Crain was outside, close to the food court entrance. Her car, couple others, that's it."

I pictured the scene. "It still seems wrong," I said. "If someone knew she did the mall regularly, that person would probably know she did schools, too. Why not wait until Friday and do it outside a school? She'd be coming out in midmorning, probably. No parents or buses around. In and out. Far smaller chance of witnesses."

O'Mara shook his head. "Maybe, but we did sniff around the school neighborhood. We thought maybe the killer had cased the area. Nobody reported any strangers hanging around."

"Why not get her at home?"

"Security," O'Mara said. "It's gated, and you oughta see the guards there. They all look like Special Forces in great suits. You want to get into that place, you better have machine guns on your fenders."

"What kind of car did Mrs. Crain have?"

"Brand-new Lexus. Had nine hundred and forty-two miles on it. I guess you marry Mo Crain, your cars don't get out of warranty."

"So it couldn't have been a carjacking."

"Shit, no. If they wanted that car, they'd have had it. Been halfway to Mexico before the blood dried."

"They just shot her, left her there, and took off," I said.

"Didn't even grab her purse."

The waitress came with O'Mara's refill. I let him take another long drink of the Harp.

"Anything fishy about her or Mo? Grudges, problems, threats?"

O'Mara sighed. "Zip," he said. "The woman was a saint, apparently. Interview anyone who knew her and they start blubbering about how wonderful she was. I got no reason to doubt it. So we focused a little more on Mo. He claimed he had no threats."

"Disgruntled employees?"

"Yeah. Well, Mo has about six hundred people working at his dealerships. He's got salesmen and mechanics and clerical and janitors and I don't know what else. Treats them right, apparently. Good pay. Great benefits. Everybody gets to be in the Christmas commercials. You know, Mo says Peace on Earth and a thousand-dollar rebate, and all the employees wave at the camera. It's like workplace heaven."

"He doesn't have much turnover?" I asked.

"Hardly any," O'Mara said. "We checked out any recent firings. You know what? Huge company like that only axed two people in the last year. Shit, we fired more cops than that just for groping women on traffic stops."

I winced, remembering how Sanchez fastened on the prettiest young women when we caught a large group of illegal immigrants. He took them away from the crowd, behind a rock or a clump of brush. "Just cut her out of the herd, like a plump little heifer," he said. Never quite enough to admit a crime, but enough to let you know what a rascal he fancied himself. The women, frightened and powerless and feeling shamed, never filed complaints.

"Anyway," O'Mara said, "the first firee was a mechanic. Drunk on the job. Pretty typical for this jerk, apparently. He goes out a week later and drives his car into a bridge abutment on the freeway. Medical examiner said his blood alcohol was point-two-six. This was in February. Mrs. Crain was alive and well, and he wasn't. So it ain't him."

"And the other one?"

"He was a used car salesman. Got canned for steering

customers to his brother's car lot down on Irvington. What a moron."

"That seems pretty thin for a murder motive," I said.

"Yeah, but it was a week before Mrs. Crain got shot," O'Mara said. "So we're chomping at the bit when we go knock on this clown's door. You had lunch yet?"

"No."

"You want to get something here? Good beer, they've probably got good food, too."

Keep him happy, I thought, and keep him talking. I asked the passing waitress for a menu.

"We get to the guy's apartment and he's packing up. Seems he got a new job in San Diego. We ask him when he had that good fortune. He says, 'I went over there and interviewed a week after I left Crain's. They just called me back to offer the job.'"

"They must not check references too carefully over there," I said.

O'Mara laughed. "California, you know, they probably just sense his aura. But the little fuck was telling the truth. Dealer there confirmed it. He had the interview one hour after Mrs. Crain got shot. Clark Kent couldn't have made it to San Diego that fast."

We felt the midday heat gathering. The overhead misters came on, providing a little relief.

"You know," I said, "if somebody wanted to hurt Mo, why not just kill *him?* He's out in public. He comes and goes from his dealerships. He would have been as easy to hit as she was."

"I think you're right," O'Mara said. "That was the first thing we thought. We put bodyguards on him as soon as he got home from Canada. After a few days, he got private security. But nothing happened. No, it was her they were after. I'd bet my pension on it. But if you find anybody who thinks she had an enemy in the world, you're doing better than I have."

"Mo have any girlfriends?" I asked.

"Ah," O'Mara said. "This top sirloin sandwich here looks pretty good, don't you think?"

"Sure."

O'Mara ordered the sirloin, rare, and another Harp. I had a club sandwich and iced tea.

"This is my day off, you know," O'Mara said. "I wouldn't partake if I was working. Ever since Gilliland, we're being real careful."

Gilliland was a police captain who wrapped his Audi around a light pole shortly after the bars closed one night. The investigating officers tried to cover for him, but it made the papers. Gilliland took early retirement.

"On the girlfriend business," O'Mara said, "*nada.* Seems that Mr. and Mrs. Crain were straight arrows. Mo Crain's sitting here with you now, he wouldn't even be checking out the college girls. At least according to his friends."

"No new women in his life since the murder?"

"Nothing," O'Mara said.

"How about their kids?"

"Forget it. Daughter was away at Stanford. Son was in Paris for a semester at the Sorbonne, wouldn't you know? Jesus, can you imagine the bills? I can barely afford Pima Community College for my kid. The daughter needed heavy counseling, I hear."

The food arrived. O'Mara tucked in hungrily and we ate without speaking for a few minutes.

"Anyway," O'Mara said, "we interviewed both the kids.

Not a hint of any trouble. If the parents were having problems, they weren't having them in front of the children."

I said, "What about insurance?"

"Nope," he said. "There was a half-mil term life policy, payable to Mo. Guys like us, that's a motive. Guy like him, it's petty cash."

"So Crain doesn't have any financial problems you know about?"

O'Mara leaned a bit closer. "Nah. Think about it. The guy sells cars, and car sales are great. He's got land all over Arizona, and that's no-lose right now, especially if all your chums are on the city councils and boards of supervisors and zoning commissions. Mo Crain's gotta be worth about thirty million bucks, Brinker. He didn't whack his wife for some insurance policy."

O'Mara finished the beer, leaned back in his chair, and patted his belly.

"You're positive about his alibi?" I asked. "No way he could have been here?"

"Absolutely not. We've got the airline tickets. We've got witnesses on the plane. You have to show picture ID to fly, and besides, we've got immigration records, for chrissakes. We've got the Canadians on the trade commission in meetings with him, all day for three days. They have this group called Westfriends. They meet several times a year for promoting trade, cultural exchange, shit like that. All serious big shots in Vancouver. Usually Mo had breakfast with one of them, dinner with another, and lunch with all of them. Mo's totally clean."

"Could he have hired somebody?"

"Could he? Anything's possible. I'll tell you, though, I've

broken the news to some supposedly bereaved hubbies over the years. I can usually tell if they're bad. Mo, I don't know. He is a kind of performer, after all. Maybe he could fool an old cop."

Of course he seems sincere, Anna had said.

O'Mara looked into his empty beer glass as if considering another.

"Let me tell you how it went," he said. "When we identified Mrs. Crain's body, we didn't know that Mo was in Canada. Figured he was at work. We went over to his office at the Carplex. His secretary tried his cell phone, but he was already in the air, and he keeps it turned off during the flight. He called his office when he got to L.A. and the secretary told him. His connecting flight arrived here at three-thirty in the afternoon. I was there, man. Mo came off the plane looking like he was the one who got killed."

"Sounds like O.J.," I said.

"Yeah, but Crain didn't leave Tucson after this murder. He was already up there in Canada for days when it happened. If he did it, he didn't do it himself."

He pushed the manila envelope over to me. "You probably want to see this stuff, but not right after lunch," he said. "Three in the face."

I nodded.

"It's ugly," O'Mara said. "The guy who did it is out there someplace. I don't care how long it takes or what I have to do. If I'm being wheeled around the old cops' home, drinking Ensure through a tube in my nose, I'm still going to get this fucker."

"I hope I help you."

He regarded me for a moment and said, "Listen, amigo. I'm

not being a glory hog, but the Tucson Police Department is who has the legal responsibility to solve this. If you find out anything, and I'm not the very first call you make, you'll wish we never met. Anything unclear about that?"

"Got it."

"Be damn sure you get it. This ain't amateur night. It's not Border Patrol cowboy shit. This is a maximum-sensitive, high-profile murder case. If you do anything, anything at all to screw it up, even your pal Avila won't be able to save your sorry ass. *Comprende* that?"

I smiled back at him.

O'Mara stood up. "Thanks for lunch."

"My pleasure," I said. I reached for the envelope and the check.

SEVEN

ACCORDING TO A PERSISTENT Tucson urban legend, Mo Crain wanted to incorporate the land his automobile megadealership occupied as the City of Crain Carplex, Arizona. Even the usually malleable politicians gagged on that one.

The place might have qualified as a city, though. It occupied more ground than some subdivisions. Despite the vastness, Crain avoided the gaudy neon overkill of his competitors. He placed small, softly lit signs at the Carplex entrances and landscaped the property with natural desert plants. Along the east end, he built a five-acre public park with swings and basketball courts.

Environmentalists protested all his plans and opposed his permit applications. After the Carplex was built, someone figured out that business would march on, regardless, and Crain was the best they could hope for. They praised his sensitivity and accepted his donations. It was vintage Mo. Trained in the trenches of car sales, he could win over almost any skeptic.

He was outside the main showroom when I arrived. Video crews moved about, positioning cameras and jockeying cars into view. For reasons that I could not fathom, the crews used bright lights on this brilliant, cloudless morning.

A young woman at an umbrella-shaded makeup table was powdering Crain's face. He left her and met me with a handshake. He had tissues tucked under his shirt collar. His white hair held its style in the breeze.

"You'll do it, won't you?" he said.

I said, "We'll need an understanding."

"We'll have one," Crain said. "Let me finish this last spot and we'll talk."

Crain walked to a position between the cameras and a new sport-utility vehicle. The makeup artist ran out to remove the tissues and apply one last quick dab of powder. She quickly withdrew, walking backward to keep an eye on her handiwork.

Two big lights snapped on, making Crain look unnaturally bright. The powerful illumination wiped out the long morning shadows, answering my question about the need for artificial light.

Someone yelled, "Rolling!" and after a second of absolute silence, Crain was suddenly into it, doing what I had seen on television thousands of times. He recited the SUV's virtues, optional features, lease terms, monthly payments. Watching him, I was impressed by the warmth and freshness that he brought to the pitch. It was easy to feel that the man loved his cars and his customers.

The spot ran thirty seconds. Crain finished with his signature line, "We make the deal that works for you! There's no pain with Mo Crain!" It was hokey and I felt embarrassed to watch a live human being, not a television image, say the words aloud. But kids could recite that slogan before they learned the Pledge of Allegiance. Mo knew what he was doing.

A crowd had formed. Not just the video crew, but the staff and most of the morning's car shoppers. Everyone applauded. Crain flashed a nothing-to-it grin and gave a little bow.

The makeup artist was standing next to me. I asked her, "Doesn't he need cards with the script on them, or a TelePrompTer or something?"

"Anyone else would, but not Mo," she said. "He just knows all that stuff and ad-libs it. He thinks it sounds more natural, more believable that way. We do new commercials every week, and nobody can remember the last time he flubbed one. We're all sure he's got a photographic memory."

As Crain walked toward us, a family stopped him. The parents smiled happily. The boy, about ten years old, I thought, looked at Crain as though he were Tiger Woods. Crain took his time with the family, chatting and answering their questions. An aide handed him a postcard-sized picture of himself. He signed it and gave it to the boy.

The mother said something that stripped the smile from Crain's face. I saw him mouth the word "No," and a few others. He shook hands with the parents, then made an elaborate show of shaking the boy's hand. "Thanks for coming by," he told them as he made his way over to me.

"Who'd have thought it?" Crain said. "A car dealer giving autographs."

"What a great country," I said. "You're a superstar."

"With no talent." He gave me that modest grin. "I buy my recognition. No complaints, though. Television serves me well."

"Where did you get the 'no pain' line? Is it just to rhyme with Crain?"

He grinned. "Market research shows that people hate to buy cars. Love to have them, love to drive them, but hate to buy them. They're terribly misinformed about salespeople. They don't trust us."

"Imagine that," I said.

Mo kept a straight face. "They dread choosing the wrong model. And they always expect the monthly payments to kill them. So we try to take the pain out of the process."

"For a minute there, that woman looked unhappy," I said. "Did she buy a lemon?"

Crain's smile vanished. "We don't use that word anymore," he said. "But if she did, I'd replace it. No jerking around. People understand that machines aren't perfect. Cars break down. But if you treat your customers right, make things okay for them, they forgive you. They come back. The good dealers figured that out years ago. Big guys like Jim Click and mom-and-pop stores like the Volvo dealer. Treat 'em right."

I said nothing as we walked toward the offices.

"But your real question," Crain said, "was, what did she say? Right?"

"Yes."

"She asked about Sandra. Did we ever find out who did it? I told her not yet, but we would. She said she'll pray for me."

In the cool office, I said, "I need to find out everything I can about the victims."

"What do you mean by victims?" Crain asked, emphasizing the "s."

"Mrs. Crain and you," I said.

Crain looked hard at me, frowning, for a long moment. Then he nodded. I thought he looked displeased, but resigned to it.

"You want to retrace the cops' footsteps? Dig around in our lives and look for problems?"

"I don't know where else to start, Mr. Crain. There's not one clue that points to the killer. If we had a suspect, we could focus on him. But we don't. So I have to begin with you and your wife, and work back from there."

Crain sighed. "All right," he said. "If anyone won't talk with you for fear of offending me, tell them to call me and I'll set their minds at ease. Okay?"

"Okay," I said. "Here's one thing I didn't get from O'Mara. Was Mrs. Crain troubled about anything lately? Had something happened, or had she seen or heard anything that bothered her?"

Crain leaned back in his leather chair and rubbed his temples with his fingertips. "If she did," he said, "she said nothing about it to me. I have to tell you, though, that would be just like Sandra."

"What do you mean?"

"Ever since we were young, first married, she tried to spare me any distractions. If she was feeling blue, or if there was some problem with the kids, or the roof leaked, she'd deal with it herself. She wanted me to be able to concentrate on my career and building this business. She liked to think things out for herself. Eventually, if she needed my help or a decision or something, she'd come to me, sure. But if something had just happened or if she were newly troubled, I probably wouldn't have known about it."

He was speaking more to himself than to me, looking at the photograph on his desk.

"I have to go back up to Canada this evening," he said. "Do you have time right now?"

I said, "Sure."

"So let me tell you about Sandra," Crain said with a wistful smile, and for two hours, he did. It was like hearing my conversation with O'Mara replayed. Crain told the story of a wonderful woman and a perfect marriage. I left with a notebook full of names, people to question, just as the police had already done.

EIGHT

DRIVING FROM THE CARPLEX to my house, I bought an afternoon paper from a street hawker. My car's outside temperature gauge said 101 degrees. No clouds broke the hard blue sky. The hawker stood on the concrete median, hammered by the desert sun, sucking up rush-hour exhaust fumes. An orange safety vest hung loosely on his scrawny frame. His working days were numbered. The city council was about to ban sales on the road medians. I gave him a dollar for the thirty-five-cent paper and rolled up my window before he could offer change. He smiled through a few dark teeth, then limped away to the next car.

The front-page headline read, "Feds Probe Patrol."

When the Broadway traffic stopped for red lights, I read bits and pieces. The story was written by Gabriela Corona and George Matson. I knew them, Gabriela pretty well and George in passing. Gabriela Corona covered border issues, smuggling, immigration, trade deals. The newspaper was too cheap to maintain a border bureau, but Gabriela spent as much time there as she could. She went bowling with the local cops and Border Patrol agents. Like so many Southern Arizonans who plied their trades on the frontier, Gabriela was bilingual, bicultural, and friendly with officials on the Mexican and American sides. George Matson was a city reporter who worked law enforcement and courts. He would know the investigators. Gabriela would know the investigated.

"A special Justice Department team will probe allegations of Border Patrol corruption and violence in Southern Arizona," the story said. "The investigations will center on reports that Border Patrol agents sexually assaulted illegal aliens in their custody, facilitated drug smuggling along the Arizona-Sonora frontier in return for bribes, and even forced aliens to serve as moving targets for pistol practice. The team will also examine allegations that Border Patrol agents routinely harass people, including U.S. citizens, who 'look Hispanic.'"

Newspapers and TV stations love government corruption. Government doesn't buy much advertising. The media can blast officialdom as hard as they like without risking a dollar. Big businesses are less attractive targets. You don't see many local news exposés of, say, car dealers.

The light was green at Jessica, so I couldn't read again until I reached the busy intersection at Wilmot. The sunburned hawker there looked disappointed when he saw the paper in my hands.

The article said that a Justice Department spokesman had "no comment on any investigation that may or may not be pending." The Border Patrol's Tucson sector chief said he welcomed any examination "of the important work we do, and the exceptionally dedicated people who perform it. If wrongdoing has occurred, we will immediately take the appropriate action."

The Wilmot light lasted long enough for me to turn to an inside page. The story continued with a highlighted section that listed activities and events under investigation. At the bottom, I saw, "Shooting of Border Patrol agent by unknown persons at the canyon known as Lovers Crossing, east of the Nogales Port of Entry. Assailants escaped into Mexico. The wounded agent survived but left the Patrol. Rumors have persisted that another agent played a role in the shooting."

Sanchez was waiting as I drove up to my house.

He wore jeans and a tight black T-shirt, showing all muscle rippling around that short body. His thick black hair was combed straight back from a low bronze brow. He rested against a gleaming white Jeep Grand Cherokee, in full view of any neighbors who might be watching from their houses on the rise above mine. If he planned trouble, it would not happen now, in plain sight.

I parked my car in its usual place. Sanchez kept his body still as I stepped out and faced him. The sun made him squint. He closed one eye more than the other, as if he were sighting me in a sniper scope. We stood twenty feet apart, two antagonists leaning against their vehicles, playing it strong and silent. If Anna Avila were here, she would claim to hear the testosterone dripping.

"You're smiling," Sanchez said. "You must not have read the paper."

"I saw it," I said.

"Could be pretty bad trouble for a lot of people, Brinker."

"Nervous? Maybe Justice would do a prisoner swap, Sanchez. We'd get back a few marijuana smokers and pistol packers from the Mexicans, and you could do your time in the Hermosillo jail."

"Funny," he said, but those hard, reptilian eyes looked as though they had never been amused by anything except other people's pain. "You're gonna be in that grand jury, too, asshole. Were you Mr. Perfect on the Patrol?"

"No such person," I said.

"You didn't let some of those señoritas keep walking north

if they'd give you a quick Lewinsky? You didn't confiscate some cash before you pushed illegals back through the fence? C'mon, Brinker. Your shit stinks like the rest of us."

"I let some people in," I said. "But not for that. I never stole. You don't care what I did, Sanchez. You're worried about what I saw. You care what I might know."

He shifted around, stared up at the nearby houses, looked down at his boots. The guy we all suspected was bent, even though we couldn't prove it. Agents gave him room and tried to avoid working with him. But someone had to, and when you got the call, you prayed not to be with him, alone in the dark desert, when his malevolent friends had you in their gun sights. Suspicion about Sanchez grew after I was shot at Lovers Crossing, but the Border Patrol's halfhearted internal reviews could not nail him. A federal grand jury would be more dangerous.

"You don't know shit," he said. "You're just a guy who got shot by smugglers and turned into a paranoid. Thinking a brother agent, a guy who helped rush you to the hospital, was trying to get you killed. Who's gonna believe that?"

"If anybody asks," I said, "we'll see who believes it."

He shrugged. "Stakes are higher these days," he said. "Lots of people gonna be seriously pissed off if you run your mouth. Good people."

I held his gaze and said, "The good people have nothing to fear from me."

Sanchez grunted. He opened the Cherokee door and climbed in. He looked at me through the open window.

"Get your head out of your ass, Brinker. I'm not going down in this thing. You're fucking sure not dragging me down. Understand what I'm saying here?"

"So long, Sanchez," I said.

"Cute kids, your friend the cop has," Sanchez said. "Nice little girls."

He spit out the window. Then he gunned the engine and drove off. The Cherokee's oversized tires churned dirt behind him.

ONCE INSIDE THE HOUSE, I called Al and told him what Sanchez had said about the girls. The line was silent for several moments when I finished.

"They're going to camp in a few days." He spoke in a soft but emphatic voice that told me he had thought it through and knew how to handle the problem. "I'll see that they're safe in the meantime. Thanks, Brink."

"Okay. I'm sorry to drag your family into this."

This time he did not hesitate. "You didn't drag us in," he said. "You and I went into that tunnel together, and I decided."

"Goddam Sanchez," I said. "I can never get rid of him."

"A man like that," Al said, "he may do himself in. He'll go just a little too far sometime, and a lot of people will be waiting to help him hit bottom."

"I hope you're right," I said.

"I'm right," he said. "The trick is for us to still be standing when he goes down."

NINE

I HAD WRITTEN in my notes about Sandra Crain, "born Nogales, Son. Came to U.S. as child. Parents worked Eberle home. Linda E (now Nelson) best friend years."

Linda Eberle Nelson lived in a foothills gated community. Tucson has a hierarchy of gates. At the low end is the empty gatehouse, an ornament to impress the gullible home buyer, while discouraging timid tourists and low-IQ burglars. High-end gatehouses are manned twenty-four hours a day by very courteous fellows wearing tailored blue blazers over guns they know how to use.

The Nelson gatehouse was in the midrange. It had a guard, an old guy with scraggly white hair and a Bank Dick nose. He called the Nelson house to say I was on my way. She was waiting at the door when I pulled up.

She wore white Bermuda-length shorts and a soft pink shirt with a little polo player stitched into the fabric. Ready for golf, maybe, or a drink at the golf club bar. She was almost six feet tall. Her hair purported to be blond, and her deep tan would make dermatologists weep.

"Thanks for seeing me, Mrs. Nelson," I said as she led me into the cool living room. The house was built up to the edge of its mountain lot. The large room's panoramic view reminded me of a national park lodge.

"It's Linda, please," she said. "Mo called before he left town and gave me carte blanche to talk about Sandra."

"Permission?" I said.

She smiled. "I don't need permission, really," she said. "But he was married to my best friend in the world. If he thinks I can help by speaking with you, I'm glad to do it."

"And if he asked you not to?"

She tilted her head and raised her eyebrows. I placed her noncommittal expression in my growing mental file on Mo Crain's influence.

"Would you like something to drink?" she asked. "I have a jar of sun tea all chilled. Or a beer?"

I accepted the iced tea. When she went to the kitchen, I looked around the living room. It was decorated in the soft desert earth tones favored in foothills homes. At first, I found it surprisingly bland. Then the interior understatement pushed my attention to the window, with its view across all of Tucson and south toward Mexico. Five or six miles away and a little west, at the base of the hills, I could see rooftops of the mall where Sandra Crain had died.

Linda Nelson returned with two tall glasses on a silver tray. She placed it on a table between easy chairs. She handed me a glass of tea and took something clear over ice for herself.

"Please, sit down," she said, "and tell me how you'd like to do this."

"I'd like to start from your first days with Mrs. Crain," I said. "I'm sorry if this takes you over the same ground the police covered."

"They didn't ask many questions," she said. "An overweight redheaded guy drank a couple of my beers, but it didn't take him long."

I smiled, remembering lunch with O'Mara.

Linda Nelson took a small sip of whatever it was and waited for me to open my notebook.

"Sandra was Mexican," she said. "She was born just over the border in Nogales. She came to this country with her parents. They worked for my folks. Her father did gardening and handyman work. Her mother was a housemaid, cook, babysitter."

"Did they have green cards?" I asked.

She answered without hesitation. "They were illegals, of course, but Tucson people hardly noticed in those days. It was viewed as a mutually beneficial arrangement. There was none of this nannygate or undocumented alien foolishness. Daddy eventually called some congressman and they all got green cards. They applied for citizenship later."

I nodded and waited for her to continue.

"Sandra lived with her parents in a little house on the back of our property. She went to school with the other children from the neighborhood. There were Anglos whose parents owned the houses and Mexican kids whose parents worked there and lived in servant quarters."

I took a few notes. I would ignore most of this later, probably, but I wanted to look interested as she got into the story. Another tip from Dolores.

"My parents were both doctors. Daddy had a private practice and Mom worked at the VA Hospital. They were busy and away from the house a lot, so Sandra's mom was like a second mother to me. Sandra and I were the same age. Naturally we became good friends. Later in life, we realized that it was strange, because outside the home we had different lives."

"How do you mean?" I asked.

"Well, she socialized with Hispanics and I never did. Sandra got my hand-me-down dresses. That must have made her feel terrible, although she never said so. Somehow, though, that gap never mattered when we were together. At least, not to me."

She smiled and said, "You have to excuse my amateur psychology, Mr. Brinker. It's just that I've been thinking a lot about Sandra lately. We had a wonderful relationship and, in some ways, it's surprising. But we were so alike, despite all our natural differences."

I thought of my own lifelong friendship with Al Avila. Race never mattered, at least not in any conscious way. Al's mother had often cared for me, but except for that, it was difficult to reconcile my experience with Linda Nelson's. Perhaps the idea of caste carried more weight in her circle than in the humbler precincts where Al and I grew up.

"It's odd how things work out," she said. "Sandra must have thought I was rich. Her family must have envied mine. But she's the one who became truly wealthy. Then she died so horribly."

"You seem to be doing fine," I said, my eyes taking in the luxurious room and the million-dollar view.

"Yes," she said. "I married a doctor, just as my mother had."

"Your father married a doctor, too."

"Good point," she said.

Her eyes seemed to lose focus for a moment. I had seen this before in wealthy clients, usually parents whose children had disappeared. Trouble triggered an unexpected suspicion that they had spent too much time concentrating on the wrong things.

She brought her gaze back to me and asked, "Where were we?"

"So much alike," I said.

"That we were," she said, smiling. "We were college roommates, even. We went to the U of A together. Daddy paid Sandra's expenses and he rented us an apartment near campus."

"She met Mo in college?"

"That's right. Sandra and I were having lunch in the student union and Mo just walked right up to us. He was Morrie Crain then, did you know that? He changed his nickname because everybody admired Mo Udall so much."

Morris Udall, known to everyone as Mo, represented Tucson in Congress for many years. He was a liberal, but even Arizona's Goldwater conservatives respected his honesty and loved his famous sense of humor.

"Mo had that salesman quality even then," Linda Nelson said. "He looked at Sandra in the most humble way, not the usual cocky college-boy thing. He said, 'You're so beautiful that I'd be honored if you'd go out with me.' I would have thrown up if he said that to me. Maybe I was cynical even then. But Sandra looked up at him and smiled and said, 'Okay.' Kismet. They were together from that moment on."

I said, "No other boyfriends? No disappointed lovers?"

"Good grief," she said. "You don't mean somebody who carried a torch for twenty-five years, then killed her?"

"Something more recent," I said.

"Not Sandra," she answered quickly. "No matter what, she would never, how should I say it? Stray."

I gave it a moment and asked, "What about Mo?"

She sat a bit straighter and said, "Are you investigating your own client, Mr. Brinker?"

"No," I said. "But if there was another person in his life, then she or somebody else might have had a motive."

"I don't know how things work in your circle," Linda Nelson said, "but up here, adultery isn't even cause for divorce, let alone murder."

"Was that a 'yes' about Mo?" I asked. But her face had gone dark and I knew that I had played one card too many.

"This isn't a very pleasant conversation," she said. "I don't think it's very productive, either."

She stood up.

"And no, it wasn't anything critical about Mo," she said. "Now I'm a bit late for an appointment."

I gave her a business card.

"I'll be in my office tomorrow morning from about eight o'clock," I said. "And you can always leave a message if you have more information."

She took the card but said no more as she showed me out.

"Could Mo have had something to do with this?" I asked at the door.

"Goodbye, Mr. Brinker," she said.

When I drove past the gatehouse, I noticed a white Chevy Lumina parked beside the public road. Tinted glass obscured the driver. Nothing unusual about that. Lots of Arizona cars have darkened windows to weaken the powerful sun. I wasn't looking for problems, anyway. People often pulled off there to admire the view of Tucson far below, or just to look at the impressive houses inside the gated subdivision.

I was a quarter mile down the hill before the Lumina eased onto the roadway and followed, keeping its distance.

I checked the Volunteer Nurse Association and the Red Cross. Just as O'Mara told me, everyone loved Sandra Crain. They found it astonishing that a woman who had so much wealth would give so much of herself.

"It's not just money, you see," said Martha Blevins, R.N. She had gray hair and the cheerful, no-baloney attitude of an efficient nurse who loved her work. "Mr. Crain gives lots of money, too. But Mrs. Crain gave time and ideas and that contagious enthusiasm of hers. She seemed grateful for the chance to help other people. Sometimes, wealthy contributors just come by for the photo opportunities, then you never see them again. I don't mean to seem ungrateful. God bless anyone who helps others. But Sandra Crain was special."

At the Tucson Unified School District's Volunteer Coordination Office, Leticia Castillo sat behind her desk in a wheelchair and almost cried when I mentioned Sandra Crain's name.

"I usually think that God must have a plan," she said, "but may the Lord forgive me, this time I wonder. That fine, kind woman getting murdered. There's nothing to justify that. Her children are all grown now, and she loved our little kids so."

Was there anything about Mrs. Crain, anything she ever said or did, that indicated trouble in her life?

Nothing.

Was there any hint of another man in her life?

"Don't be ridiculous," Ms. Castillo snapped.

NOGALES, ARIZONA, WAS AN hour away, so I telephoned the center for abused children there. The woman who answered the phone said her name was Elena Grijalva, the director and only paid staff member. She spoke like a person without enough time in the day.

"Sandra was kind and caring," she said. "She wasn't like some of the wealthy people who give some money, volunteer once, then go to Hawaii. She was here every other Tuesday, as promised, and worked most of the day. Sometimes she just dropped in, even if she wasn't scheduled to be here. Nursing, diaper changing, nothing bothered her. Everyone loved her. Her financial contributions were nice, but if she hadn't had a dime, she would have enriched us just by being here."

Two days of this, and I had checked off every name on the list that Mo Crain had given me. Friends and relatives, community contacts, former employers and professors. Sandra Crain had been killed by person or persons unknown, perhaps even to her, for reasons that no one could possibly imagine.

Coming out of the school district office, I spotted the white Lumina sedan again. Perfect for a tail; half the cars in this urban desert seem to be light-colored, midsized sedans. It was parked on Tenth Street, three vehicles behind the entrance to the lot where I left my car. The driver had a clear view of anyone leaving the schools building. When I started walking toward him, he put the Lumina in reverse, then made a quick U-turn. We don't use front license plates in Arizona. There was mud on the rear plate.

I remembered a Border Patrol agent who showed me the ropes soon after I came back to Arizona from the academy in Georgia. His name was Collins, a skinny, straw-haired Texan with calluses on his hands and in his voice. He had eight years on the job.

"Sometimes it gets nasty out there," he rasped, kneeling down behind our Jeep and drinking from a can of Dr Pepper. "Rough stuff. Can't always do things strictly by the book. You get my drift here, son?"

I nodded, although I wasn't quite sure that I understood him. Or wanted to.

"Times like that," he said, "it helps if your tags is a little hard to read." He scooped up a handful of dirt, poured some

Dr Pepper into it, and rubbed the mixture on the license plate. Then he sloshed some on the vehicle numbers stenciled on the Jeep's side.

"Damn desert," he said, shaking his head. "I wash this sucker every day. Still can't keep it clean."

I watched the Lumina speed down Tenth Street. The license plate looked muddy and I couldn't make out the number.

It hadn't rained in a month.

TEN

GABRIELA CORONA agreed to meet me at an elementary school on the south side, not far from the newspaper building.

"It's a dog and pony show with the state superintendent and some Tucson educrats," she said. "This school gets a lot of immigrant kids and the district is making a pitch for more federal money. The news conference starts at noon so they can get live shots on the TV news. Lots of videotape of little brown faces in need of dollars. I should be bored comatose by twelve-ten and done by twelve-thirty."

A television news van was pulling away as I drove into the school parking lot. I recognized the state superintendent, a telegenic woman who reportedly had a new job lined up with the feds in Washington. As she eased into the back seat of her state car, she waved mechanically at a few teachers, but saved her best smile for another news crew that was still taping. The official sedan had a Mo Crain license plate frame.

Gabriela walked over and shook my hand.

"Rescue me," she said.

I had to think about that one for a moment.

"Fontella Bass," I finally said, "1963. Sixty-four, maybe."

"I can never get you," she said. It was a game we had started playing when I was still on the Patrol and she was hanging around the agents in Nogales, looking for stories. She liked sixties music and so did I. We had been greeting each other that way ever since. One called out a song title and the other tried to name the artist.

"I really could have used a rescue during that little photo op, though," she said. "It's amazing how much self-serving claptrap these people can cram into a half hour."

We sat on a bench near the school office. The superintendent and the TV crews were gone and nobody else was out front.

"So, Brinker," she said. "I thought I'd be calling you, instead of vice versa."

"How come?"

"George Matson and I are working the Patrol investigation story together. I've got the Beep and he's got the grand jury." The Border Patrol was the Beep in law enforcement and journalistic shorthand, in the same way that the FBI had become the Feebs.

Gabriela said, "Your name seems to be coming up at both ends."

"I saw your story," I said, "but I didn't see my name."

"That's because we're a newspaper of great discretion, compassion, and principle," she said, laughing. "We wouldn't dream of making anyone uncomfortable with our coverage. The feds won't name you on the record as a witness, so I can't report that. And you're not indicted, as far as I know. Although they probably wouldn't tell me that anyway."

"I'm grateful for small favors."

"It's going to come out pretty soon, so don't be feeling too lucky."

"What's coming out?" I asked.

Gabriela was tiny, maybe four-foot-nine, with small bones and the lean, healthy look of a person who kept moving. Agents liked her because she wrote fairly about them when the Patrol made bad news. No agents expected special treatment, but they didn't fear getting gratuitously slimed in her stories, either. She stared down the school hallway, watching the dust rise from the playground beyond, thinking about how much to say next.

"George says the INS supervisor they brought in, Rosen? He's hot to get Sanchez. So there's been a lot of attention paid to anything where Sanchez's name comes up. More than one agent will get flushed, but Sanchez is the one they really want."

"Good," I said.

"I hope it's good for you. What I heard this week is that Sanchez is still being bad. Maybe some new sleazy business. George says the feds are going slow on that, building a case. That's why they haven't brought him in yet. Meantime they're checking you out."

"How come?"

"If they indict Sanchez for being part of your getting shot," Gabriela said, "you're the star witness, right?"

"I'd have to testify, sure," I said. "I can't pin it on him, though."

She nodded. "You ever do anything down there that you don't want on the front page?"

I trusted Gabriela, but I was not about to tell her the story of Al and Alicia and me in the tunnel. And I decided to keep Sanchez's visit to myself. If she thought it was a social call, she would be suspicious. If she knew that he made threats, she would push for an on-the-record interview now.

"You need to look good," she said. "No nasty surprises?"

I shook my head. "He can't have anything that bad on me," I said. "Gabriela, you've spent lots of time down there. Everybody bent some regulations. Al and I took you out on runs sometimes without an okay from the boss. That was against the rules. That kind of thing, sure. But I never stole, I never smuggled, I never hurt anybody on purpose."

"I know all that," she said. "The U.S. attorneys think they know something else."

We sat for a few minutes, savoring the quiet. Maybe it was nap time in the nearby classrooms. I wondered if Sandra Crain had come to a school like this for her health clinics. Maybe she sat on a bench like this, enjoying the silence or the children's laughter when it came, as it surely would.

Gabriela and I got up and walked toward the parking lot.

"So how's your life?" I asked her.

"Could be worse. They don't have me writing about recipes yet, or adoptable bunnies for the neighborhood sections."

"Maybe you'll get a Pulitzer out of the grand jury story," I said.

"I hope you're not the headline, Brinker." She said it with genuine kindness in her voice.

"How about your real life? Away from the paper."

She laughed. "Dull as dirt. The TV babes get all the interesting guys."

"Baloney," I said. She cocked her head and flashed me a small mysterious smile. By the time I met her, Dolores and I were together, so romance was never an issue. But I liked that smile.

At her car, we shook hands. I held hers for an extra second.

"Thank you for the information," I said. "And the encouragement."

"Thank me by keeping in touch on this."

"Okay."

"And if I hear anything, and it doesn't compromise the story…," she began.

"Call me," I said.

She smiled.

"Chris Montez, 1966," she said. "Gotcha."

ELEVEN

MO CRAIN CALLED my cell phone as I drove to Al and Anna's house.

"Any luck?" he asked.

"Slow going," I said. "Mostly confirming what the cops had."

"I figured," he said.

"I won't bill you for the last hour," I said, remembering the talk with Gabriela. "I learned more about me than about your case."

"That's like selling cars," he said. "You learn things about yourself. The way other people see you. How far you'll go to close the deal. Keep me posted, Brinker."

A blue and yellow decorative tile on the Avilas' door read, MI CASA ES SU CASA. I knocked lightly with one hand while opening the door with the other. Dolores had come straight from the television station. She was putting together more videotapes of her work to take to New York. She, Al, and Anna were standing at the window, watching the girls play in the yard beside the house.

"Did we ever have that kind of energy?" I said, and they turned to greet me. Dolores was smiling and laughing. Her little nieces had that effect.

Al gave me a beer. We all sank into chairs around a heavy old wooden coffee table covered with the girls' toys.

"How's the big case?" Anna asked.

We were in the family room that Al and Anna built several years ago, when Al made lieutenant and the school district promoted Anna to principal. They still lived in the house they bought when we graduated from college.

"Weird," I said. "The murderer just vanished. It's as if he pulled the trigger, then fell off the planet."

I told them what I knew. It didn't take long.

"Time for a happier topic," Anna said.

"Amen," Dolores said.

"Look what I found in the scrapbook today," Al said. "I'm going to have this blown up and framed."

He held up a photograph of three young people standing at a beachside bar.

"Who is that handsome devil?" I said, pointing to the picture of my younger self.

"And where was I?" Dolores asked.

"Mom wouldn't let you come with us," Anna said. "In fact, she wasn't too thrilled about my going."

"We were mature college students," I said. "You were a high school kid."

"As a police officer, I must tell you," Al said, "if Brink had taken you across an international border for immoral purposes, he would have been subject to arrest."

"Sure," Dolores said. "They're really strict about that at spring break in Rocky Point."

Rocky Point is Puerto Peñasco, a beach town in Mexico, four or five hours west of Tucson.

"God's gift to the Tucson police," Al said. "We have a university with twenty-five thousand students and hardly any spring break problem here. All the worst rowdies are in another sovereign nation. I don't want to go there anymore, but I love the place."

"What about you guys?" Dolores asked. "Were you rowdies?"

"I conducted myself in a manner befitting a future law enforcement officer," Al said.

"Oh, yeah, right," Anna broke in. "In fact, these two clowns pretty much tied for the Corona chugging championship. I also heard reports of inappropriate sexual activity."

"Reports?" Al said. "You were there."

Anna gave him an obvious kick under the table.

"More things were inappropriate in those days," Anna said. "When Al and I got married, I didn't get my driver's license changed for a few weeks. Some motel clerk in San Diego actually asked us for ID and gave us grief about the different names. He didn't believe we were married. Now nobody cares."

Dolores turned to me and said, "And you? Were you a wild man?"

"Never arrested," I said.

"The *Star* did a story on spring break last year," Anna said. "The kids figure it's Mexico, so the rules didn't apply. The cops look the other way because the college students and other American tourists keep the place solvent. So it's like renting a different life for a week, then giving it back at the border when you come home. You could do anything down there. None of it mattered."

Anita and Alicia came running in.

"Speaking of rowdies," I said. I grabbed both girls and gave them TV-wrestling hugs, complete with exaggerated grunts. They kicked and wriggled and giggled, half trying to break away from me. I had an arm around each little waist, ready to hoist each girl. But the shoulder sent me a warning pain.

"You can't do that anymore!" Anita hollered. "We're too big."

"I work out with your dad," I said. "I lift little dumbbells all the time."

"We're not dumbbells!" Alicia shouted.

"Yeah, you are, but it's not your fault," I said. "It's hereditary."

"What's 'hereddy' mean?" Alicia asked.

She still had a hint of Mexico in her voice, but it attracted no special notice. Many children born in Tucson sound the same way. The cheerful, healthy child was an Avila kid now, outwardly showing no sign of the tunnels.

"It means we're a lot like our parents," I told her.

Alicia put her arms around Al's leg. She looked up at him and said, "So I'm like you and Mommy?"

"That's it," Al said. "We're the 'A' Team."

"Okay," she said happily, and proceeded to wrestle the six-foot cop to the floor.

Al looked up from the carpet and caught me smiling at the two of them.

"Crime pays," he said.

Anna had gone into the kitchen and now she reappeared to move us toward the dinner table.

"You should have kids. You'll be a good daddy," Anna said.

"Don't look at me," I told her. "Dolores is the one who's leaving town."

"Anna's always been like that," Dolores said. "She moves fast."

"True. I snagged Al in the first grade," Anna said.

Arf, the Avilas' golden retriever, came sniffing around to see if the squealing girls were okay. I released them. The dog ran down the hall, looking back to be sure the girls followed him.

"Bet they don't have entertainment like this in New York," I said to Dolores.

"No," she said. "Just Broadway."

Over dinner, we made small talk and ignored the Crain case. Anna kept looking at Dolores, then at me, gauging the state of the relationship, I suppose. At ten o'clock, with the girls put to bed and the dishes washed and drying, we turned on the news. The station was one of Dolores's competitors, so we laughed at the anchors' phony banter.

"Ugh," Dolores said. "Small stories and big hair."

"Why do we watch this junk?" I asked.

Dolores said, "I read an interview with some network executive. He believed that viewers just want to know two things. Is the world safe and is my family safe? Once you've told them that, you can put anything on."

"What was the top story tonight?" Al asked.

"Bus accident in Michigan," I said.

"Guess we're safe, then," Al said.

"When I first went private," I said, "I had a missing kid case. The father was a newspaper manager. He told me that the only things anybody reads in the paper now are the sports and Dear Abby."

"And Mo Crain's ads," Al said. "Somebody must read 'em, and watch 'em on TV, because he keeps buying 'em."

Anna sighed. "No Mo tonight. It's so grim."

I stood up. "No more anything tonight. I've got an early start tomorrow."

Dolores and I said our thanks and good nights. We had each parked in the Avila driveway and we walked out there together.

"I don't remember that story about the newspaper manager," she said.

"I told you. You were pretty busy with a special report then, I think."

"What happened to the kid?" she asked.

I remembered perfectly. It had been my first case, and for a brief, shining moment there, I was batting a thousand.

"Found her," I said. "She was fifteen years old and she went to live in Los Angeles with some guy she met at a club downtown. He said he knew a lot of movie stars. Turned out he was a part-time parking lot attendant at a restaurant in North Hollywood. Full-time drug dealer. He beat her up and shared her with his cokehead pals."

Dolores stood rigid by her car.

"You don't remember this?" I asked.

She shook her head.

I said, "The good news is, this poor kid had one moment when she needed to reach out. She phoned a girlfriend back here and told her the whole story. She wouldn't say where she was, but she gave the girlfriend a number to call her back."

"Needed some human contact," Dolores said.

"Exactly. I showed up two hours later to interview the girlfriend. Talk about beginner's luck. She handed me the phone number the minute I told her what I wanted. I didn't have to cut through any teenage solidarity bull. She was scared for her friend and she wanted grown-up help. Al traced the number for me. Then I went over there and picked her up. She said her boyfriend went off with some other woman. She was alone in this crappy apartment with no food and no money. I drove her home to Tucson. She cried all the way, but she never asked to go back. She never tried to get away. And when we got home, you should have seen her parents' faces. They were almost overcome with joy and gratitude."

We stood quietly on the drive for a moment.

"When you were in high school," I asked her, "did you ever have the cops come for career day?"

"Probably," she said. "I went to the media career rooms, though."

"Al and I went to the cops' talks. One year, a couple of homicide detectives came. They told us about their nastiest cases. Didn't leave much out. Exit wounds and maggots and all the really revolting things. And some smart-ass kid raised his hand and said, 'I hear a lot of cops kill themselves because you see so much horrible stuff. How come you guys haven't killed yourselves?'

"Everybody laughed, kind of embarrassed by this kid, but they realized that beneath the attitude, he had a meaningful question. How can cops stand twenty, twenty-five years of poking around in dead bodies and people's grief? And this big, gruff cop looked right at him, and said very quietly, 'Because if we succeed, we get to tell people what happened. Maybe why it happened. We can bring them a little peace.' Even kids understood that. Nobody said another word.

"Sometimes," I said, "I think that's why I stayed in work like this. The look on those parents' faces, even on the girl's. I brought them a little peace. Maybe I can even do that for Mo Crain."

Dolores was biting her lip. She seemed to be holding her breath.

"See you at home," I said.

She got into her car and I let her back out first. I turned to the house window and waved good night to Anna. She stood there with the living room curtain parted just a little, watching with a big sister's gentle smile.

TWELVE

I WAS THINKING, last time in a long time, and Dolores picked it up.

"I'll be back in a few days," she said. "Nothing is decided until then."

"Dolores," I said, "it's okay. We both know you're going."

She moved closer and buried her head against my neck, but did not answer.

"What do you want to do tomorrow, before the plane?" I asked.

"La misa en Español," she said. "Come with me?"

"I'll pray that your flight is canceled. Bad weather. Like in *L.A. Story.*"

She laughed softly, her breath on my throat. "This is Tucson," she said. "Even in bad weather, we still have fifty miles' visibility."

"There could be clear-air turbulence at New York," I said. "You can't see it in advance."

"Point taken," Dolores said. "How about mass?"

"I'll go with you," I said.

SAN AGUSTÍN WAS the patron saint of Tucson. The cathedral name had been Anglicized to St. Augustine's, but two of its five Sunday masses were in Spanish. The eight o'clock mass featured mariachi music. It was more than a curiosity for tourists. Someone had the idea in the 1960s: use Mexican music to bring the faithful back to a central city church. It worked. The sanctuary was almost full, even on this summer morning.

"You know the joke about the Spanish-language mass here?" Dolores asked as we entered. She took my arm, moved close, spoke softly. "My mother told me this. She said, 'First, the mass was in Latin. Only the priests could understand it. Then they switched to English, and only the priests could understand it.'"

"Not completely true," I said, laughing.

Dolores smiled. "True enough to be funny, Mama thought."

"Welcome to the new Southwest," I said. "They switched to Spanish and got five hundred people this morning."

"Four hundred, maybe," Dolores said. "You old ex-law enforcement guys always overestimate crowds."

An usher led us to a pew about halfway down the long center aisle. He was an old Mexican man with a deeply burnt tan and widely bowed legs. His western-cut suit had grown tight around the midsection and the slacks rode low beneath his belly. I wondered if his grandsons still drove cattle on a ranch near town. We sat in front of an old woman with a stern, pious face. A black lace mantilla covered her white hair.

This was Dolores's territory, not mine. She and Anna had come here with their parents. Every few months, and always at difficult times, Dolores was drawn back to this church. She knelt at the rail to pray. I sat, looking at the slender stained-glass windows, always vividly backlit in the Arizona sun, and colorful Mexican-Indian tapestries hung high on the walls. When I turned to see the windows behind me, the woman in the mantilla was smiling at Dolores. She frowned at me.

Dolores rose and stood beside me as the trumpet sounded the first notes of "Las Mañanitas." The priest's procession moved forward to the altar while a mariachi's clear voice sang in Spanish of a perfect day's beginning:

Qué linda está la mañana
How beautiful is the morning
en que vengo a saludarte…
in which I come to greet you…

Dolores knew the words and sang along, as I translated silently. Two rows ahead of us, a very young woman ran her fingers affectionately through the shiny black hair of a little boy who looked much like her. The child paid no attention to the mass and wriggled in his Sunday-best clothes, but stayed on his good behavior. The woman did not look old enough to be his mother, although an expression of utter devotion gave her away.

During the prayers and hymns, Dolores stared around the cathedral, watching the Hispanic faces with their hints of Tohono O'odham and Pasqua Yaqui, visages she would not see in New York. Several times, she smiled when her gaze settled on older parishioners. I realized that they must have been members here with her parents.

Finally, the priest began the familiar benediction:

Que el Señor nos bendiga y nos guarde…
May the Lord bless us and keep us…
y conceda su paz.
and give us Your peace.

We followed the procession out. Dolores looked back one final time as we reached the rear of the sanctuary. Then we stepped into the morning sun and San Agustín's bells rang as we walked away.

AT THE AIRPORT, we held hands and said little.

"The station is sending a car and driver to pick me up at LaGuardia," Dolores said. "Can you believe that?"

"I'll be here to drive you home," I said.

"Maybe I could put you on my expenses," she said.

When her flight was called, Dolores stood up quickly. "Better go," she said.

"You could board last," I said.

"They said first class could board now."

"Dolores," I said, "with what the station paid for that ticket, you can board whenever you want."

"I get nervous. I know it's silly, but I'm always afraid they'll leave without me."

"Just don't miss the one coming home."

"Wish me well, Brink."

"*Que te vaya bien,*" I told her.

We hugged. Her eyes glistened as she pulled away from me and walked to the jetway door. I was vaguely aware of other passengers boarding and the plane pushing back from the terminal building and taxiing away.

In a few moments, it raced back into view. It used most of the runway before lumbering up into the steamy head wind. Like everything else about Dolores's leaving, this was over before I realized it. The jet bored through the summer haze. I caught one quick flash of sunlight on the fuselage, then she was gone.

THIRTEEN

MY OFFICE IS DOWNTOWN. Tucson was once a Spanish presidio, a walled encampment built to protect the inhabitants from intruders. Of course, if you ask the Indians, the Spanish were the intruders. Hohokams farmed the Santa Cruz valley almost two thousand years ago. According to one version of history, Indians gave Tucson its name, Chuk-son, which roughly means "at the foot of a dark mountain." Today, the dark mountain has a huge *A* painted on it, whitewashed by University of Arizona freshmen, painted green for St. Patrick's Day, and set ablaze by the fireworks show on the Fourth of July.

The garrison walls crumbled centuries ago. Lunkhead municipal planning keeps people away now. The sleepy, rundown centro houses mainly law firms and government offices. Hopeful antique and art galleries come and go, replaced by others with equally dreary prospects. Downtown once boasted a first-class restaurant, but its landlord, a second-class museum, wanted more space. The evicted chef reluctantly took his toque to the booming suburban foothills, where he prospered.

At the edge of El Presidio Historic District, lawyers had converted old *casitas*—little houses—into offices. The adobe walls were painted, the wooden interiors restored. The better firms built carports for their partners and clients. As I drove into the Allejandro & Katz lot, a man in khaki slacks and a blue and yellow golf shirt was leaning against a new forest-green Mercedes, watching me. His license plate read JOINTZ.

"Good morning," I said, as he stepped away from his car and started toward the law firm's rear entrance.

"Are you Brinker?" the man asked. He clenched both hands by his sides.

I stopped. He was tall, with the righteously thin look of a serious runner. His light brown hair was cut very close. The skin held tight under his chin. His car and clothes indicated a man of substance, but his eyes glowed unnaturally and his body language rang alarm bells. My gut tightened and I wished for a gun.

"I'm Carl Nelson," the man said. "I came down here this morning to tell you politely and once only. Do not bother my wife. Keep your nose out of things that are not your business."

He spoke in the loud voice and flat tone of a man trying desperately to sound confident.

"Doctor," I said, "I called your wife for an interview. She invited me to see her. When she ended our conversation, I left. Maybe she's bothered by something, but not by me."

"Don't get smart with me, mister," Nelson said. Now his face reddened with anger. "You want to talk to my wife or come into my home, you get my permission. You don't clear it with some glorified car salesman."

"You seem awfully perturbed about a short conversation with your wife," I said.

"You heard me," Nelson said.

"Well, thanks for your input," I said. I turned again toward the rear entrance.

Nelson moved fast and got between me and the door. I tried to watch the man's eyes and hands for a signal of violence.

"Just stay back, mister," Nelson said. "You're in way over your head here. And your rich and famous client won't be able to help you, because he and a lot of other people could get hurt. I'm warning you. Let this thing go. Tell Mo Crain to let it go."

He stormed back to his car, then turned and shouted, "I'm doing you a favor! Stay out of it!" He slammed the door hard when he got in, and drove off too fast for the narrow streets. I realized that Mercedes was one of the few car lines that Mo Crain did not sell.

Inside, I asked David Katz if he knew Dr. Nelson.

"Carl Nelson," Katz said. "Medium player in the local medical establishment. Not a superstar, but he has a very successful orthopedic surgery practice. He's on a few artsy and charity committees in town. Shows up at some of the right parties."

"Is he in the same league as Crain?" I asked.

"Nobody's in Mo's league." Katz smiled. He reminded me of a hip Buddha, with his round body and sly, knowing smile beneath a bald dome. He and his partner, Rubén Allejandro, made quite a pair. Katz, smooth and bookish, resplendent in tailored suits. Allejandro, a jeans-and-aloha-shirt guy with his Pancho Villa moustache and all the sweetness of a cornered javelina. But he was even better than his reputation. He delivered for Al and Anna—and me, for that matter—in the days after we pulled Alicia out of the Nogales tunnel. What he called "productive contact" with authorities on the Mexican side generated the paperwork for a thoroughly legal adoption in Arizona.

"'Productive contact'?" I asked him.

"Hey, amigo," he replied, in the tone you say "friend" to

someone who isn't. "You work your patch of the border, and I'll work mine."

But if he held indelicate probing against me, he never showed it. When I asked him for a job, as many ex-cops and Border Patrol agents did, he steered me down the hall to his partner.

I asked Katz now, "You know anything about Mrs. Nelson?"

"A dish, but a little flaky," Katz said. "Since neither Mo nor she is my client, I can gossip freely. Rumor has it, not from any lawyers, mind you..."

"Of course not."

"Rumor has it the Nelsons experienced some marital difficulties and recently sought counsel, but decided against pursuing legal solutions."

I said, "Do the rumors suggest what their troubles were?"

"Person or persons unknown occupying a Nelson bed," Katz said. "I heard that the doc was, shall we say, extramaritally active. Does he still have that JOINTZ vanity plate? That apparently speaks to his social life as well as his surgical specialty."

Katz chuckled at his own joke.

"My wife says she heard similar stories about Mrs. Nelson. Could be a gender gap in the reporting, or maybe they're both fooling around. Or maybe it's all bullshit."

I liked Katz's local knowledge. It filled in the gaps for me after several years down at the border. Even better, I appreciated his lawyer's habit of qualifying information. Katz loved rumors, but he knew how to distinguish them from facts. I tried to provide equally complete reports in the investigations I handled for Katz's firm. It was a solid partnership. I got office space and a steady retainer. The lawyers got dependable information.

"Why would he say I'm in over my head?"

Katz thought about it for a moment.

"You know," he said, "I once tried a products liability case against the manufacturer of a single-engine airplane that crashed and killed my client's husband. To be sure I understood piloting and the plane involved, I took flying lessons. The instructors had a joke. They said, Who's the most dangerous person in the world? And most people would say Saddam Hussein or Bill Gates or someone similarly notorious or powerful. The answer was: the most dangerous person in the world is a doctor with two hundred hours in a Beech Baron."

"I don't get it," I said.

"Neither did I, at first," Katz said. "It's an in-joke. It took forty hours of flight time to get a private pilot's license, as I recall. So when a pilot has two hundred hours of experience, five times the minimum, he thinks he's pretty good. He may become overconfident and careless. If he's a doctor, he has enough money to buy a hot little plane like a Baron. The moral is, put a highly confident person—like a surgeon—in something he can't quite handle, and he'll be too proud to admit his inadequacy. With aviation, that means he flies when he shouldn't. In bad weather, for example, or when he's not fully alert. Or perhaps he hasn't mastered control of a high-performance airplane. He might try to bluff his way through. He doesn't think he can fail. It's a prescription for disaster."

I took a mint from the Baccarat candy jar on Katz's desk.

"The point is," he said, "Dr. Nelson may be the one who is in over his head. And it's making him act foolishly."

"Nelson did seem close to some sort of crash," I said.

"He may well be," Katz said. "Considering the circumstances, his problem may be at home. It certainly sounds connected to Mo Crain's situation. Maybe both. Watch your back, my boy. And if he threatens you on my property again, tell me at once. He'll find out what being in over one's head really means."

"Thanks," I said.

"You're welcome. Now, if you have time between Unsolved Mysteries, I have a little more prosaic investigation for you. A scoundrel is trying to separate one of my favorite insurance companies from its money. If my tip is correct, you should be able to nail this greedy fool before lunch."

RICHARD W. SMITH'S SWING was ungainly but aggressive. He could lift engine and transmission parts for eight hours a day. His thick arms and large hands seemed too big for the golf club, even with its long shaft and oversized metal head. No finesse game for him, I thought. Mr. Smith liked power golf. He lashed at the ball as if it were his enemy.

Which was true, as things were working out.

I took his picture. The 300mm lens, propped on the car window frame, showed Smith's smile as his supple upper body pivoted into the shot. He was claiming severe back injuries, suing a well-insured motorist for $400,000.

Greedy fool, indeed, I thought. Doctors weren't the only people who thought they could trick the world. This mechanic had his scam. Sandra Crain's murderer had one. But so far, the killer was right about being smarter than everyone else.

I switched from the still camera to video. In the viewfinder, Smith bent over easily to pick up balls on the putting green, then ran after the cart as his partners moved to the first tee. I turned off the camera and returned to my car, the day's insurance defense done. It's strange work. I felt like a grubby snoop and a righteous avenger at the same time.

The dashboard clock said 11:05 a.m. David Katz was right again.

FOURTEEN

I SPENT THE AFTERNOON looking through case materials in O'Mara's manila envelope. Making fun of the free-drinking, freeloading cop was easy, but the files revealed a thorough detective. He had pounded plenty of pavement since Mrs. Crain was killed. The envelope contained three months of credit card receipts and phone bills for Mo and Sandra. "Nothing," O'Mara had written, suggesting that he found no suspicious expenses or contacts.

He followed up every reasonable lead and even the goofy tips that plague any high-profile murder case. UFOs landed in the parking lot and aliens shot her when she refused to return with them to their planet. She knew the truth about all the Kennedy deaths. They committed suicide. The caller saw it happen. O'Mara left careful notes and comments on each contact.

Sandra Crain had been hit by three .22-caliber bullets. Crime scene investigators found shell casings on the pavement near her body. The killer was either a rank amateur or, more likely, a pro who had no fear of being matched with a murder weapon. He ditched the gun fast. If it were ever found, it would be out in the desert with no fingerprints. Robbery was not even an issue, with $84 and change in a $250 purse, and a brand-new Lexus not taken.

O'Mara had been more meticulous with Linda Nelson than she realized. His notes indicated that she was at her allergist's office when Sandra Crain was murdered. She said that her husband had gone to a medical convention in Scottsdale, about a hundred miles away. O'Mara had checked and learned that Dr. Nelson did, in fact, attend. He could not confirm Nelson's exact whereabouts at the time of the murder. Hundreds of docs were drifting in and out of seminars and meetings.

Without expecting to find anything useful, I read O'Mara's record of telephone calls confirming Crain's presence in Vancouver. Mo had arrived at midday on Monday and was met at the airport by Catharine Richard ("ree-SHARD," O'Mara had scribbled), the executive director of Westfriends, the western Canadian business liaison to United States business. She dropped him off at his hotel, the Four Seasons on Howe Street. From his suite, Crain spoke for fifteen minutes by phone with Richard (O'Mara wrote "RICH-ard") Cannington, a Vancouver banker who served as chairman of Westfriends. That evening, Crain dined with Catharine Richard and discussed the week's agenda.

Tuesday and Wednesday were jammed with meetings. He conferred with the Downtown Business Association. He lunched with Jock Proctor, described in O'Mara's notes as "big car dlr, MC of BC," which I took to mean the Mo Crain of British Columbia. He met with the Greater Vancouver Auto Dealers Association. On Wednesday afternoon, he conferred with Cannington at the banker's office. He took a cab from the Four Seasons to the airport on Thursday morning, checked into the United Red Carpet Lounge, and waited there for his flight. Catharine Richard, Richard Cannington, Jock Proctor, and the hotel and airline employees could account for virtually every moment of Crain's time in Vancouver.

As Al Avila had said, the alibi was solid gold. Mo could not have killed his wife. At least not by himself.

O'Mara even checked the Canadian witnesses' whereabouts at the time of the murder. This struck me as an absurdly long shot, but the detective apparently had reached the point where you try your wildest guesses. He had the daily calendars of Richard Cannington, Jock Proctor, and some other Vancouver members of Westfriends. Catharine Richard had gone to New York City on business Tuesday night. O'Mara had confirmed her journey with the airline and the Plaza Hotel. Overkill, I thought, but CYA is a survival skill in the police bureaucracy. No cop commander would be able to fault him.

By four o'clock, the case was a blur. I had that nagging feeling, so familiar to investigators, that some tiny fact lurked there. It was waiting to be discovered, but I couldn't spot it.

I was locking O'Mara's papers in the desk when Al called.

"I just got a heads-up from a pal at county," he said. "Sheriff's deputies took a domestic abuse call in the foothills. Guess who got beat up today?"

AL MET ME AT the University Medical Center emergency room. He took us through the AUTHORIZED MEDICAL PERSONNEL ONLY swinging doors. When he showed his badge to the head nurse, she led us to a row of curtained-off recovery cubicles. She looked inside one, spoke very softly to the woman there, then nodded permission for us to enter.

"I paged O'Mara," Al said. "He hasn't called back. Maybe he'll want it, maybe not. County may have told him already. Anyway, this gives you a few minutes."

I thanked him. He walked away toward the lobby. I parted the curtain and stepped inside.

When I saw her last, she was the fashionable foothills lady

with a strained social smile and a deep tan. Now the smile was gone, replaced by a cut lip. She had a black left eye. The tan failed to conceal an interior pallor of pain. Her left wrist was wrapped in an Ace bandage.

"I'm so sorry, Mrs. Nelson," I said.

"Not your fault," she said. Her voice was thick and her cut mouth labored to get the words right.

"Your husband came to my office. He was angry about our talk. I should have called to warn you. I just had no idea that he'd take it out on you."

"I've had that idea for a long time," she said. "He's angry about everything. If it hadn't been this, it would have been something else."

"Where is he now?" I asked.

She shrugged. "For all I know, he's right here in the hospital," she said. "Healing someone."

"Did you file a complaint with the deputies?"

She shifted on the examination table. She winced and held her abdomen.

"There are hurts you can't see," she said.

"What about the complaint?" I asked.

She shook her head. "I have to go back there," she said. "I have to live with him."

"Do you?"

"Oh, God, don't give me the battered spouse speech. I got that from the deputies already. I'm going home."

"Are you sure? How about a hotel?"

"He won't come home tonight," she said. "I know the routine."

The nurse parted the curtain and stepped inside.

"Mr. Brinker? Lieutenant Avila asked me tell you that Detective O'Mara can't come tonight. He'll arrange to see Mrs. Nelson sometime tomorrow."

When the nurse left, I said, "I can take you home."

"No," she said. "I'll take a cab."

"It's no trouble."

"I'll take a cab."

"Okay."

She pulled a cardigan sweater over her shoulders. It was still hot outside, but the sweater covered little spots of blood on her blouse.

"Mrs. Nelson, I need to ask you one thing," I said. "Did this have anything to do with Sandra Crain's murder?"

She tried looking around the tiny cubicle but there was nothing to see. Her eyes came back to mine.

"May I borrow twenty dollars?" she asked.

I gave her the money. She held my arm as we walked to the cab stand. I helped her in and gave the driver her address, up in the safe and exclusive gated community.

I went across the street to Nelson's office building. He had his own suite, not affiliated with the university's teaching orthopedic surgeons. Three women sat behind the reception desk, answering phones, filling out insurance forms, and looking anxious. I approached the woman whose window said APPOINTMENTS and asked to see Nelson.

"Oh, I'm sorry," she said. "I thought we called everyone. Dr. Nelson had to cancel his appointments today. What was your name, sir?"

"I didn't have an appointment," I said. "Did he say why he canceled?"

She looked stricken. One apparently didn't question a physician's actions.

"I'm sorry," she said, gracing me with a frosty smile. "Did you wish to make a later appointment?"

"How about tomorrow?"

"Oh, he's fully booked tomorrow. Let's see." She clicked her computer keys. "He does have an hour available two weeks from tomorrow."

"Never mind," I said. "I'll find him."

He won't come home, Linda Nelson had said. With a lucrative medical practice, neither would he vanish over a "mere" wife beating. Shame might keep him away for a day or two, but at his fees, not much longer.

I checked the hotel closest to the hospital. The small outdoor parking lot was easy to cruise. No sign of the green Mercedes with its vanity plate. The university garage by the Marriott had a few cars in the hotel guest section, but not Nelson's.

Tucson is a tourist capital and a major way point on Interstate 10. The area has more than a hundred hotels, motels, and guest houses. There was no chance of driving to even a fraction of them. That meant calling the registration desks.

I ruled out the expensive resorts—he might run into friends there—and decided to concentrate on the impersonal chain motels. Nelson would probably have credit cards and use his own name. I stopped at the University Boulevard Starbucks for takeout coffee, then drove to my office and began working the phones. Two hours later, no hotel or motel had acknowledged having Carl Nelson registered.

One more call.

Linda Nelson answered on the second ring.

"I just wanted to see if you're okay," I said.

"It could be worse," she said. Her voice was still thick from pain and medicine and tears.

"Yeah," I said. "He could have killed you."

"I'm not sure that would be worse," she said.

"Have you heard from him?"

"No. I won't tonight. Tomorrow he'll come back acting as though nothing happened."

"Do you need anything?"

"No."

I took a deep breath. "Could he be with someone tonight?"

"If he is," she said, "I don't want to know about it."

"I'll say good night, then. I really need to talk to you soon about what happened."

"Good night," she said. And after a pause, "Thank you."

I hung up and thought about Dr. Nelson's bizarre behavior. Something I had told Dolores came back to me. It was the abuser of a runaway girl I found. *He beat her up and shared her with his cokehead pals,* I remembered. Drugs. Maybe enough to make Nelson beat up his wife…but enough to kill someone?

Not much of a lead, I thought. But as the song says, a little bit is better than *nada*.

FIFTEEN

AL AND I STOOD in the batting cage at Pitch-and-Putt. Anna was walking the girls around the miniature golf course. The pitching machine threw anemic fastballs, waist-high. Al crushed every one into the canvas backstop, grunting and grinning as he made contact.

"Barry Bonds's muscle and Sammy Sosa's smile," I said.

"Right," he said, laughing. "Now if TPD would just give me a three-year deal for forty-two million."

He smashed the next pitch. Extra bases to center field, probably.

"You know one thing I keep wondering about in the Crain case?" Al asked.

I took the bat and stepped into the box. "What?"

"Suppose it was anybody else who got killed. Not Mrs. Crain. What's the first thing we'd all think of?"

"Drogas," I said.

"Sure," he said. "Quick hit, clean getaway, no apparent motive. If the victim had been anybody else, we'd be thinking drugs."

I hit my first pitch late and pushed it to the fence that would be right field. My strength and arm speed had never completely returned since the shooting at Lovers Crossing.

"O'Mara checked," I said. "Obviously Sandra wasn't doing drugs, and Mo comes up clean on everything."

"I know, I know," Al said. "But that's just it. The idea is so far out. Homicide never gave it a hard look."

The next pitch seemed slower, or maybe I was just catching on. I met it solid, but it still flew to the right corner. The hard contact rippled from my hands to my sore shoulder. Foul ball, probably. I wondered if Monica Seles ever got all her racket speed back.

"It's always drugs now, isn't it?" I said.

"Most of the time," Al said.

"Did we waste all those years on the Patrol, Al?"

"No," he said emphatically. "It was a good job when we started. We protected the borders. We even helped out the immigrants when we could."

Off to our right, Anita was crying and stomping her feet because she couldn't hit her blue golf ball through the moving windmill. The younger Alicia watched with amused tolerance, as if to say, This isn't what I'd call a problem, sister.

I said, "We did help, didn't we?"

"Yep," Al said. "But things changed on us, *hermano*. Changed despite us. No more rules on the border anymore. Too much poverty and corruption down there. Too much money and corruption up here. Drug war and cheap labor are making a lot of people rich."

"When you and I got out of the academy and started at Nogales, I remember the first people I stopped," I said. "A mother and father and a little girl. They had come all the way up from Guatemala. The girl was maybe four, and she looked exactly like her mother. They both had little moles in the same spot on their chins, and they both had this crooked little smile."

"Didn't even process them, did you?" Al said.

"No. We couldn't arrest them, because there was no place

to hold families. So we'd just write them citations and say, be in court on whatever day. And of course, they'd head for Tucson or Phoenix or L.A. and get lost. They never showed up."

"I had a bunch of those myself," Al said.

"So one day, I'm on patrol north of Nogales with Sally Moreno. You remember her?"

"Yeah. Didn't she marry a DEA guy and move to Miami?"

"Right. This time I'm thinking about, she was new on the Patrol. We see a couple trudging north along the old highway. It's July, about a hundred and ten outside already, and this couple is carrying a baby. The little guy couldn't have been a year old, and they're dragging him through the Arizona desert in summer. They'd all have been dead in an hour."

Al was nodding, probably remembering a bunch of those, too.

"So we stop them," I said. "They were out of water. The baby was crying. They looked almost grateful to be picked up. It was the family rule again. No arrest, just tell them to show up in court. They said okay, and they asked us for a ride back to Nogales. While we're driving, Sally leans over the seat to go gitchey-goo with the little boy. She plays with him for a minute and then gets quiet. Finally she says, 'Brink, I've never seen this couple before, but I have seen this baby. A week ago.'"

The pitching machine had been still for a while. Nobody was waiting, so Al and I stood there, leaning on the fence, watching Anna and the girls struggle with number 12, the double humpback hole.

I said, "Sally started in on this couple, firing questions about the baby. They caved in right away. The smugglers were renting babies to the illegals."

"Renting babies?" Al said.

"Yeah. The deal was, you'd take a baby, cross the border, and turn yourself in to the first Border Patrol agent you saw. You say you're a family, so you get a ticket and you're allowed to stay in the States until your court date. Then you meet the smuggler, give back the baby, and go to wherever you're headed."

"After my time," Al said. "I never heard about that one."

"Turns out they were doing it in Texas, too," I said. "It even made the paper down there, but nobody told us to watch for it. Typical INS screwup."

Al asked, "Where did they get the babies?"

"Sometimes the parents were smugglers and used their own babies," I said. "Sometimes the smugglers just bought babies. Their mothers couldn't afford to keep them. Some guy comes along, gives a poor girl a couple of hundred dollars, and says the baby gets to grow up in the States. What's the girl going to do?"

"What happened to the babies?"

"They got recycled, mostly, I guess. Used again. We know that happened with the one that Sally spotted. But you know, in the desert, when we found bodies, some of them were babies."

He stood there, in that still way of his, looking into the distance.

"There's an even bigger business now," I said. "Smuggling babies out for good. Mexican kids are winding up in New York and Chicago and God knows where. They get some phony papers, have a woman say she's the mother, and carry the baby right across the border. Then they set up an adoption."

"Like I say," Al said, "things changed on us."

"Well," I said, "we got out alive and fairly honest. And we got Alicia out of the tunnels. That should count for something."

Al put more money in the pitching machine. "You still in touch with Hector?" he asked.

"Not someone I want to be in touch with," I said.

"He's still The Man with drugs down there, isn't he?"

"That's what I hear."

"So if this Crain thing has a drug connection, he'd probably know."

"Maybe."

"Does he still owe you a favor?"

"I suppose. I hadn't really planned on collecting anything from him, Al. I get caught cozying up to a drug dealer and the state will yank my ticket in a split second."

"Yeah, I agree. Anna and Dolores won't like it, either."

"I'd be unemployed and unloved," I said.

"Yeah. It's probably the worst plan of the year," Al said. "Got any better ideas?"

"Nope," I said. "Not a damn one."

SIXTEEN

HECTOR ORTIZ insisted on meeting on home ground, in Mexico.

"Things are a little warm along the fence these days," he said when I phoned him. "I really don't want to try going through the migra station into the States." I knew that he came often, but this was his play. "You're the one wants to talk, Brinker. You come down here to Pee Wee's playhouse."

His friends called him Pee Wee because he had been a shortstop when he played high school baseball in Tucson. He reminded a sportswriter of Pee Wee Reese, the Hall of Fame shortstop for the Brooklyn Dodgers. After it appeared in the newspaper, the name stuck.

He laughed. "Hey, it's no problem down here. We have strict gun control. Keeps us safe from you dangerous gringos."

The Mexican police had recently arrested a Phoenix man for bringing a pistol into the country. He had left it in his car's glove compartment and forgotten about it when he crossed the border. The man was thrown into a Sonoran prison and would not be released until the right people were bribed. The gun law reeked of hypocrisy, for Mexico's corrupt cops and *narcotraficantes* and muggers were rich with arms. American hunters with Mexican connections routinely got permission to bring in powerful weapons. But every few months, an unwary motorist from gun-friendly Arizona fell into the trap.

Mexico finally eased the rule, but nobody bets on reasonable law enforcement there. I locked my gun in David Katz's office safe and drove seventy miles south to Nogales. Most American auto insurance is no good in Mexico, so I parked in a tourist lot near the McDonald's on the U.S. side and took the pedestrian walkway around the pink stucco Port of Entry building that separated the two nations.

Out of the first world, into the third, just like that.

An indolent Mexican policeman in rumpled khaki leaned against a souvenir shop, watching the tourists stroll in. He wore a gun but no badge. I figured that if I asked him about it, he would give me the Fred C. Dobbs treatment. I kept moving and he paid me no attention. So much for immigration control.

Hector Ortiz's restaurant was a five-minute walk down Avenida Obregón. The street took its name from a revolutionary war general who twice outmaneuvered rivals for the presidency. He became known as a reformer, at least by Mexican government standards. Some people think he engineered the murder of his old rival, Pancho Villa. Just before Obregón's second term began, he was assassinated by a religious fanatic. Reform hasn't fared much better since.

Along Obregón's namesake street in Nogales, two relentlessly friendly young men pursued me for a block, offering absolutely genuine gold Rolexes for forty bucks. A special bargain just for me, they said. It's guaranteed, man.

Shops selling T-shirts and cheap curios dominated the sidewalks, their goods priced for haggling in American dollars. Several places had serapes, the traditional woven Mexican blankets, with National Football League team logos. Every other storefront sign advertised a discount doctor, dentist, or pharmacy.

In the restaurant lobby, a muscular guy who was not a waiter nodded his head toward the dining room. I let my eyes adjust to the dim light and walked in. Hector Ortiz sat at a corner booth, his back to a multicolored serape hanging on the wall. He was the only person in there. He kept a clear view of the lobby and the kitchen and rest room doors. I went back and sat down. We did not shake hands.

He took a cigar from his mouth and smiled, a laughing, toothy grin beneath a lush black moustache. Hector was handsome, and still a young man. Mid-twenties by now, I figured. He was like Mo Crain, in a perverse way: the dominant figure of his town's leading industry.

"You must want something bad, to come slumming down here," he said. His English was good and he liked to show off with Americans. He had spent two years in Tucson, illegally registered at a high school that wanted a good shortstop. Sonora produces fine young ball players. After graduation, he tried out for the Dodgers and Padres, but didn't make it.

"I need some information, Hector," I said. "I figure if anybody in Mexico has it, you do."

"Could be," he said. He pulled a fresh cigar from his shirt pocket. "You want a real cigar? Fidel's finest. Gotta smoke it here, though, or your old customs pals will bust your ass when you go home."

"Those things give you mouth cancer," I said. "I have enough medical problems from the last time I was down here."

He gave me the great smile again. "Yeah, you forgot to duck. Hey, your good friend Sanchez is still around, you know. Keeps the border safe for truth, justice, and the American way."

"If you know something about that," I said, "I'd like to hear it."

"I never did like that guy," Hector said. "Well, if I knew something about him, it might be good to save it until it could really help me. You know, like if I got arrested, maybe that information would be a get-out-of-jail card."

He laughed. "Course, if you ever need somebody to nail him in court for being part of your little accident, let me know. I have some friends I could get to testify, explain things your way."

"Hector," I said, "I don't think drug dealers perjuring themselves would help me much."

"Maybe it wouldn't be perjury," he said, watching me and smiling.

A waiter brought a bottle of dark gold tequila and two shot glasses. He placed them on the table without speaking. Hector poured.

"*Conmemorativo,*" he said. "Best there is." He raised his glass in a toast. "Here's to family values."

We drank and he filled the glasses again. The tequila was thick and rich, with none of the bitter burn of a cheap brand.

"How come they still let you work in Tourist Town?" I asked. "I heard they're cracking down."

Hector laughed. "I heard that, too," he said. "But I'm an upstanding citizen. I just paid for two new baseball fields in the city park. Grandstands, scoreboards, everything. Don't get my name on a plaque or anything, but people know."

"Mo Crain," I prompted.

"The car guy up in Tucson?"

"Yeah."

"What about him?"

"You know his wife was murdered a few months ago? Got shot down in the mall parking lot. No apparent motive."

Ortiz held up both hands. "Hey, man," he said. "I got nothing to do with that. Killing a woman that way, I would never even think of it. That's nasty shit, man. Colombians, Jamaicans, crazy fuckers, they do that. Not us."

"Remember that massacre in Ensenada a couple of years ago?" I asked. "Women, little babies, even."

"C'mon, man," Hector said. "Okay, some Mexicans, too. There are some bad people in every business. But those guys are locos. Not us. No way."

He downed the second tequila. I sipped mine and waited while he thought.

"Besides," he said, "we have no business with that Crain guy. Wish I did. Lot of American cars get assembled down here. Some interesting shipping possibilities there for my product, you know? But I never even met him."

"How about a doctor named Carl Nelson? Any of your people in Tucson do business with him?"

"I never heard of him," Hector said. "You want, I'll ask around. He a customer or what?"

"Maybe a customer," I said.

"Well, if he's just a street-level, I wouldn't know about him. We get a lot of doctors, though."

Another dead end, I thought. I drained the tequila glass. Ortiz poured another before I could stop him.

"Think the Dodgers can do it this year?" he asked.

"They need a shortstop," I said.

"They had their chance," he said. "Couple more years, maybe I'll buy the team, huh?"

I pushed back my chair. "Thanks," I said. "We'll call it even now, okay?"

He frowned and put his hand on my arm. "Wait a minute," he said. "I ain't done notheen for you yet, man."

He said it like an old Cheech and Chong routine, the accent exaggerated, so I'd know that he knew the English was wrong.

He hauled himself out of the booth and walked toward the lobby. He said something to the guy who had shown me in. The man produced a cell phone from his jacket pocket. Ortiz took it, turned away, and dialed a number. After a few moments, he began speaking softly. He listened for a long while, said something else, then hung up and gave the phone back to the other man.

"*Gracias a Dios* the U.S. cell phones work on this side," he said. "If I had to use the Telmex phone here, it would take an hour to get Mexico City. Cost a fortune. And I'd be lucky to hear anything."

"Don't the feds tap you?"

"Sure, but we have other phones for the heavy business stuff. And we switch the cell phones every few days. This one's brand-new. It has unlimited long-distance minutes in the States."

He slipped back into the booth and said, "Nothing about Mo Crain or Nelson."

"Okay," I said.

"Some rumors, though. My friends in Mexico City watch out for things happening up here in Sonora. Good market here, you know. We like to stay informed. Keep that competitive edge."

"What do you hear?"

"Somebody is spending a little money and asking unusual questions. Few months ago, someone bought a big house on the beach at Rocky Point. It was done through a Mexican company. And somebody involved in that deal wants to know how to come into Mexico without any problems, and how to go up to Tucson without the usual immigration checks."

"Your friends say who?" I asked.

"No," Hector said. "Only so much information available on short notice, for free."

Nothing about Hector's rumor seemed connected to the Crain case. The timing was right, though. The money activity started a few months ago, probably about when Mrs. Crain was murdered.

I knew two more things that made the story intriguing. Mexico had been a good place to run to, a country where well-placed dollars could keep the law off your back. And if the charge was murder, Mexico had an even greater value. It has no death penalty and refuses to extradite wanted criminals who face capital punishment. Mrs. Crain's killer would be a candidate for lethal injection in Arizona, but state prosecutors usually must promise not to seek the death penalty if they want a murder suspect extradited from Mexico. So even if the new Mexican politicians cleaned up government and bribery no longer kept you free, Mexican law might keep you alive.

"One thing," Hector said. "Some of this is being handled by a lawyer up in Tucson named Logan. William Logan. You know him?"

"He's been in the papers, I think. He might be one of Mo Crain's lawyers. That would be interesting."

"Logan is maybe doing stuff in his name, so the real player doesn't have to go public. Then if anybody wants to know, he can use that lawyer-client thing. That's a good rule, you know?"

"How do you get stuff like this?" I asked Hector. "I walk in here, hit you cold, and you come back from one call with an international business report."

He touched his glass to mine. "The value of an American high school education," he said.

I stood up and said, "Thanks for the favor. Now we're even."

"Naah," Ortiz said. "This was a little favor. I still owe you a big one."

When I reached the dining room door, Hector called to me.

"You're hobbling, man," he said. "That from getting shot?"

"Just a little stiff when I stand up," I said.

"I can get you some really excellent pain relief," he said. "Perc, codeine, cox-2 inhibitors, you name it, amigo. Free for you."

I laughed and left, walking back Avenida Obregón to the fence. It was twelve feet high, a rusty brown hue, made of interlaced steel beams. The Nogales government tried to cover parts of it with colorful signs and banners, but nothing could conceal its Berlin Wall ugliness.

Inside the pedestrian checkpoint, I watched for Sanchez. Border Patrol agents didn't hang around here, but I watched for Sanchez everywhere. A young customs officer I didn't recognize looked at my Anglo face and empty hands. He waved me through with no questions. Outside the building, members of the Joint Counter-Narcotics Task Force, wearing combat fatigues and JCNTF baseball caps, led their German shepherd through the auto lanes. The excited dog was on olfactory overload, darting happily from one car trunk to another.

Most JCNTF troops were advertised as Arizona Army National Guardsmen, but they didn't look like weekend warriors to me. Their quick eyes scanned the streets. They moved with the tight muscular glide of Green Berets. I watched them until they started watching me, then I headed back to my car.

SEVENTEEN

THAT NIGHT, Dolores called from New York. I was sitting outside, drinking a beer, with an empty chair beside me.

"Where are you staying?" I asked.

"The Plaza Athénée," she said. "It's right near Central Park. They got me a suite. It must cost a thousand dollars a night."

"Bet it doesn't have a sunset like I just watched."

"They don't even have sun in New York," she said. "I read an interview with Woody Allen. He said he likes gray days because they give more uniform light for filming street scenes. I have to remember that for my stories."

"Good," I said, laughing. "Start doing news stories like Woody Allen movies and you'll be working out here again."

"Oh, Brink, let me have some fun. They're treating me like a queen. This hotel, all *ricos* staying here, except me. And the car that met me at the airport, it was a stretch Lincoln, just for me. It was almost as big as your house. I felt ridiculous, but I loved it."

Your house, she said.

"Enjoy it while you can, Dolores. Once they have you under contract, they put you in a Motel 6 when you travel. You'll have to bunk with a makeup woman who snores."

"You're just trying to discourage me," she said.

"True."

"It went really well today, in case you were going to ask. I had an audition with the anchorman who's been here forever. We seemed to hit it off. The station manager was beaming afterward. Good chemistry, he said."

"Can't trust those guys," I said.

She laughed and said, "Come on. What have you been up to?"

"Went to Mexico today," I said. "Called in a favor from a drug dealer named Hector Ortiz."

Dolores was quiet for a moment, then spoke in a wary tone. "Let me get this straight," she said. "A drug dealer owed you a favor."

"Right," I said.

"Do I want to hear why a drug dealer owes you? This isn't something I might have to tell, say, a grand jury?"

"No," I said. "You know how Al and I go to ball games a lot?"

"Do I ever," she said. "Anna and I felt like baseball widows when spring training's in town."

Felt, she said. Past tense, already.

"You remember we even go to high school games sometimes," I said. "Years ago, before you and I got together, I heard about this hot kid playing shortstop for one of the 4-A teams. He was batting .500 and hitting a homer almost every game. That was Hector Ortiz. Al and I went out to see him. He was terrific. Went four for five that night. He had a homer and two doubles, I think. Smooth fielder, too. If you stay out here, you could come to those games with us."

"Brink, I'll have the Yankees."

"Umm. Anyway, a few months later, I'm on nights at the I-19 checkpoint. Hector Ortiz comes through, driving a tan Ford Explorer with Arizona plates, registered to somebody named Ortiz in Tucson. Daddy's car, I figured, and the boy's just been out for a prowl on the Mexican side. He acted a little nervous, but I was near the end of my shift, and I recognized him, so I waved him through."

"So," Dolores said, "if I wanted to smuggle some drugs, I should do it at the end of a work shift?"

I laughed. "We switch the schedules around," I said. "You never know when somebody's going home."

"So you sent this kid through."

"Right. My relief agent showed up then," I said. "I got my stuff together, signed out, and headed up I-19 to Tucson. It's dark. About ten miles from the checkpoint, I see a tan Explorer and another car pulled off on the shoulder. I wondered if it was Hector. I stopped, and when I got out, I heard scuffling and yelling in a culvert below the roadway. I ran down there and these two guys are beating the hell out him. I was still in uniform and I had my gun, so I ran into the culvert. They heard me coming and took off across the desert. Didn't even try to get to their car."

Over the phone line, I heard a pop from a bottle of something fizzy.

"Perrier?" I asked.

"You're psychic," she said. "I can do that. You're out on the patio. I'll bet you have a Dos Equis."

I smiled and drank some.

"Hector was hurting pretty bad. He kept looking at his right hand, his throwing hand. I helped him up to my car and took him back to the hospital in Nogales. He had broken ribs and some bad blows to the head. But his hand was only bruised."

"Lucky," Dolores said.

"I think they just wanted to hurt him, scare him," I said.

"If they planned a killing, they would have had a gun or a baseball bat. They probably would have done it by the time I got there."

I carried the wireless phone inside to find my ibuprofen.

"Next day, I went back to the hospital and asked him to tell me what happened. He wouldn't say anything. He said he appreciated what I did, but he couldn't tell me anything. You do this work for a while and you know when they mean it. So I said okay, and told him to watch who he hung out with, and good luck the next season. When I started out the door, he said, 'Thanks, man. I owe you.' And he remembered."

"What was it all about, do you suppose?" Dolores asked.

"I never found out. The whole thing could have been over a girl, for all I know. Or maybe he was getting his feet wet in the drug trade."

There was a rustling sound on the line. I pictured Dolores rolling over on the bed, maybe propping herself up on the pillows the way she did when she talked on the phone.

"Do you think it's right to ask him for help, when you know what he is now?" she asked.

"It's not comfortable," I said. "If solid citizens had answers, I'd ask them."

I heard a soft chime.

"It's the other line," Dolores said. "Hold on a second, Brink."

I took a couple of ibuprofen while I waited. They were big ones and I was over my limit for the day, but the walk through Nogales seemed to have irritated my hip.

The phone clicked and Dolores said, "Hi, again."

"Could you steal that phone?" I asked. "I like the nice little 'pong' sound it made."

"I'll look for one at Wal-Mart when I get home," she said. "So what's up?"

"That was the production manager," Dolores said. "He wants to set up the taping schedule for tomorrow morning. I said I'll call him back."

"I better let you go," I said.

"Yes," she said.

I was silent for a moment and she asked, "A penny for your thoughts?"

I told her.

"You could get arrested for thoughts like that," she said, sounding happy.

"Only if I'm reported," I said.

"Well, I'm a reporter," she said, "but I'm willing to suppress some news if it's to my advantage."

"You'll fit right in at the network," I said.

She laughed and said, "*Hasta mañana,* sourpuss."

EIGHTEEN

THE NEXT DAY, Dr. Nelson still didn't show up. When I called the hospital, I got a recording. "Dr. Nelson's office is closed for the rest of the week," the voice said. "We apologize for any inconvenience. We will contact you soon to reschedule appointments." It gave the number of another physician to call for emergencies.

O'Mara came by my office. He had reinterviewed Linda Nelson, but she would say nothing about her beating or a possible connection to the Crain case. He had to let it go because the abuse was out of his jurisdiction. She still refused to file a complaint or a missing persons report with the county sheriff.

The cop was about to leave when his beeper went off. I pushed my phone across the desk. He made his call, listened for a moment, then said, "Okay. Fifteen minutes." He hung up, pushed the phone back to me, and sighed.

"I was going to hit you up for another beer," he said. "But I think you and I should run out to the airport instead."

O'Mara didn't use the blue lights or siren, but he drove fast. He said nothing. We swung into the road that circles in front of the airport terminal building. At the long-term lot, a police cruiser blocked the entrance. The gate arm was up. The young patrolman directing traffic waved us through.

About fifty yards into the lot, we saw five more police cars parked around a large sedan. As we drew closer, I recognized the forest-green Mercedes. The trunk was open. Several plainclothes officers blocked the rear of the car, but I knew that the license plate would be JOINTZ.

"The plot thickens," O'Mara said.

Dr. Carl Nelson was in the trunk, of course. I couldn't see his face, but I recognized his blue and yellow golf shirt from our parking lot encounter. The smell was bad, but not as horrible as I expected. I have not found many bodies in trunks, thank God. He could not have been there long.

"How'd you find him?" O'Mara asked a young man in blue jeans and T-shirt with a rookie cop's short haircut.

"I was taking my mom to catch her flight home to Cleveland," the man said. "Lieutenant Avila had told us to keep an eye open for a Mercedes with the vanity plates. Nothing official, you know, but just to watch for it. I thought I saw it when I drove past here. So after Mom's flight took off, I walked out to the long-term lot to check it. One smell, you know, pretty much told the story. I went back to the terminal and called it in."

"What's your name?" O'Mara asked.

"Riley," the kid said.

"I shoulda known," O'Mara said. "Force has a future, we get a few more good Irish cops." The kid laughed. O'Mara patted him on the back and affected a brogue. "I'll tell your boss, lad. And I'll buy you a drink next time I see you."

The young officer beamed as if his promotion had just been hastened by a year. Maybe it was. O'Mara dismissed him and turned to the Mercedes. He spoke quietly with two crime scene guys, then looked over their shoulders at the body in the trunk.

"I'll be damned," he said.

He turned back to me.

"It ain't a suicide," he said.

"Don't tell me," I said. "Shot in the face."

"Not quite," O'Mara said. "Back of the head."

"Not like Mrs. Crain, then," I said.

"Close enough to arouse my curiosity," O'Mara replied. "Time for me to call on Linda Nelson again. The widow Nelson."

"No way she did this," I said.

"Don't give me that 'no way' bullshit," he said. "You feel guilty and protective because she got beat up after you talked to her. Well, maybe she snapped. Maybe she decided that was the last time. Maybe the doc was porking Sandra Crain and lovely Linda got 'em both. I don't know if she did it or not, but don't you tell me 'no way,' Brinker. I keep telling you, this ain't amateur night."

He stormed to his car and drove away. I walked to the terminal building and caught a cab.

NINETEEN

WILLIAM LOGAN practiced law in Logan Square, a warren of Santa Fe–style professional suites on Tanque Verde, ten miles east of the downtown courthouse. It was the office of a lawyer who kept his clients and himself out of court whenever possible. His waiting room sported about fifty thousand dollars' worth of leather furniture, current copies of *Architectural Digest* and the financial weeklies, and a sleek, sleepy-eyed receptionist who looked right out of a TV soap. She offered coffee, then took me without announcement into Logan's room.

He rose to greet me, walking around a desk that was cluttered with documents and tablets of yellow writing paper. The man had retained a preppy look into his sixties. He was tall, six-foot-three at least, and thin. Unruly hair, a mix of blond and gray, topped a slightly daffy expression that I assumed was misleading. He wore a starched white shirt and a silk tie, dark blue with a pattern of little gold tennis rackets.

We shook hands and made small talk until Sleepy brought the coffee. Logan carried his cup behind his desk and motioned me to a chair facing him. It gave me a nice view of diplomas from Harvard College, the Wharton School, and Yale Law.

"When David Katz called," Logan said, "he mentioned that you're working on Sandra Crain's murder."

"That's right," I said.

He waited a moment and said, "I called Mo, of course."

"Ah," I said. The coffee was strong and delicious as only just-brewed coffee can be.

"Mo doesn't seem to mind if I tell you everything about his legal affairs. I find that ridiculous and I told him so. Still, he asked me to be open with you."

"Thank you," I said.

"Don't thank me yet. Many of Mo's legal matters involve other people. Business associates, in the main. Some of those people are clients of mine, with the same rights that Mo has. My duty of confidentiality to them is unaffected by Mo's spirit of openness."

"You know what happened, Mr. Logan. You know why this means more to Mo than preserving a little confidentiality. In fact, he's asked many of his friends to help me as much as possible."

He raised the coffee cup to his lips. He didn't actually look down his nose at me, but I got the idea.

"They haven't told me," he said.

"Would it make any difference if you could help with an investigation of the murder of Mrs. Crain?"

"Regrettably," he said, "no."

"The police are stuck, Mr. Logan."

"You mean they haven't solved it yet."

"No," I said. "There's a difference. They're not getting any closer to solving it. And they don't know what to try next."

"And you do?"

"I'm trying this. I'm trying you."

Logan pursed his lips and raised his chin and fingered the knot of his necktie.

"Let me ask this in a hypothetical way," I said. He gave me an indulgent "yeah, right" smile, but I plunged ahead.

"Suppose that someone came to you for help with an investment in the Arizona-Sonora region." His expression did not change. Just that skeptical smile and nothing else. "Would you handle something like that?"

"I handle all kinds of business matters," he said. "It's what most lawyers do."

"And suppose the client's goal included buying real estate in Mexico. Could you handle that?"

"Of course I could. These aren't even questions," he said. "They're simply confirmations of the obvious. And they're not truly hypothetical, Mr. Brinker."

I shifted in my chair and leaned closer to his desk. "Okay," I said, "let's try it this way. The request for investment help comes around the time that Mrs. Crain is murdered," I continued. "Mo Crain's name gets attached to these investments because you're Mo's lawyer. Isn't that something you'd want to clear up, in fairness to Mo and the other client?"

He didn't miss a beat. "You have four untenable premises there," he said. "First, a knowledgeable client would deal directly with a Mexican attorney. An intermediary American lawyer would not necessarily be needed. Second, if there were no American lawyer involved, there would be no reason to attach Mo's name to this supposed transaction. Third, therefore, nothing needs to be cleared up. And fourth, I would feel no obligation to reveal client confidences to a private investigator who, in my judgment, has no legitimate business in a murder case, anyway."

Pretty slick, I thought. If I ever have a kid, I'm springing for Harvard, Wharton, and Yale.

"I'll grant you number four," I said. "The other three happened, Mr. Logan. I have it on absolutely reliable authority." Hector Ortiz. What the hell.

"Whose authority?" he asked.

"No way," I said. "Lawyers aren't the only people who respect confidentiality."

"If push comes to shove," he said, "we're the only ones who can invoke it as our clients' privilege. Unless you're working on this for David Katz, which you're not."

"Can't we avoid the push?"

He leaned back in his chair and said, "I really don't see how."

We sat silently for a moment, Logan looking confident and me feeling lost.

I stood up. "Thanks for your time, then," I said.

He stayed seated.

"I feel comfortable telling you one thing," he said. "I think it's appropriate for me to deny a client's involvement in something, as long as his noninvolvement doesn't impact his interests negatively. Mo Crain is not a party to any transaction such as the one you described, and he knows nothing about any such transaction by any other person. I can give you my personal assurance that he made no such transaction through me or this office."

"Did anyone else?"

"I do cross-border land transactions," Logan said. "I am working on some now, which is likely why you heard my name mentioned. But Mo Crain is not involved in anything in Mexico at the moment."

"Who is?" I asked.

"Now, now," Logan said.

"Richard Cannington?" I knew the name only from O'Mara's report, but it was worth a try.

Either he never heard of Cannington, either, or he had the best poker face in the State Bar of Arizona.

"Catharine Richard?"

"Mr. Brinker…"

"How about Dr. Carl Nelson or Linda Nelson?"

"I do not know the first two people you mentioned. I know Dr. and Mrs. Nelson socially, but only slightly. Neither is my client."

He stood and offered his hand. "Mr. Brinker," he said, "it's been a pleasure to meet you."

TWENTY

O'MARA HAD LEFT a message on my cell phone while I was talking to Logan. I called him back before leaving the lawyer's parking lot.

"Guess what, Dick Tracy?" he said. "Whoever took out Dr. Nelson used a different gun than the Sandra Crain shooter. That and the different styles, I think we've got separate perps here. Weird fucking coincidence, but it happens."

"The question is, why?" I said.

"The ME found cocaine in his blood," O'Mara said. "The hardworking physician's controlled substance of choice, you know."

"Has Mrs. Nelson heard about this?"

"No, and you're not going to tell her. I want to give her the news. See if she has an interesting reaction, or maybe some information about his habits."

"They'd been fighting. Maybe when he took off, he went looking to score some coke, and got jammed up with a dealer."

"We're sniffing around now," O'Mara said. "If that particular Mercedes was cruising down South Sixth or some other hot spot, then I think we've got ourselves a scenario. This is going to take some time, because I'm short-handed. Goddam city councilmen all make speeches about crime, but they don't give us any money for cops. You want to go down there, ask around, I won't complain."

"So," I said, "since we have different shooters, does this let Mrs. Nelson off the hook?"

"For one of them, I suppose," he said, sounding disappointed.

"Maybe both."

"Maybe," he said. "Oh, hell, probably."

DRIVING SOUTH ON Sixth was like entering Mexico. Past St. Augustine Cathedral and the police headquarters, signs quickly turned to Spanish. Bony dogs dozed in dusty vacant lots. Little kids smiled and waved. Teenagers looked away or met my glance with hostile stares.

Neighborhood guys liked to gather at a ramshackle tire repair shop just off Sixth. It was a place to talk about cars and girls and, for some of them, drugs. As I drove by, two Hispanic men were standing against a new blue Mercedes sedan parked at the curb. One of them, short and muscled with close-cropped black hair, looked familiar. I turned right and drove around the block, pulling in across the street from the two men.

One guy took off the moment he saw me. The familiar man just stood there, leaning against his car. Sounds of salsa rap blared from a radio somewhere as I walked across the street.

"Frankie Dominguez, right?"

He looked at me, trying to place the face. Then he got it.

"Oh, man. Brinker, from *la migra,* right?" he said. "I heard you got killed."

"Not quite," I said. "But I quit the Patrol. How many times did I pick you up, Frankie?"

He could laugh a little at that. "Ten, maybe," he said. "I don't know what it was. Seems like half the times I tried to come across, you were on duty."

"Did I ever treat you bad, Frankie?"

"Sent me back."

"Besides that?" I asked. "I ever beat you up or steal from you?"

He thought for a minute, perhaps to avoid confusing me with some other agent.

"No," he said. "You never did. Most of you guys were okay."

"One time out by Arivaca," I said. "That was you, wasn't it? You and four other guys? Middle of August, it was. You recall whose canteen you drank from that day, Frankie?"

"Yeah."

"Saved your ass, right?"

"Okay, okay, you're a saint," he said. "What, you a cop now?"

"Nice car," I said.

"I got a good job."

"What do you do, Frankie?"

"Sales," he said.

He was looking over my left shoulder. I turned to see a huge man walking across the street toward us. He looked Samoan, with honey-colored skin and a body built for sumo wrestling. He weighed at least three hundred pounds, but seemed light on his feet.

"Goin' on?" he asked in the rich, mellow voice of a Polynesian singer.

"I'm just having a conversation with my old friend Frankie," I said.

"Oh, yeah?" the big man said.

"Can you help us out, give us a little privacy here?" I said, trying to sound friendly.

"I'll help him out," the Samoan said, pointing a meaty finger at Frankie. "Don't give a shit about you."

I turned to Frankie. "Look, Frankie, I'm not *la migra* anymore and I'm not DEA. I'm no law at all. I want to give you a chance to earn some points with the cops, though."

Frankie chewed it over, then nodded at the behemoth. Without a word, the man turned and walked away toward Sixth.

"Saved your ass, right?" Frankie said, with a smug smile.

"Who was that guy?" I asked, watching the man turn the corner.

"That's Percy," Frankie said. "We call him No Mercy Percy. He's my, what do you say, *socio?*"

"Your business partner?"

"Yeah, that's what he is. We're partners."

"Okay, Frankie, here's the deal," I said. "Your car caught my eye, because a guy who drove a car like this got shot the other night. I'm wondering if maybe he was driving around down here and you, being a Mercedes owner yourself, noticed the car."

For the first time, he looked worried, as though this might be worse than the usual hassle with an Anglo who could hurt him.

"Oh, man, you're not talking about that doctor on the news?"

"That's the guy," I said. "Had a sedan, almost exactly like this one, only green. They found it at the airport with him in the trunk."

"Goddam," he said. "I saw that on TV, the car with the trunk open. I didn't know whose it was. I wondered about the car, but I never put it together."

Bingo, I thought. "So you did see it here."

"I saw it. Funny license plate, right? 'Joint,' or something."

"That was it, Frankie. What was he doing?"

"What do you think? Rich Anglo guy down here?"

"Did he hook up with a dealer?"

Frankie licked his lips and looked up and down the block. "Yeah, he did."

"Who?"

Now he shook his head. "I'm not going to tell you that, man. You get me deported, that's okay. I'll come back, you know? But there's other people can do stuff I don't come back from."

On the Patrol, you learn to read the characters like Frankie. I could tell when they were bullshitting or bargaining and when they really had finished talking.

"Okay," I said. "Forget the names. What do you think happened?"

There was some loose gravel on the street. Frankie pawed at it with the toes of his new Nikes.

"Word is, the guy scored some coke and picked up a *puta*. They went to the motel, couple of blocks down from here. He beat her up pretty bad. Crazy guy, I hear. Her pimp was driving by when she ran out of the room naked, screaming like crazy. Pimp went in, grabbed the guy, threw him in the Mercedes. They drove off. That's the last anyone saw."

Frankie got into his car. He started the engine, rolled down all four power windows, and kicked up the air conditioner.

He leaned his head out the driver's window and said, "You treated me fair on the border. Don't change your style now, Brinker. Keep me out of this. I'm getting established in my business. It's not fair if I get screwed over something I got nothing to do with."

"Nelson's supplier wasn't your *socio,* too, was he, Frankie?" I asked.

"C'mon, man," he said. "Do I look like a crook to you?"

"Frankie," I said, "what does a crook look like?"

He laughed, adjusted the rearview mirror, and finger-combed his short hair. He drove off to do business.

TWENTY-ONE

I WAS DRIVING up the hill to Linda Nelson's house when Mo called.

"Anything?" he asked.

"No," I said. "I'm going to see Mrs. Nelson. Her husband freaked out with me, warning me off the case. Then he turns up dead. Maybe she can give me some idea what that was all about."

I expected Mo to jump in with "Give her my sympathy" or "Keep me posted," but he was quiet for an oddly long time.

Finally he said, "Carl Nelson was a difficult, bitter man. You should tread carefully when you talk to Linda. She must be in terrible pain and very confused about all this."

"I'll be careful," I said.

"Good," he said, without much conviction.

THE GUARD MADE his call, got the okay, then waved me through the gate. Linda Nelson waited at her front door. She had seemed like a decent person, trapped in her husband's strange, secret life. I had given her a few days while I cleared a few routine jobs for David Katz, and now it seemed like a good time to see her.

Her gray slacks and blue cotton shirt looked rumpled and too large for her. Her face was thinner than before. She managed only a polite smile as she led me to the living room.

"Let me read your mind," she said. "I look like shit, right?"

"That's not how I'd have put it," I said.

"It's what you thought."

"Don't be hard on yourself," I said. "You've had an awful time."

"It's hot," she said. "Let me get us some cold drinks."

I stood by the panoramic picture window and watched central Tucson shimmer in the overheated haze. A brown layer of pollution sat at ground level, the product of too many cars, too much sun, and too little breeze. Mo probably had a pollution expert and a lobbyist who would disagree with me about the cars. Everyone in town already longed for rain, but the cleansing summer storms—the monsoons, we called them—had not materialized yet.

Linda Nelson handed me a glass of iced tea. Again today, her drink was something clear, with lots of ice and a slice of lime.

"How are you holding up?" I asked.

"It's pretty lonely here, to tell you the truth," she said. "Once you get past the ritual condolences, nobody comes around."

She pointed me to a sofa with the nice view, then took a chair facing me, with her back to the window. We sipped our drinks and looked at each other until she spoke.

"Even when my other friends quit calling or dropping in," she said, "Sandra would have been here for me."

I gave her time. She took a lot of it, drawing long drinks from her tall glass.

Finally, she said, "I'm going to tell you something I swore to myself I would never repeat. But now the whole world is upside down, and the only thing I know for sure is that Sandra deserves the best I can do for her. That's not a whole hell of a lot, but she deserves that much."

She looked at me carefully, making one last appraisal before speaking.

"About five years ago," she said, "Sandra had terrible depression. I don't mean just mood swings or that empty feeling that anybody can get in middle age. This was a serious, clinical thing. Can't get out of bed, can't eat, can't sleep. That kind of illness."

She drank, closed her eyes, swallowed slowly.

"I went over there every day. Mo got her the best of care, naturally. Twenty-four-hour nurses. Psychiatrists making house calls, can you believe it? Anything for Mo Crain. But I think just having a friend in the room helped Sandra. We didn't talk much. Some days, she didn't talk at all. Once in a while, she'd reach over and take my hand and just hold it for an hour."

"Do you know what caused this?" I asked.

"No. It lasted about six weeks. When it was over, she never spoke about it. I never asked."

She carried our drinks into the kitchen. I heard ice cubes clink. Soon she returned with full glasses, tea for me and whatever for her. She sat down, her back very straight in the chair.

"One day," she said, "maybe a month into it, I had planned to go over to see Sandra in the afternoon. But I hurt my wrist on the golf course and had to find a doctor."

"That would have been your husband's field, wouldn't it?"

"Yes, but Carl was away in Boston for a medical convention. I didn't want to go all the way down to the hospital, so I had my internist look at it. Her office is just down the hill. It took an hour to get in, and she spent quite a while with me. By the time I was bandaged up and got home, it was almost evening. I had a sandwich, then decided to make up the visit to Sandra that night."

Now I sat a little straighter.

"When I got to the Crains' house," she said, "a doctor was leaving. Sandra had a bad day, apparently. He gave her a shot for sleep. Mo took me into her room. I sat with her for a few minutes, but she was completely knocked out. Mo said the doctor expected her to stay that way all night."

She tried to draw a deep breath, like a mountain trail hiker straining at an unfamiliar altitude.

"I went back to the living room. Mo made me a drink. We talked about Sandra and her treatment. I said to him, 'This must be agonizing for you, too.' He said yes, it was. Then he sat beside me on the sofa. He said the last month had been like living alone. Solitary confinement, he called it.

"I was sitting with my hands folded in my lap. He reached over and put his hand on mine, then kind of moved it around so that his hand was in my lap. I was absolutely stunned. Speechless. Maybe he took that as encouragement, because he said, 'I know you care about both of us,' and then he leaned over to kiss me, and he put his other hand on my breast.

"That finally snapped me back to reality. I jumped up and moved away from him, but I still could barely speak. I was so shocked. I managed to tell him that I was leaving. He went to the door with me and apologized as I left. I was shaking so badly, it's a miracle I didn't have a wreck on the way home."

She took a handkerchief from her pocket and dabbed at her eyes. "I sat in this chair," she said, "and cried. I cursed myself for not cursing him. I mean, it was hardly a rape, was it? He stopped the instant I got up, and he apologized. But it was such a horrible violation even to think that I would be part of that. His wife, my best friend, was terribly ill and drugged into sleep down the hall. It was so selfish and heartless. He did it, but I was the one who felt cheap and used. Can you understand that?"

"Women have told me that," I said, "even about actual rape. They were victims of really vicious attacks, and somehow they felt that they did something wrong."

Now, I realized, she was being used again. I wanted to keep her going, revealing secrets about the Crains that might help me.

"Carl came home the next afternoon. We had a pretty good marriage then, I thought. So I told him what happened."

She reached for her drink, but pulled back her hand before picking up the glass. "He went into a rage. He yelled about going over to the Carplex right then and killing Mo. I talked him out of it. Eventually, he seemed to calm down. But that was the end of everything. He wanted revenge on Mo, but he took his revenge on me. He started up with other women. The beating began then.

"After that night in Mo and Sandra's house, everything was different. And I wonder who else's life might have been changed."

"Or ended?" I asked.

She shook her head. "I don't know. I've given up looking for sensible answers."

"It's strange," I said. "When I asked Mo for people who could tell me about Sandra, yours was the first name he gave me. It's as if he had nothing to hide."

She gave me that lost waif smile, small and rueful. "He could be in denial. Or he could understand his own power. Mo knows that his confidences will be respected," she said. "Look at me. Even with a murder, I didn't want to tell anyone else. Not many people who move in a certain circle want to cross

Mo. All his money and influence can put you on the 'A' list in this town. Or knock you off it."

"Why did you tell me today?"

"You were kind to me," she said. "You'd be amazed at how much that means. And Sandra deserves to have her killer caught. I think that's why you're still involved. I know you aren't doing it for Mo's money."

I gave her a moment, then asked, "What do you think happened?"

She shrugged her shoulders. "I don't know. I can hardly bear to think about it."

Linda Nelson stood up. Her eyes were moist and her face looked even more drawn than it had when I arrived.

"I've had enough for today," she said.

At the door, I asked, "Do you have more to tell me?"

"There's one more thing," she said. "It isn't anything I know for sure, but Carl told me something."

"Something more about Mo?"

"Yes," she said. "Carl was at a medical conference in Los Angeles. It was at some fancy hotel near the beach. He said he was leaving the hotel bar one night, going back to his room. He said he saw Mo with a woman who looked a little like Sandra, but wasn't. This was before my problem with Mo, so Carl was actually about to say hello to them when he realized that it wasn't Sandra."

"It wasn't just business, or some casual acquaintance?"

She smiled without pleasure. "They were nuzzling, Carl said. That's the word he used. Nuzzling. He thought it was funny at the time, like he could say 'gotcha' to the great Mo Crain if he ever had to."

"It might be something," I said.

With her hand on my arm, she eased me onto the front step. She reached into her pocket and brought out a twenty-dollar bill.

"For the cab from the emergency room," she said.

I started to protest, but she pressed the bill into my hand. She turned away and closed the door softly behind me.

TWENTY-TWO

AT THE AVILAS' HOUSE, Anna gave me comfort food, hot coffee and freshly fried sopapillas with warm honey.

"This case is a shitstorm in a stationary front," I said. "Mrs. Crain gets shot. Mo hires me. I talk to Linda Nelson and she gets beaten up. Her husband threatens me, then he gets murdered. Now she tells me that Mo, good old saintly Mo, hit on her. What a mess. This is worse than the Border Patrol."

Anna said, "Take it from a spouse. Nothing is worse than the Border Patrol."

Al spooned honey into the center of his sopapilla. "I still wonder if Mrs. Nelson knows anything more about Mrs. Crain," he said. "What did David Katz tell you? The Nelsons screwing around?"

"He said it was strictly rumor," I said. "But there was talk that one or both of them was fooling around. And Linda Nelson got a little touchy when I wondered if one of the Crains had something on the side."

"Which might mean," Anna said, "that some of the funny business involved a Crain and a Nelson together."

Al poured fresh coffee for all of us. "Did you ask Mo about that?" he said.

"No," I said. "O'Mara checked the romantic triangle possibility pretty well. He said that was one of the first things that occurred to him, but it came up empty."

Anna said, "Let's make a list. Start with stuff we don't know, then add what we do." She pulled a pad of ruled paper from a drawer near the telephone.

"You on my payroll, Anna?" I asked.

"Well, you're dogged and determined," she said, "but somebody has to supply the intellect."

"Thank you," I said.

"Start with motive," she said.

"Unknown," I said. "But it wasn't drug-related and wasn't money."

"Which means," Anna said, "it's something personal. I don't care what O'Mara thinks. It could still be a marriage problem or something like that."

"Maybe," Al said.

"Any better ideas?" Anna asked.

"No," Al said. "But it isn't necessarily personal. It could be something that we don't understand because there are no obvious signs. Maybe the people that O'Mara and Brink have questioned don't even realize that they know something important."

Anna shrugged. "Okay. Let's say it was only maybe something personal. That brings us back to the Nelson-Crain affair."

"If any," Al said.

"Well, of course." Anna poked him in the side. "Either way, what did Dr. Nelson know?"

"Something," I said. "He told me that a lot of people could get hurt. He specifically mentioned Mo."

"Okay, good," Anna said. "Next question."

"Why the mall?" I asked. "That still bugs me. Of all places, why did the killer choose that? Did he have several possible locations in mind, and that looked good before the others?"

Anna put down her pencil. "You guys laugh at me," she

said. "But I think the mall argues for a hitman." Al and I groaned, but she pressed on. "Look. A guy gets hired to kill Mrs. Crain. Some guy named Vinny or Guido from Detroit."

"It's great to be assimilated, isn't it?" Al said. "Now we can make the ethnic jokes."

"Oh, all right," Anna said. "Call him Pedro from El Paso. I don't care. He flies in. He sets aside a couple of days to do the deed. He knows where Mrs. Crain goes, so he has several possible locations in mind. His plan is to strike at the first good opportunity, then get out of Dodge. Why is this so dumb?"

I said, "Anna, I don't think it's dumb. Since we've ruled out all the local players as actual triggermen, maybe hiring somebody isn't as far out as it seemed."

"Yes!" she said.

"Anna," Al said, "how does he know where Mrs. Crain goes?"

"Easy. He follows her around and chooses his moment. Or somebody who knew her movements very well tells him. The somebody who wanted her dead."

We let that hang there for a moment.

Anna said, "You think I'm just twisting the argument back to Mo, don't you?"

"Yep," I said.

"Who else could have hired a killer?" Anna asked. "Who with a better motive than Mo, and who with better resources?"

Al and I thought about it.

"Why not?" she said. "And even though O'Mara says Mo is in the clear, isn't it weird that he's off in Canada when that Dr. Nelson was killed, too?"

"Something was bothering me about the two cases," I said. "Maybe that was it. Mo was out of the country both times."

"Come on, you two," Al said. "Having an identical alibi

would be a red flag for homicide. Two deaths, same Canadian trip both times."

"That's a loose end, even if the Nelson murder isn't connected," I said. "Nobody has really talked to the Canadians, up close and personal. O'Mara got Mo's alibi confirmed by phone. But it's strange that he was there when both murders went down. Maybe someone up there is involved."

"Pretty long shot," Anna said. "Canadians don't kill people, do they?"

"You'd also be investigating your own client," Al said.

"Not necessarily. I might get some little bit of information that helps. Anything."

"So what's next?" Anna asked.

"Maybe I'll go up to Canada," I said. "While I'm getting that set up, I'll see what Mo is up to."

Al and Anna gave me their "we know you" smiles.

"I've got those pictures of Mrs. Crain in my head," I said. "I can't just let it go."

Anna looked away, down the hallway toward her daughters' bedroom. "I guess you can't," she said. "That's always been your problem." She gave me a kiss on the cheek and said, "*Buena suerte,* honey."

TWENTY-THREE

ON THE OLDIES STATION, Harry Chapin sang about circles as I drove out Broadway to the Crain Carplex. The case seemed to be going around in circles. My only idea now was to follow him. He had secrets—how deep or dark, I did not know—and with his guard down, he might reveal them.

While I circled Mo, Sanchez would be circling me. Hunters waiting to see if the hunted would make a mistake.

I got there at seven o'clock and parked across the street. The spot gave me a clear view of the showroom-office building. Cars were lined up for their morning appointments at the service entrance. Mo pulled in at seven-ten, ever the early-rising, hardworking owner. He chatted with a young man who was washing windshields of cars on the lot. The kid had very long, stringy hair and a thin, empty face that showed surprise when Mo spoke to him. I wondered if he hoped to work his way up in the Crain organization. Mo walked over to the repair area and greeted his service managers. They wore crisp khaki pants and blue shirts with his name and picture embroidered over the left breast pocket. He moved back along the line of cars and said hello to customers. At last, with no more friends to make, he went to the showroom and headed for the stairs leading to the upstairs offices.

It was nearly eight o'clock. Mo's secretary arrived, followed soon by other employees. Salespeople trickled in after nine, carrying coffee cups, sporting their indefatigable smiles. A few service customers drifted from the waiting room to look over the latest-model cars and SUVs.

At nine o'clock sharp, a new Lexus pulled up to the office building. A tall, slender man stepped out, adjusted his tie knot, grabbed a black leather attaché case from the back seat, and walked into the showroom. It was William Logan, the attorney. At eleven-thirty, he and Mo emerged together, shook hands, and went to their cars. Two and a half hours with his lawyer. It seemed like a lifetime to me, but I had no empire to run.

I followed Mo west on Broadway toward downtown. He pulled into the parking lot at El Parador and hurried inside. It was almost noon. The restaurant's marquee read, BIENVENIDOS CHAMBER OF COMMERCE LUNCHEON 12:00. Parking was not allowed on Broadway, so I backed into a neighboring store's space facing the restaurant. I had good views of El Parador's front door and Mo's car.

The next hour passed in tedium. I thought of Gene Hackman in *The French Connection.* Poor Gene stood shivering across the street from a fancy Manhattan restaurant, wolfing takeout pizza and drinking bad coffee out of Styrofoam cups, watching a drug lord dine at leisure and sip fine wines. At least I wasn't shivering. The temperature was pushing a hundred. I kept the engine running and the air conditioner on.

Mo emerged at one forty-five, laughing with several well-dressed, upbeat Chamber of Commerce folks. He drove north to Sixth Street and west to Mansfeld Middle School, by the university. The school had a marquee, too. It read, WELCOME MAYOR RAUL IGNACIO AND MR. MO CRAIN! HONORS ASSEMBLY TODAY. A tall black woman wearing a blue suit and white blouse, surrounded by five children in their blue and white school uniforms, met him at the entrance and led him inside.

He was out by two-thirty. He headed south on Campbell and east on Broadway, so I figured it was back-to-work time. When he pulled into the Carplex, I took up my old position across the street.

At four-fifteen an old, battered van arrived. Four women got out and began looking at new vans lined up in the "Family Fun Vehicles" section of the lot. The women wore identical light gray skirts, white blouses, and white Keds. It took me a moment to realize that they were nuns.

A salesman came out to greet them. He showed them features on several models. One of the nuns pointed to their old rustbucket. The salesman took a small book from his shirt pocket, thumbed through it, and said something to the group. All four of them frowned.

Mo, wearing tuxedo pants and shirt and carrying the matching black jacket over his shoulder, strode out of the main building. He started for his car, but saw the nuns at the van section, and detoured to greet them. The salesman pointed to one of the new vans, then to the nuns' old one. Mo nodded gravely, then smiled and said something to the group. Two of the nuns clapped their hands. All four smiled so broadly that I felt their happiness from across the street. I could not read lips, but one nun surely said, "God bless you, Mr. Crain."

He scribbled something on a business card and gave it to the salesman. Probably an okay for the manager to give them the new van and skip the hustle for undercoating and extended warranty.

With his TV grin and a presidential wave, Mo got into his car and went north to the Catalina Foothills. At Ventana Canyon Resort, he left the car at valet parking and strolled into the hotel lobby. I drove up the hill to the free self-parking. When I walked down and peeked through the first doorway in the main building, I spotted Mo among a crowd of tuxedoed gents and evening-gowned ladies.

"Nice-looking party," I said to a passing waiter. "What's the occasion?"

"United Charities benefit," he said. He checked out my clothes and calculated that I, too, would be envious. "Three hundred bucks each for drinks and dinner. Must be a tough life, huh?"

"Must be," I said. I fetched my car from the free self-parking lot and drove toward home, laughing at my day.

TWENTY-FOUR

"*CABEZUDO*," DOLORES OFTEN called me, using the Chicano Spanish word for a hopelessly stubborn guy, a hardhead.

So I was back at the Carplex, parked across the street, when Mo arrived the next morning. Today, I figured, he would cure cancer and pick up a Nobel prize for honest auto dealing. But there I sat. *Cabezudo.*

He came in at seven-ten again, chatted with a gardener who was fussing over a barrel cactus by the front door, then headed to his office. That was the last I saw of him for hours.

About eleven, I remembered something Dolores had told Al and Anna and me. There was only one thing a man had that she wanted, she said. We all had fun guessing until she told us. A big bladder, for stakeouts. Waiting around for some newsmaker to do something interesting, she always had to pee more often than the guys.

At eleven forty-five, Mo came out of the office building and walked to the service area. I could observe most of the service bays. Mo schmoozed with his mechanics for a few minutes. He left just after noon and went to the small cafeteria next to the showroom. Thirty minutes later, he walked back to his office, stopping to shake hands with customers along the way.

I was almost dozing in my car when Mo's Lexus zipped off the Carplex lot and headed west. This time, he turned south on Kolb, cruising past the airplane graveyard at Davis-Monthan Air Force Base, then west on Valencia. This looked like a ride to Tucson International Airport.

It was. At the terminal road, Mo pulled into long-term parking. He was leaving, rather than meeting someone. I zipped into short-term, parked, and trotted to the terminal building before he covered the greater distance from his lot. He carried a small case, just enough for a few overnight things but not likely for a longer journey.

I ducked behind the welcome desk and watched him take the escalator to Departures. At the ticket counter, Mo got plenty of fawning and groveling as he moved into the first-class line. His ticket was waiting. He showed ID but the clerk barely glanced at it. Ah, fame. He took the ticket folder and headed up the concourse to his gate.

The information board showed only one flight leaving soon. It went to Los Angeles. Mo could be stopping there or connecting to anyplace in the world. The small bag argued for L.A. as the final destination. Tucson businesspeople made hundreds of quick trips like that every week.

Mo had taken a seat by the terminal window, looking out to the runways, with his back to the gate area. I sat across the hallway until he and the other passengers had boarded. The ticket agents were left alone to finish their departure duties.

I walked to the podium, mustering my best *gee-whiz* attitude.

"Say," I said to the agent, "wasn't that Mo Crain getting on this flight?"

"Sure was," the agent said. She sounded proud. "He's one of our most frequent fliers. Runs over to Los Angeles all the time."

"If I had all that money, I'd keep going to Hawaii or someplace," I said with an admiring smile.

"He does that, too," she whispered, "but not this time. Has to come home tomorrow afternoon and earn some more, I guess."

"Well, thanks," I said.

"Have a nice day, sir," she said, gathering up her passenger lists and heading back to the ticket counter.

The next day, I watched from across the concourse as the afternoon shuttle arrived from L.A. Mo came off first, greeting a few fans who were meeting other passengers or waiting for the outbound flight. I followed him to the parking lot and fell in two cars behind him as we approached the cashier's booth. The attendant took his ticket and his payment. Even from a distance, I saw the young woman smile broadly at her famous customer. She reached out from her window to give him change and shake his hand.

FROM MY OFFICE AT Allejandro & Katz, I called Tommy O'Mara at home. He sounded as though he'd had a few pre-dinner cocktails.

"What do you want?" he said.

"I was at the airport today and it reminded me of something," I said. "The airlines have passenger lists. Did you happen to check departures in the hours after Mrs. Crain was killed?"

There was a silence, then a sigh. "Brinker," O'Mara said, "how stupid do you think we are? Of course we checked. In fact, we checked Phoenix departures, too."

"What did you look for?"

"Christ," he said. "Are you getting remedial education credit for this call? What do you think we looked for?"

"Any names that jumped out at you. People connected to

the Crains. Maybe some known bad guys. Maybe an FBI list of organized crime gunmen."

"That's real original thinking," he said. I heard ice cubes clink in a glass. "Yeah, Brinker, we did all that shit within twelve hours. I spent one whole day on the phone, calling OC guys I know in other departments. New York, Chicago, Detroit, L.A. Not to mention Phoenix and Albuquerque."

Anna's theory. A hitman, a mob shooter brought in for a quick, anonymous job. It had occurred to O'Mara, too. Anna would be pleased.

"So don't worry, hotshot," O'Mara said. "We civil servants aren't total retards. We looked at the manifests. That's what the airlines call passenger lists, by the way, case you didn't know. We checked for relatives, friends, your good buddy Linda Nelson. Even her late hubby, who wasn't late back then. We checked for Mo's business competitors. We even checked for all those Canadians who alibied him. Waste of time that was, but the point is, Brinker, we didn't miss a fucking thing. We did everything right and then some. Any other bright ideas?"

"Thanks, O'Mara," I said.

"Yeah, right," he said, and slammed down the phone.

TWENTY-FIVE

TWENTY-FIVE MILES southeast of Vancouver, our 757 broke through the solid cloud cover and eased down into a gray Canadian afternoon. The pilot announced that we had just passed the international border.

I had expected a familiar feeling of crossing boundaries, but this view from above generated something quite different: a shock of nonrecognition. The Mexico-U.S. frontier is an arid, hostile place, with ugly iron fences and armies of agents to hold back the poor and the drug carriers. The desert teems with rattlesnakes and automatic weapons. But below me now were fields of green, rivers of actual water, tidy democratic towns full of well-fed people with health insurance and safe streets. Why the subtle shudder as I flew four miles above an almost imaginary dividing line?

The airport immigration officers behind their elevated kiosks looked like English teenagers with sun-starved skin, little rosy patches on their cheeks, and sandy hair. They glanced at our landing cards and sped us—the Americans, at least—along with a smiling, "Enjoy your stay." A Chinese family, looking lost and clutching their dark blue British passports for dear life, got shuttled to another desk for more questions.

With only a carry-on garment bag, I walked straight through the baggage hall to the green line and outside. I took a great breath of cool, damp air and thought, Brinker, you're not in Nogales anymore.

The cabdriver maneuvered off the airport's island and headed north on Granville Street. He wore a white shirt with a very old knit necktie. A tweed cap was planted atop his gray hair.

"How long to downtown?" I asked.

"About a half hour, sir," he said, "absent delays." The "about" sounded like "a boot," but otherwise his accent was little different from an Arizona Anglo's. I tried to remember if I had ever heard a Tucson taxi driver say, "absent delays." Or, for that matter, "sir."

We passed signs for Queen Elizabeth Park and crossed a road called King Edward Avenue. A bridge took us above a spot of land that the cabbie identified as Granville Island. The buildings appeared to be renovated warehouses, with lots of worn brick and colorful banners.

"Nice restaurants and shops down there, sir," the driver said. "On fair nights, pretty girls come after work to drink wine and watch the sunset." He looked at me in the rearview mirror and smiled discreetly. "So I'm told," he added. I had a feeling that winking would be un-Canadian.

Jock Proctor's office was on Hastings Street, in the kind of close-to-downtown salesroom that most U.S. dealerships abandoned years ago. He had Cadillacs, Buicks, Oldsmobiles, and GMC trucks under one roof. I wondered how many he sold in this neighborhood. It looked oddly empty of prosperous customers.

I paid the cabbie and walked into the showroom, carrying my garment bag. A salesman raised his eyes from the receptionist he was chatting up. He said, "You'd be Mr. Brinker for

Jock, I'll bet." I told him yes and he said, "Right up the stairs. First door on your left."

A secretary in a white woolen sweater and red plaid skirt took my bag, then showed me into a large office with burnished wood paneling and a thick carpet the color of burgundy. It had the feeling of a venerable gentlemen's club. The window gave a striking view of the harbor and, across it, North Vancouver. Proctor rose from his desk chair and strode around to meet me, his hand outstretched. He was a tall man, thin but robust. He wore a gray wool suit that looked old and well made. His hair was patrician gray and thick, longish, with a luster and careful combing that suggested pride in his enduring good looks. I suspected that he was older than he appeared.

"Thanks for seeing me, Mr. Proctor," I said.

"Please," he said, "I'm Jock to everybody. Have a seat." There was a trace of Scotland in his voice, barely enough to justify his first name. He had the same easy, instantly friendly manner about him as Mo Crain. I wondered if successful car people were born that way or if they went to some school for it.

"Terrible about Mo's wife," he said. "That sort of thing seldom happens here. Not that we don't have crime. Murders, even. We'll probably have tong wars if things keep changing the way they are. But this business of a woman's being shot down in a parking lot, for no reason, I can scarcely imagine it."

"It's produced even more grief lately," I said. I told him about the Nelsons, her beating and the doctor's death, but admitted that no connection seemed apparent yet.

"Dear God," Proctor said, shaking his head. "Well, I can't imagine how I can help you, but I'll do anything possible. You want a drink?"

"I wouldn't mind," I said.

In a rear corner of the office, I saw a beautiful teak chest with glassware, an ice bucket, and napkins. I expected him to walk over there to mix drinks, but he reached into his desk drawer. He pulled out a bottle of Glenlivet and two heavy crystal glasses.

He caught my smile and said, "Some things should be close at hand." He poured two generous drinks, neat, and handed one glass to me.

"Face the devil," he toasted. "Robert Burns, of course."

I sipped the rich, smooth scotch. Jock took a much longer pull at his, then sat back in his chair. He held the glass in both hands, the way some people hold a coffee mug for its warmth.

"Keeps a man young," he said, the eyes twinkling. "My doctor disagreed, but he died."

Proctor grinned, perhaps to assure me that it wasn't true.

"My father used to tell an old joke," I said. "A man goes to the doctor and asks, 'Is it true that men who don't smoke or drink or chase women live longer?' And the doctor says, 'No, it only seems longer.'"

He laughed with me. "I think my father told that one," he said, "and I'm much older than you."

"Jock," I said, "about this case. There's very little to go on. So I'm revisiting information we already have. Maybe we'll catch something that we missed before. It's a long shot, but frankly, we're down to long shots."

"I understand," he said. "You're here to ask about Mo."

"Yes."

"You can't possibly think he had anything to do with it."

"I just wonder if something about him or his business, something he doesn't even realize, provoked the killer."

He took another drink and shook his head. "I can't imagine what," he said. "And I certainly can't imagine anything here. He flies up, meets with businesspeople like myself, wines and dines a bit. On his last trip, I took him to Whistler Mountain for a couple of days of golf. Good for him, I thought. He seemed terribly agitated. Who can blame the poor man? But usually for all of us, it's business, then home."

"Does he have social friends in Vancouver?"

"Not that I know of. You see, when we make these Westfriends trips, we're not getting paid. We leave our businesses untended. Heaven knows they may be better off without us sometimes. We get nervous, though, like parents leaving the kids at home. Consequently we do our work in the shortest time possible, then come back to where we belong. It's business at breakfast, lunch, and dinner. I'm the same way in Tucson. I hardly know a soul down there, except Mo."

"So who would be his contacts here?"

"Well," Proctor said, "there's Dick Cannington, of course. He's very much the leading light of Westfriends. Started it, in fact, mainly to give us a piece of the action in the States. Quite forward thinking, especially now that we have the NAFTA. You have an appointment with Dick tomorrow, as I understand it."

The Maple Leaf grapevine, I thought.

"Then there's Catharine Richard," he said. He pronounced it "ree-SHARD," with the accent on the second syllable, just as O'Mara had written. "She's the one who actually runs things. Does all the real work. The executive director, you know. We business folks just show up and try to look important. But Catharine does the research, schedules the meetings, offers recommendations, brokers the deals. Anything important goes by Dick, of course. In fact, he gives Westfriends office space in his building, so they work quite closely."

"What exactly does Westfriends do?"

"I sometimes ask myself that question," he said. "A newspaper columnist here, writes for one of those weekly things that's given away, he called us 'a bunch of old farts who conspire to fatten their already considerable portfolios.'"

I laughed and Jock went on, "I thought that was a bit unfair. If we make business healthier, we create jobs and increase tax revenue and all of that. We brainstorm ideas to improve international business cooperation. Rather different ways of doing business, you know, here and in the States. And now that Mexico's more in the picture, well, it's a different language of business in more ways than one. So we help businessmen, oops, businesspersons from all three countries form alliances, make proposals and deals, and we offer suggestions to smooth the regulatory procedures a bit. One country's red tape is bad enough. When you get three, well, that's just frightful."

I finished the Glenlivet and put the glass on the table next to my armchair. "Well, Jock," I said at last, "I'm dancing around one of my main concerns here. Could Mo have been involved in some romantic triangle up here? Provoked an irate husband?"

"Good Lord, no," Proctor said. "The only woman he sees much of here is Catharine. We should have more businesswomen in the group, I suppose, but we don't. A bit behind the times there, I'm afraid. Catharine is long divorced, I think, so there's no irate husband. Not that Catharine wouldn't turn any man's head." He smiled kindly, as a nice old man might when he imagines a pretty girl.

"Anyway," he said, "Mo's not that kind of fellow, I wouldn't think. Up here, we've pretty much decided Mrs.

Crain's death must be one of those uniquely American acts of random violence. Forgive me for saying that, but heaven knows what can happen down there with all those drugs and guns. Especially around the Mexican border."

He looked out the window for a moment and said, "We shouldn't be too smug, I suppose. With the Hong Kong influx, this city is being changed by loose money and customs with which we're not familiar."

I thanked him for the drink and for his time.

"Glad to help," he said, standing and walking me to the door. "Truth be told, I'm often looking for something interesting to do. My sons run the business these days, so I'm not as busy as I used to be."

"Do you do your own commercials?" I asked.

"Me?" he said. "No. In earlier years, yes, but I'm too old for that now. The boys do them. Youthful vigor and modern style, that's the ticket in the car business these days."

"I thought you might do them, because somebody described you as the Mo Crain of British Columbia."

Proctor laughed. "That's because we're large and diversified. Thank heaven I was a little greedy thirty, forty years ago, because you must be big to survive today. We have twenty-three dealerships. All different makes, all around the province."

"Well, that's just like Mo," I said. "Strength through size."

"The gospel truth in business," Jock Proctor said. "But it can't protect you from rotten luck in life, can it?"

THE HOTEL VANCOUVER was one of the stolid old Canadian railroad hotels, brick and limestone, sitting firmly on a whole city block. It looked as if it could survive a nuclear attack, if anyone ever concocted a reason to attack Canada. Inside, the lobby resembled Jock Proctor's office. Wood panels gleamed. The carpet was rich and springy. Stylish, colorful banners hung from the ceiling. The hotel obviously worked hard to keep a traditional, luxurious look without turning off more modern, casual customers. The reception clerk handed me a key card. She asked if I needed help with luggage. I declined and she directed me to the elevator.

The phone rang as soon as I entered the room.

"Mr. Brinker, this is Catharine Richard from Westfriends." She said "ree-SHARD," too. "Welcome to Vancouver."

"Well, thank you," I said. I was not expecting the VIP treatment. Maybe this explained the two-room suite at a discount rate. "I just arrived at the hotel."

"Yes," she said. "Reception called me. I just wanted to be sure that you've settled in, and inquire as to whether I can do anything for you before we meet tomorrow." Her voice was mellow and pleasant, with no accent that I could identify. She spoke in a quick, clipped fashion, as if she were checking points off a list.

"I'm fine," I said. "It's been a long day. I think I'll have a beer and dinner at the hotel and maybe stroll around downtown this evening."

"The downstairs restaurant there has wonderful fresh salmon," she said. "Try the Okanagan Pale Ale. It's a British Columbian beer and they have it on draft. The place is informal, so you won't feel strange dining alone. Quite nice, really."

"Sounds perfect," I said.

"If you like an ambitious walk, you might enjoy Granville Island. Lots of lively spots. On fair nights, I sometimes go there after work to watch the sunset."

"Somehow I knew that," I said.

"Really? Well, have a pleasant evening, Mr. Brinker, and we'll see you tomorrow. Mr. Cannington has made a few moments available at eleven forty-five, and you and I shall have our meeting over lunch, if that's convenient."

Nice time management for the big guy, I thought. I said, "I'll look forward to it," and tried to imagine a face to go with the voice.

TWENTY-SIX

THREE BLOCKS FROM my hotel, the Pan-Canadian Mercantile Bank rose fifty-three stories, one for each year of the bank's existence at the time this headquarters building was erected. It was all silver metal and glass. The hotel concierge, with a sly smile, had told me that everyone called it the Pan-Can. I asked for Mr. Cannington and found myself wondering what everyone called him.

The security guard wore a dark blue suit and crisp white shirt. He looked more like a bank executive himself than a rent-a-cop. He took my name, checked an appointment book, and transformed himself from wary sentry to humble servant.

"The chairman is expecting you, Mr. Brinker," he said. "Please take the private elevator on the right. I'll send you directly to fifty-three"

The elevator door opened as I approached it. It closed as I stepped in. The FIFTY-THREE button lit without my touch and the cab whooshed smoothly upward. When the doors opened, a middle-aged woman with a Margaret Thatcher accent and a sergeant major's attitude was waiting. Her jaw was square and her frame was squat. She wore sensible brown shoes and, despite the promise of a warm day, a brown tweed suit. She said the chairman would see me at once. We marched back to Cannington's suite. She left me in a clubby room with Norwegian black leather chairs, a gleaming stainless steel and glass table, and a heart-stopping view of Stanley Park. I could see all thousand acres from this altitude, and the Lion's Gate Bridge beyond, and even the road to Whistler Mountain.

"You picked a good time to visit," said a voice behind me. "Rain and clouds all last week. Couldn't see a thing until today."

Cannington was small but muscular, a little guy who kept fighting-fit. I figured him for mid-forties, young to run a big bank, but perhaps the executive track was faster in Canada. Or maybe he was just very bright. He wore a blue oxford cloth shirt, sleeves rolled up, with a blue-gray silk tie knotted smartly beneath his buttoned collar. His black hair was cut short and had a little cowlick, the sort of minor disarray that looks perfect with a Bahamas tan. He radiated that coiled-spring intensity that you see in top corporate types. He shook hands firmly and directed me to one of the facing chairs.

"We're both busy men, Mr. Brinker," Cannington said, "so I won't waste time. All of us here are making ourselves available out of respect for Mo Crain. Leave no stone unturned, as they say. But nobody at Westfriends can tell you anything about Mrs. Crain's death. I know this because we've discussed it, as you can imagine. No signs of marital difficulties were apparent to us. Mo spent considerable time with Catharine Richard and she assures us that his conduct with her was never inappropriate. There were no business intrigues that we knew of. Certainly Mo's home area would be a more likely venue for that sort of thing anyway. To the best of my knowledge, Mo Crain is a businessman and a gentleman above reproach. And to my certain knowledge, everyone he met with here is of equal caliber."

He glanced at his watch. It was very thin and very gold. "Now," he said, "how can I help you?"

"Did you ever meet his wife?" I asked.

"Once here in Vancouver, and a few times in Tucson," Cannington said. "Simply a lovely woman. She was quite striking, as you know, and very nice as well."

"She only came here once?"

"As far as I know. Nothing unusual there. Spouses don't often come on the Westfriends trips. Frankly, if I weren't in business, our meetings would bore me to tears. Mrs. Crain was of Spanish descent, I believe."

"Mexican," I said.

"Yes. Well, perhaps she found it too cool and dreary up here. Some people do."

He moved restlessly in his chair and stole glances at the office door. "I'm sorry to hurry things, Mr. Brinker," he said, "but today is even busier than I expected. If you don't mind, I'll put you together with Catharine now."

I must have looked surprised.

"You're better off with her, actually," Cannington said, "where the subject of discussion is Westfriends."

He stood and opened the office door. Margaret Thatcher was there in a flash. She led me down the hall to another suite with a discreet WESTFRIENDS sign at the entrance, past a secretary, and into another office. The plaque on the door read V. CATHARINE RICHARD, EXECUTIVE DIRECTOR.

"Mr. Brinker, Ms. Richard," Margaret Thatcher said.

Catharine Richard walked from behind her desk with an all-business stride that matched her voice on the phone. Her face was framed by black hair done in a practical style that reminded me a little of Sandra Crain's. I had expected a Galic look, something like the dark and sensuous quality of a Parisian movie star. But she had the flawless, creamy complexion of English royalty's prettier branches, the ones who marry into the family. I wondered if her French surname was by marriage. Ms. Richard's dark skirt was cut shorter than any Tucson businesswoman would dare. I had heard that urban Canadians liked European high fashion. If this was it, so did I.

She extended her hand. Her grasp was firm and business-like. Her eyes, almost level with mine, had that bemused little sparkle that I often noticed in very bright people.

"What would you like for lunch?" she asked. None of the time-wasting "hello how are you" foolishness.

"Nothing fancy," I said. "Something Vancouverish."

She smiled and called to her secretary. "Lil, ring Thomas's pub. Ask them to save us a window table in about thirty minutes."

"I don't think they take lunch reservations," Lil protested.

"Ask for Thomas," Catharine Richard said as she moved us toward the door. "Tell him I'll owe him a big wet kiss."

I was laughing as we walked to the elevator. She said, "I didn't mean that, you understand, but it seldom fails."

At the curb, she raised her arm and taxis raced to us. "SeaBus," she told the winning driver. He dropped us by the harbor at a building that looked like a railway station. I followed her through an airy transit terminal area. She bought two tickets from a machine and led me down a long, enclosed gangway to a waiting passenger ferry. We entered just as the automatic doors shut. As the name suggested, it was a seagoing bus, a wide enclosed vessel with long rows of seats and thick glass windows all around.

"I've been to Tucson," she said. "I thought someplace with water would be a nice change for you."

The SeaBus eased out of its mooring and throttled up for the short run to North Vancouver.

"Look behind you," she said.

The harborside vista fell away from the SeaBus windows, as if we were pulling back a wide-angle lens. The Expo '86 site and convention center gleamed white in the foreground, with downtown's skyscrapers reaching to a cloudless blue backdrop. We rode in silence, feeling privileged on public transportation, watching little boats bob out to Burrard Inlet.

The vessel docked at a complex called Lonsdale Quay. Catharine Richard led me inside on the ground floor, a Westernized bazaar of specialty food markets. I smelled fruit and rich coffee. Busy vendors offered prime aged beef and gleaming fresh fish. A stand by the stairwell had candy from Scotland and tea from Sri Lanka.

"What did Sri Lanka used to be?" I asked.

"Ceylon," she answered without hesitation. "Its Arabic name was Serendip. Do you believe in serendipity, Mr. Brinker?"

I thought of Alicia and Al and me in a tunnel that might have been in a universe separate from this place.

"Oh, yes," I said, watching her start up the stairs. Stepping briskly in her dark blue skirt, white blouse, and high heels, Catharine Richard stood out dramatically from the casually dressed tourists and grocery shoppers. We left the stairway at the second floor and walked into a modern pub, all polished wood and brass, with sunlight pouring in through waterfront glass. She waved at the barman. He blew her a kiss and raised his eyebrows expectantly.

"Thomas?" I asked.

"Hope springs eternal," she said.

We walked without waiting to the best window table. It had

a knockout view of Vancouver. A hand-lettered card, propped against the saltshaker, read RESERVED.

"Sit here," she said, giving me the view. She faced back into the dining room. With the city skyline as a backdrop and her face in the foreground, I awarded the place five stars for ambience.

"You drive a good welcome wagon, Ms. Richard," I said.

"It's Catharine, please," she said. "You're my job this afternoon. Not that I mind a bit, but the word is, this is Be Nice to Mr. Brinker Day."

"You can start by losing that 'Mister.' Everybody calls me Brinker, or Brink."

"Okay, Brinker. Do you have a first name, or are you like Inspector Morse, endeavoring always to conceal it?" Her eyes twinkled and I wondered if I had missed some little joke.

"It's Roscoe," I said.

"Ah," she said. "I understand, then."

A waitress came and took drink orders. I asked for a pint of the Okanagan Ale, Catharine's recommendation last night. She joined me with a half pint.

"I'd have thought Chardonnay," I said.

She laughed. Her quick smile and short dark hair reminded me again of Sandra Crain in the picture on Mo's desk.

"I love a bit of beer," she said. "It means an extra hour's exercise, but it's worth it."

When the drinks arrived, she picked up the glass in her left hand. She wore no rings.

"So, you were explaining about Be Nice to Me Day," I said.

"That is because everyone here feels so terrible about poor Mo. If there's any way we can help you, and get your investigation on track, we're eager to do so. He said that if you came up here, we should help you. He didn't sound happy about it, but he thought that you would keep bothering us until we spoke with you."

His reach did not stop at the border, I realized.

"Are you bothersome, Brinker?"

"Persistent," I said.

She smiled.

"How long have you known Mo?" I asked.

"About two years. I had worked in tourism for a while. Dick Cannington was on the local tourism board. He asked me to join Westfriends and I met Mo shortly after that."

"And his wife?"

"I never met her," she said, looking down at her menu. "I understand that she came up once, when Westfriends first started, but our paths didn't cross."

The waitress brought our food. Bangers and mash for me, a salade niçoise for Catharine Richard.

"Tell me about Mo's trip the week she was killed," I said.

"I wasn't here for all of it," she said. "He arrived at mid-afternoon Monday, as I recall. I met him at the airport and drove him to his hotel. He always stays at the Four Seasons, just down the street from Pan-Can. We had dinner at the hotel restaurant that night. It's wonderful, by the way, especially if someone else pays. I briefed him on the week's activities and issues. He had meetings with the Westfriends directors and several business organizations over the next two days. I can't help you with details of those, because I had to go to New York on Tuesday. I didn't come back until Sunday, and of course by then, these terrible things had happened."

"How did you find out about it?"

"It was on the news in Vancouver the night it happened. A Thursday, wasn't it? Dick Cannington telephoned me in New

York the instant he saw the story." She smiled. "He forgot the time difference. His call woke me up at two-thirty in the morning. Very unlike Dick, to call anyone outside business hours. He doesn't show much emotion, but he must have been stricken by the news."

I took a long drink of beer. "Cannington blew me off pretty quickly," I said.

"Welcome to the club," she said. "Everyone is getting that treatment this week. Don't take it personally. Or professionally, either. It has nothing to do with your case. There's merger talk flying around the Pan-Can. If it's true, Dick is consumed by the deal-making. Actually, you're lucky to have had the five minutes. That's more than I'm getting all this week."

I'd rather be here, anyway, I thought.

"Did Mo ever confide in you about personal things?" I asked.

"If they were personal, and he confided, I wouldn't tell you," she said. Her voice was neither defiant nor offended.

"You know what I'm getting at, Catharine," I said. "Was there any sign of trouble between the Crains?"

She sighed and shook her head. "Surely you don't think Mo had something to do with it?"

"Did he ever make a pass at you?"

"Oh, really, now," she said.

"What do you think happened?" I asked.

"Not much is certain in this life, Brinker," she said. "But here's one absolute truth for you. Mo Crain didn't have his wife killed. I know that any self-respecting Sherlock wants to rule out the impossible. Well, Mo as a killer is impossible."

I raised my beer glass to her and said, "I hope you're right."

And I realized that she had not quite answered my question.

At the SeaBus terminal in Vancouver, I said, "Would you like to have dinner tonight?"

"I'm sorry," she said. "Dinner meeting with some visiting politicians from Alberta."

"Sounds like great fun."

"Actually, I'd prefer a new edition of the Spanish Inquisition, as 'Enry 'Iggins said." She laughed. "But duty calls."

"Well, then," I said, "thanks for the lunch and the information."

"I'm sorry it isn't more. Are you going back tomorrow?"

"Nine o'clock plane."

"Give yourself extra time leaving the hotel," she said. "Morning traffic is terrible. And you must clear U.S. Customs and Immigration at Vancouver Airport. It moves quite slowly. If you buy a Cuban cigar here, don't try to take it home. Your government is moronic on that subject. Do you have an airport lounge membership?"

"Afraid not. I'm an infrequent flier."

"You're lucky. I just got back from Los Angeles yesterday and I'm off to Montreal next week. I'm so weary of planes and airports. Anyway, go to the lounge and ask for Sylvia. I'll call her this afternoon and arrange a guest pass. It's much more comfortable in there. In fact, Sylvia might even manage an upgrade on the flight."

"I'll do that," I said. "Thank you."

"Did you get to Granville Island?" she asked.

"No, I didn't."

"You really should. It's so pleasant on a summer night, and we finally have a nice forecast."

"Maybe I will." I wrote my home address and phone on the back of my business card and gave it to her. "If you think of anything that might help me on the case, please contact me."

"I will."

"Well, then. Goodbye, Catharine."

"*Au revoir,* Brinker," she said.

TWENTY-SEVEN

JUST AFTER TEN that night, the taxi dropped me near a restaurant with an expansive waterside patio. Table umbrellas, with their insignia of European liqueur and mineral water companies, were connected by strings of small white lights. The place was jammed. It drew a young crowd, drinking, talking hockey and movies, laughingly planning to buy the $7 million high-rise condos across the water.

I had a beer, then another. I watched passengers board the tiny shuttle boat for the short ride off the island. I eavesdropped on conversations about Tories and Liberals and New Democrats and dollar exchange. Just when I despaired for my intuition, she came up beside me.

"So," she said. "You spotted the clue."

"I was hoping that *au revoir* didn't mean goodbye."

Catharine Richard wore a soft, fresh perfume that hinted at plumeria. The scent seemed incongruous so far from the tropics, but I liked it. The twinkly umbrella lights were reflected in her gleaming dark hair, like tiny stars.

"The wish was father to the thought," I said.

"Shakespeare?" she asked.

"J. Edgar Hoover," I said. "He used it whenever people asked him if he planned to retire. Maybe he stole it from Shakespeare."

She took a sip of my beer and said, "You're the only man who ever quoted J. Edgar Hoover to me in the moonlight."

"Well, you're Canadian," I said. "In the States, we do it all the time. It's considered very clever."

"And you think we're odd," she said.

We were stumbling through this idiot conversation without looking at each other. We leaned against the rail and watched the shuttle boat putt-putt across the water. Auto traffic hummed along the Granville Avenue bridge above us.

"I would have expected to find you in Quebec," I said.

"Drinking Chardonnay?"

I laughed. She didn't forget much.

"Your name. Everybody made a point of telling me to pronounce it the French way. Ree-SHARD."

"Ah. I moved here from Montreal after my divorce. Get away, clean break, and all that. Richard is my ex-husband's surname. Pierre Richard, a Quebecer to the core. Would you believe my maiden name was London? Occasionally I wish I had changed it back. Some Anglophone Canadians dislike anything French."

"What's the 'V' for? The sign on your door said V. Catharine Richard."

She laughed. "You have Roscoe and I have Victoria. How's that name for English? Victoria London. I sounded like a railway station. But when I was six, I saw a picture of old Queen Victoria. I thought she was terribly frumpy, so I insisted on using my middle name. Catharine. My parents were heartbroken, I think."

"You seem to be doing well," I said, "even without the English name."

"Vancouver's fairly cosmopolitan," she said. "Anyway, the Hong Kong Chinese get most of the cultural resentment these days."

"Someone plays that role everywhere," I said. "But it's a beautiful town, and everything seems to work so smoothly."

"We hope so," she said. "Peter Ustinov said Toronto is like New York run by the Swiss. Vancouver is like that, too, I think."

Two young men walked past us, holding hands and laughing softly.

"What about you?" Catharine asked. "Single, married, polygamous?"

"Never married."

"That could be considered an ambiguous answer, Brinker. You didn't say 'single.' Does that mean you're unmarried but with someone?"

I wondered what Dolores was doing tonight.

"Someone left," I said. It was true, but saying it, I felt too easily disloyal to Dolores. She was leaving town, but whether she had left me was a question we had not dared to answer.

"We're a long way from Tucson," Catharine Richard said. "Distance can give a body freedom, don't you think?"

I felt a surprising little catch in my heartbeat. "Nice way of putting it," I said.

"You did come here tonight to meet me?" she asked.

"I heard that pretty girls came here to watch the sunset."

She smiled and took my arm. "I don't know about pretty, and it's too late for sunset," she said. "But my apartment faces east. Would you settle for a sunrise?"

"Wow," I said. "What a friendly country."

"That was not what I'd call a passionate acceptance," she said.

"I guess it wasn't," I said.

"Well, then," she said, and slowly slipped her hand from my arm.

"When I came over here tonight," I said, "that's what I was thinking of. I imagined being with you."

"But?"

"But, when I get right there, I can't. Some unresolved issues back home, I think."

"Oh, dear," she said. "Unresolved issues. I'm rejected with chat-show babble."

I laughed.

"I said it badly," I said. "I don't mean to be pompous, Catharine. There are some people I care about. Someone I've been with for a couple of years. We've known each other since we were kids. Her sister Anna is married to my best friend. She just left. It wasn't officially a breakup. I don't know exactly what it was. She went to New York to interview for a job. But I think she's ready to leave. Maybe it's the right thing for her to do."

"Why?" Catharine asked.

"She hasn't been happy with the way I live. I was on the Border Patrol for a long time. It can be dangerous, and I did get shot once."

"They should have assigned you to Blaine, Washington," Catharine said. "Not many shootings there. Occasionally someone accidentally drives through the express lane with an expired sticker, but that's about as ugly as Canadian border crossers get."

"Then when I left the Patrol," I said, "she wanted me to do something safe. Go to law school or veterinary school or something that didn't involve getting shot at, or rocks thrown at me."

"I'm not sure law school would have achieved that," she said.

I laughed. "Maybe not. But I went into investigations. It

seemed all right. Not as dangerous as the cops, which would have been my other logical choice. I found some missing kids. Nailed some insurance crooks. Then this Crain case came along, and that seemed to bring danger back into the picture. I guess it's coincidence, but she seemed to pull back from the moment I took this on."

"What's her name? May I ask?"

"It's Dolores. Dolores Gonzales."

"In French," Catharine said, "*douleur* means pain. Is it something like that in Spanish?"

"You're right," I said. "It's *dolor*."

"Well, you can't judge someone by her name, but maybe she is a sad person. Maybe she always feels some, what is it? *Dolor?* I've known people like that, who find it difficult to be happy, no matter what."

"I never thought of her that way. She's certainly happy in her work. Maybe I caused personal pain and didn't realize it."

"You still care about her. You don't take her lightly. That's not a bad thing, Brinker."

"You're learning my life story," I said. "I don't know much about you."

"My story isn't very exciting. Just an ordinary businesswoman in boring, conventional Canada. No gunplay. And I think that I get over sadness more quickly than your friend Dolores. When my husband dumped me, I promised myself never to be hurt like that again."

"Don't be too thick-skinned," I said. "You won't feel anything."

"I think I've struck the right balance," she said. "I go after what I want, but I don't hang on to impossible dreams."

"Is anything impossible for you, Catharine?"

"You, apparently," she said.

"Anna tells me that I hang on too long. When I decide that something is right, she says I can't be pulled away."

"Too bad," Catharine said.

I FLEW HOME the next day. Despite getting turned down, Catharine kept her promise to smooth my departure. Her friend Sylvia showed me to an easy chair in the VIP lounge. She exchanged my boarding pass for a new one, handing it over with a conspiratorial smile. When the flight was called, I took a spacious leather seat, 3A, in the quiet front cabin. The flight attendant brought Bloody Marys after takeoff, and sweet fresh fruit on a small china plate. I felt weightless as gauzy clouds parted to reveal the Space Needle gliding by below. A fire burned in the forests of Oregon. Lunch was poached salmon with a California sauvignon blanc. At Los Angeles, we landed on instruments in sickening gray smog. Approaching Tucson, the pilot said visibility was forty miles and the temperature was 112 degrees.

I had barely noticed any of these things.

I looked out toward the rising desert, wondering if Dolores, too, could resist the thrill of the new in a distant place.

I recalled how Catharine Richard, when I first saw her, looked a little like Sandra Crain. I wondered if Catharine had been nuzzling with Mo in Los Angeles.

And when I closed my eyes, I imagined her skin against my fingertips.

TWENTY-EIGHT

ON A WINTER NIGHT when I was ten years old, the house two doors away caught fire. Someone called in the alarm and the firefighters arrived quickly, but the house was ruined before they could get water on it. A boy who played with Al and me, Billy Flynn, lived there with his parents. The family was away on vacation. This happened years before cell phones and e-mail and even widespread use of answering machines, so the family had no idea that their house had burned. As time passed, the fire faded from my mind, but I never forgot the shocked looks of those people when they returned two days later, or the bereft cry of my playmate's mother when she saw the blackened shell of her home.

From that day on, whenever I came home, I felt a tug of anxiety. Even if I had been gone only for a day of work or an hour of shopping. And certainly that day when I returned from the trip to Canada.

Speeding through the curves as I neared the house, I had to swerve around a parked pickup truck. It sat just off the road where a wash ran behind my property. I took the final couple of turns and pulled into my long driveway. The house was still standing. I felt the familiar little rush of relief.

That's probably why my guard was down.

I parked outside and let myself in through the front door. At the threshold, I paused to listen. It was another tic of the nervous homecomer. The air conditioner hummed. A house finch tapped on window glass somewhere.

Garment bag in hand, I headed for the bedroom at the end of the hallway. That's when they got me.

Two of them, nailing me as I walked through the bedroom door. They must have worked it out when they heard me arrive, for one grabbed me from behind and twisted me toward the second man. He drove a fist into my gut. It doubled me over. I heard my own cry of surprise and pain. Inside my head, it sounded like a car backfiring. I braced for a punch in the face, but the second blow was an uppercut to my shoulder, the one wounded at Lovers Crossing.

I tried to raise my head. No good. Goon One had bent over to push my upper body down. Goon Two drove his knee up into my wounded hip. It turned my legs to spaghetti. He kicked them out from under me and I hit the floor face first.

Get a look at them, I thought.

But it was too late for that. I could see the shadow of Goon Two lunging down toward me. A sharp pain tore the back of my head, and a bright, billowing flash—like an old movie of an atom bomb test—blew out my vision.

If I was unconscious, it was only for a second. I managed to turn my head toward the open bedroom door. Two men were racing into the backyard and out the open gate, toward the wash. Probably making for the pickup truck that I had barely registered when I sped by.

It took several minutes for me to sit up and regain my bearings. The intruders had trashed the bedroom dresser, the bedside tables, and the closet. When I could finally lumber around the room to check the tossed places, though, nothing seemed to be missing.

I moved down the hall to a spare bedroom that Dolores and I used as an office. File cabinets were opened and dumped out. The desk drawers were emptied, their contents thrown around the floor.

"You want me to send an ambulance?" Al asked when I reached him at home.

"No," I said. "They didn't break any bones. I'll be all right."

"What did they get?"

"Nothing, as far as I can tell," I said. "The TVs and the audio stuff are untouched. Same with the computer."

"Not your basic burglars," Al said.

"No way. These guys were looking for something in my files. It has to be the Crain case or the Border Patrol stuff."

"You think you surprised them, or did they know you were coming back today?"

"No way to tell. But they knew how to hurt me. They knew where I got shot. Rang those bells hard."

"Sanchez," Al said.

"I don't think he was one of them. These guys were taller, thinner. But he could have put them on to me."

"Tell you what," Al said. "Let me call county and get a deputy over there. They won't be able to do much, but you should put a report on file. If this is connected to the Patrol investigation, it's probably federal obstruction of justice. One more to lay on Sanchez when the time comes."

"Okay," I said.

I grabbed some ibuprofen from the bathroom medicine cabinet, carried it to the kitchen, and took a beer from the refrigerator. The kitchen seemed untouched by the intruders, until I saw the small corkboard where Anita and Alicia had pinned together a collage of Avila family pictures.

The biggest photograph was an 81/2-by-11 of Al and Anna and the girls, standing with Dolores and me in front of the elephant enclosure at the San Diego Zoo. A friendly passerby had snapped the shot for us. Anita and Alicia were holding on to my legs, mugging for the camera. All the adults were laughing with them.

Someone had taken a paring knife from an open drawer and driven it into the picture. It was stuck there, held fast by the cork backing. The blade was lodged in Dolores's heart.

TWENTY-NINE

AL SAID, "These are the times I wish I were back on the street. I should be over at your place with an evidence kit."

"The county guys seemed pretty sharp," I said. "If there was anything to find, they'd have found it. Besides, if you were back in a squad, we wouldn't have your brilliant leadership to fight crime."

"Right," Al said. "I don't know if I rid our community of any crime today, but I gave two mighty fine speeches."

Anita said, "Four score and seven years ago. We're learning that speech in history class."

"That's not what Daddy talked about," Alicia said. "That was Abraham Lincoln."

"I talked to high school students this morning," Al said. "I told them about jobs on the police department."

"If they came to work at the police station, would you get to boss them around?" Alicia asked.

"I guess I would," Al said.

"Would you tell them not to give Uncle Brink a ticket when he drives too fast?"

"Nope. If he speeds, he gets a ticket, like everybody else."

"No danger of that," I said. "I can't go any slower on this case."

"You can get a ticket for going too slow," Anita said. "McGruff the Crime Dog told us that."

"I'm in trouble, then," I said.

The girls went running to tell Anna that I was in trouble with McGruff.

"They're wonderful," I said.

"No argument from me," Al said, smiling.

"You'd never know what Alicia went through."

He looked toward the kitchen. We could hear the girls chattering happily to Anna.

"Last Christmas," Al said, "we were watching TV. One of the newscasts did a story on the poorest of the poor down in Nogales. The Mexican side. They were doing one of those charity tie-ins they always have at holidays. They showed these people living in tin sheds with no electricity or plumbing. One family's house really was made of cardboard. In a big rain, it's almost like no shelter at all. The kids have colds that they never get over."

"Dolores did that story for a couple of years," I said. "One year, she went back to the place she had been the Christmas before, to see how the people were doing after a year. She asked about a little boy who had been real sick. His mother said he had died in January. Pneumonia."

Al nodded, remembering. "Alicia sat there and watched this newscast and didn't say a word. You know how she usually jabbers, whether it's the news or one of her cartoons or whatever. She just sat there. When it was over, she got up and went to her room. I went back there and she was sitting on her bed. Not crying or anything, just sitting there. I asked her if she was okay, and she said, *'Sí.'* She never speaks Spanish with us, because she's so determined to learn perfect English. But it was like she was transported back to the tunnels and whatever else her life was then. And then she gave me this great big hug. I left her there, and about ten minutes later, she was back laughing and playing with Anita again."

We sat there awhile in the easy silence of friends who don't need to fill every minute with talk.

"Alicia's life was possible because we were out there, doing work we liked," Al said. "These days, I wonder if I accomplish anything. I drove all the way across town to the east side for that high school career day. Then back to headquarters for a staff meeting with the chief, then back across town to Tanque Verde for a lunch speech. I probably racked up a hundred miles today."

"City vehicle," I said. "You don't have to pay for it." When Al had his occasional moments of bureaucrat's frustration, I tried to make light of them.

"I know," he said. "It's just the time spent on stuff that doesn't seem much like police work. Days like this, I actually miss the Patrol. God and Anna forgive me. But it was good to be outside, help people, catch a bad guy once in a while."

"Dodge rattlers," I said. "Collect that measly paycheck."

"Yeah," Al said. "Nothing's perfect."

Alicia chased Anna through the room, giggling, with Arf in pursuit.

I leaned forward on the couch. Al looked at me and raised his eyebrows, as if to say, What?

"Something you said just now. You drove around all day and maybe put a hundred miles on the car."

"Well, maybe not a hundred. Eighty, though, I'll bet."

"How long would it take to put nine hundred miles on a car?"

"Depends on where you go," Al said. "Up to Phoenix and back is two hundred or more. Do that Monday through Friday and you hit a thousand miles in a week."

"But what if it's just around town?" I asked. "Go from the east side to a school downtown, go to lunch, hit the mall. Maybe down to Nogales once."

"You thinking about buying an extended warranty, or what?"

"Sandra Crain," I said. "Her car had nine hundred forty, nine hundred fifty miles on it, O'Mara said. But Mo told me that she only had it for a week when she was killed."

Al thought about it.

"Demonstrator, maybe," he said. "Isn't that what they call them? Demonstrators? Maybe customers took it on test drives, or some salesman used it before Mrs. Crain got it."

"Mo said brand-new." I thought back to my first conversation with him. "He meant it that way, I think. Brand-new, like just arrived from Japan. So it would have just a few miles. On and off the trucks and the boat. Around the dealership. I don't think Mo meant an old demo. I don't think that's what he'd give his wife."

Al nodded. "You better share this with O'Mara," he said. "If Mrs. Crain drove nine hundred miles in a week, maybe there's some things we don't know about her."

O'MARA DIDN'T LIKE IT when I called, but he dug out his case file.

"I went over those credit card receipts at the very beginning," he said. "She bought almost all her gas at the Circle K not far from her house. Pumped her own gas. If she was out of town, like down at Nogales for that kid stuff she did, she'd buy there. Last three months, there's maybe two receipts from down there. One from Scottsdale. That was a shopping trip with some girlfriends. We checked that one out."

I thought about it, jotting notes on a yellow legal pad from David Katz's office.

"When was the last gas receipt from Nogales?" I asked.

I heard him shuffle some papers and mutter as he checked the list of receipts.

"Here you go," he said. "The 76 station by the freeway, just north of town. This was two days before she was murdered. I remember this one now. It matched up with her regular visit down there. Same day of the week she always went. And the woman there at the kids center, she confirmed that Mrs. Crain was there that morning and stayed to help with lunch. The receipt says two-thirteen p.m. So she must have gassed up when she started home."

"When's the next one?" I asked.

Once again, O'Mara ruffled papers as he searched for the receipt.

"Uh-oh," he said.

"What?"

"She bought gas again the next night. Stopped at her regular place near her house. Got twelve gallons."

"What did she average in that car, you suppose?"

"Probably fifteen in town, twenty on the road, give or take," he said. "I'm not real familiar with luxury car mileage."

"Say seventeen, then," I said. I scribbled numbers on the back of a Tucson Electric Power envelope. "That would be about two hundred ten, two hundred twenty miles between leaving Nogales on Tuesday and gassing up again on Wednesday."

"It's seventy miles down there, give or take," he said. "So she came home, then made another round trip on Wednesday. And it wasn't to the kid center, because that Grijalva woman said Mrs. Crain's last visit there was on the Tuesday."

"Exactly," I said.

"I have no fucking clue how this ties in to my case, Brinker."

"Wouldn't you like to find out?"

There was silence on the line for a moment.

"Yeah," he said. "I would. It's your lucky day, Brinker. I'm still jammed up here like you can't believe. I have to be in court tomorrow, for two days maybe. You got time to take a ride down there?"

"Tomorrow morning," I said. "There's somebody I want to check up on tonight."

EITHER SANDRA CRAIN kept something from her husband, or Mo knew but kept it from me. I had no idea which. Until I could search for an answer in Nogales, my only source of information was Mo. Late that afternoon, I parked across the street from the Crain Carplex. Mo's sedan was in its usual place beside the showroom. The temperature topped one hundred again. I kept the engine running, the air on, and Linda Ronstadt's *Canciones de mi padre* CD playing.

Mo kept me waiting until six o'clock. He came out looking fresh, wearing crisp khaki pants and a pastel floral-patterned Hawaiian shirt, tucked in. He looked happier than I had seen him before, sharing the salesman's smile with everyone between the showroom door and his car.

I gave him a head start, let another car get behind him, and followed west on Broadway. He took it all the way to Campbell and headed north, past the university entrance and across Speedway. When he turned right on Elm, my heart sank. He was going to the Arizona Inn. It would be hard to lose myself in the small lobby or the dining room and bar area.

It was worth a try. I thought Mo would leave his car with a doorman, but he drove into one of the small parking lots across the street. I rolled past and found a spot by a curb painted red. There was no fire hydrant around, so I parked without guilt. In my rearview mirror, I saw Mo walk across the street. He was carrying what looked like a wine or liquor bottle in a brown paper bag. He did not go the hotel entrance. Instead, he stepped through a small gate that I knew opened to the hotel grounds. Either he was taking the back way to the bar or visiting a guest staying in one of the pink casitas. I ruled out the bar. You don't bring your own booze to a bar at the city's best hotel.

The inn is a peaceful old place, built in the 1930s by an Arizona congresswoman. Al, Anna, Dolores, and I come every winter to admire the beautifully trimmed giant Christmas tree in the library. Even in the busy tourist season, there is none of the frenetic pace of a glitzy new resort. I followed Mo through the little gate, staying about fifty feet back and keeping in the shadows, trying to look casual and rich.

As I expected, he walked past the bar and across the wide lawn, heading toward a cluster of casitas at the rear of the grounds. This is not a big deal, I told myself. Just another tedious tail with no payoff. Wealthy Tucsonans often have friends or business associates stay here. Mo was probably greeting some visiting car dealer, or a motor company executive from Detroit or Tokyo.

At a bungalow near the swimming pool, Mo rang a doorbell. The door opened almost instantly. The woman who answered threw her arms around him. I could see her hand move behind his neck and through the telegenic white hair. The sight was electrifying because the woman looked at first like Sandra Crain, with short dark hair and a bright smile. They stood there for a long moment, pressed close together, until Mo broke away, put his arm around her waist, and guided her into the room. The interior light went off almost at once.

It was not a Westfriends business meeting. Seeing Mo Crain and Catharine Richard made me wonder if anything either of them had told me was true. I walked through the shadows to their room, pushed my business card under the door, and left them there alone. *I go after what I want,* she had told me in Canada, and I wondered how far she would go.

THIRTY

ELENA GRIJALVA agreed to give me ten minutes if I made it to Nogales by ten forty-five. Noon was lunchtime at the center. As usual, she said, the place had too many kids and too little help.

I took the freeway to the end and parked at one of the tourist lots below the city streets, hard by the border fence. A couple stood behind their station wagon, Kansas plates, arguing about the six-dollar parking fee. The man wanted to park at McDonald's for free, get a quarter pounder, then walk across the border.

"There was a tow-away sign in the McDonald's lot when we were there yesterday," the woman said. "It said you can park while dining only."

"I didn't see it," the man said. "We coulda parked and eaten for six dollars."

"Plus the tow charge," the woman said. "Fifty dollars, or heaven knows what they hold you up for in Mexico."

"We're not in Mexico here," the man said.

"Well," the woman snapped, "it's almost the same thing." They plodded off sullenly to score their second day of bargains on the Sonora side.

I walked across the street to a hilly residential neighborhood that overlooked the fence. The children's center was a converted adobe house, big but not fancy. Like many on that block, it probably was built in the 1950s for a large family of modest means. The faded, cracked red tile roof looked like original equipment that would soon lose its lifelong battle with the sun. But the front yard was well tended, the walk was swept clean, and a little brown smiley face sign by the doorbell said BIENVENIDOS A TODOS.

Elena Grijalva said, "Brinker, right?" and stood aside to let me enter. She was short and compact. She shook hands assertively and moved quickly as she led me back to the kitchen. Her skin was pale, like that of many desert dwellers who guard against all sun. Her black hair had gone mostly gray. She pulled it back in a ponytail held by a red rubber band.

She busied herself at the counter, removing loaves of bread from their wrappers and setting the slices in a row.

"I'll work while we talk, if you don't mind," she said.

"Can I help?"

"Peanut butter and jelly sandwich-making is a prized skill around here," she said, handing me a knife and pushing a jar my way.

"All the basic food groups," I said.

She turned and glared. "Some of these kids were starving last week, or giving blow jobs for a tortilla. Peanut butter isn't so bad."

"I'm sorry," I said.

"Aw, hell, I'm sorry, too," she said. "Ignore me. There are days when I even bitch at the nuns who come to help. Too much grief down here. We'll never catch up."

"Who are these children?" I asked.

"Kids from the American side with bad trouble at home, mostly. Runaways. Abused kids who just try to get out of the house for a while. Can you imagine that? They'd rather live on the street than in their so-called homes. Doing God knows what to survive."

"Any from Mexico?"

"Maybe. We don't check papers here. If a kid comes in, we help. We start asking questions, they won't come back. I don't give one tiny damn which side of the fence they were born on."

She slapped some peanut butter on a slice of bread, spread it around, and pushed the slice to me. I put grape jelly on a second slice, slapped the two pieces together, and put the sandwich on a plate.

"I don't know what I can tell you about Sandra," she said.

"We've run into something that puzzles us," I told her. "We think she came down here several times in the last week or so of her life."

"She was killed on a Thursday, wasn't she?"

"Yes."

"She was here on the Tuesday. She came every other week and that was her week. I remember that."

"You mentioned on the phone that she sometimes dropped in unexpectedly. Did she do that in the days before she died, other than the regular visit?"

"Well, she did, come to think of it. It must have been the Monday. Yes, it was Monday. She brought a couple of gallons of milk. Oh, would you look in the fridge and see how much milk we have?"

I opened the big refrigerator door. "Looks like one gallon. Not quite full."

"Ten kids are coming today, that I know about," she said. "Maybe more. When we're done here, you're going over to the grocery store for me. My honorarium for helping you."

"Glad to," I said.

"I remember wondering about it, that visit on Monday. She wouldn't come all the way to Nogales from Tucson to deliver two gallons of milk. Especially if she was coming the next day, anyway. But it's like she was here, so she decided to do us a favor before she went home. Typical of Sandra to do that. Always looking for ways to help."

"But she didn't say what brought her to town?"

"No."

"And she wasn't back again, except for Tuesday?"

"Not here at the center."

"What do you mean?" I asked.

"She was in town. I saw her in front of the convenience store on Grand, using the pay phone. That would have been the Friday before she was killed. God, I never even thought about that until this minute. But it was Sandra, all right. That beautiful new car of hers was parked right there, and she was talking on the phone."

"But she didn't come here?"

"Not that day."

"I wonder why she used the pay phone," I said. "She had a cell phone."

"Maybe it didn't work down here," she said. "Some of them don't. No roaming, or whatever they call it."

"It worked. I saw her bills. The cops looked them over and so did I. She used the same cellular company I do, and mine works fine here. Even across the border for a short distance." I thought of Hector, who used cell phones from a Tucson company to avoid the Mexican phone system.

"Do you remember her acting strange in any way? Troubled or scared or anything other than normal?"

"No. She might have been a little more quiet than usual. Not enough that I noticed, though."

I heard the front door open and the laughter of children.

"Now that I think of it," Elena Grijalva said, "somebody else might know something. Excuse me a minute. I want to say hi and check on the kids. Keep up the excellent work on those sandwiches."

I built some more PB&Js. Sounds of television came from the next room. The kids had chosen a soccer match with Spanish-speaking announcers.

She came back into the kitchen with her arm over the shoulder of a little boy. I'm not good at guessing children's ages, but I put this boy at seven or eight. His jeans and T-shirt were rumpled and a little dirty, but his hands and face were clean. He kept his eyes on the floor, sneaking an occasional look at the sandwiches.

"This is Pedro," Elena Grijalva said. "Pedro, *es señor* Brinker. Mr. Brinker, do you speak Spanish?"

I smiled and said, "*Sí.*"

Switching to Spanish, then, she said, "Pedro was good friends with Mrs. Crain, weren't you, Pedro?"

The boy nodded. He smiled for a moment, remembering a kind American lady, perhaps, but his expression quickly turned sad.

"Pedro, would you like to help Mrs. Crain's family find out who did such a bad thing to her?"

"Yes," he said.

"Mr. Brinker is trying to help Mrs. Crain's husband. You know Mr. Crain from the television? The nice man who sells the cars?"

Pedro brightened and nodded again. Good move, Ms. Grijalva, I thought. She mentioned nothing about police, only *familia* and *amigos*.

"Mr. Brinker would like to ask you some questions. Would that be all right?"

The boy kept looking at the floor, but nodded yes.

I knelt down to Pedro's eye level. He seemed to like that.

"Pedro, do you remember the last few times you saw Mrs. Crain?" I asked in Spanish.

"Yes, sir," he said.

"Did she say anything or do anything unusual? Something you remember?"

"No, sir."

"Was she happy about anything? Or sad?"

"She said I should be happy that Elena is here."

"Well," I said, "that's sure true, isn't it?"

"Yes, sir. Elena is nice." Pedro looked as though he would like to hold on to Elena's leg, the way little kids do, but didn't know if he should.

He did seem to warm to the subject. "She said some children from Nogales don't have any home and they get sent far away."

"What did she mean, Pedro? Do you know?"

"No, sir," he said. "Lots of Mexican children don't have homes. You can see them out there in the barrios or in the tunnels. They look sad."

"I know," I said. I thought of Alicia. I found myself admiring little Pedro. He was here because he had troubles of his own, but he felt sadness for other children.

"Mrs. Crain said she was going to help," Pedro said. "But then she died."

"How was she going to help, Pedro?"

"I don't know," he said.

"Is that why she was coming to Nogales so often?"

"I don't know."

Elena Grijalva said in English, "I think he's given you all he has, Mr. Brinker. The grocery is two blocks down. Take your car and you could pick up about five gallons of milk."

"Fair enough," I said.

"We could use some more bread, too," she said.

I walked down the hill to claim my car from the parking lot, drove to the store, and returned with the groceries that Elena Grijalva wanted. I thanked her and headed for the door. Pedro stopped me, tugging timidly on my trouser leg.

"Hi, Pedro," I said.

"I think Mrs. Crain was waiting for someone," he said.

"Waiting?"

"Yes. Come here. I'll show you."

The boy led me through the house and outside. He walked to the edge of the backyard and said, "Look there."

I joined him. We looked down on the two cities of Nogales, the big iron fence dividing them.

"She was in her car down there," Pedro said. "She was parked right across the street from the house next to the church. She was looking at the house. I saw her when I was walking here one day. I said hello to her. She said she would see me later here. Then she watched the house some more."

"Do you know who lives there, Pedro?"

"No, sir."

"How about the priests from the church?"

"No," he said quickly, proud of his knowledge. "They live on the other side of the church. You see, that house by the corner."

I thanked him and promised to visit the center again. I drove down the hill and found the street that Pedro told me about. It was a mixed-use street, common in southwestern neighborhoods, with homes and little businesses side by side. An accountant, a hairdresser, and the inevitable immigration lawyer shared the block with the church and four or five homes. Streets like this often looked neglected, with weeds in the yards and trash on the roadway and sidewalk. This one was well kept. It wasn't a busy or prosperous-looking neighborhood, but the city and the residents were taking care of it.

Nothing stirred at the house where Pedro had seen Sandra Crain waiting. I wrote the address in my notebook.

As I drove back to Tucson, the sun pounded the freeway with white light. A mirage on the pavement kept receding, no matter how fast I drove.

"FRONTERA RESIDENTIAL Rentals Limited Partnership," O'Mara said. He had agreed to run an ownership check on the property. "They have a few apartment buildings and some rental houses down there. My friend on Nogales PD says Frontera bought 'em cheap in the nineties when the peso tanked and the economy went to hell. Nothing funny about the company. Just some local businesspeople with okay reputations making investments."

"Who's the renter?" I asked.

"Frontera says they have it as just Mrs. L. Enrique. Doesn't narrow it down much in Nogales, does it?"

"I'll find out," I said.

There was a message from Mo on my cell phone, but I didn't call him back.

THIRTY-ONE

NORTH OF NOGALES, I stopped at a sandwich shop in a mini-mall and bought a twelve-inch sub and a large 7UP to go. In town, I drove past the children's center and found a parking space on high ground with a clear view of the house that Sandra Crain had watched. My binoculars and a portable CD player rested on the seat.

Alicia, who had lived in the sewer tunnel not two hundred yards from that house, made music for me. One night at the Avilas' home, I told Al how much I liked an old Cal Tjader record, *Breeze from the East,* that he was playing. It was a mint 331/3 RPM, long out of production. Alicia heard us talking. On her own, she transferred the record to the girls' home computer, then burned a CD and proudly presented it to me on my birthday. Anna mumbled something about teaching children that copying wasn't right, but she was not going to deflate her daughter's pride of accomplishment that day.

The street below me showed little life. At noon, a priest walked from the church to his residence next door. Lunchtime, probably. I opened my sandwich and took a few bites.

A young woman parked at the curb in front of the hair-dresser's and went inside. I drank some 7UP and remembered Dolores's first requirement for reporter stakeouts: a big bladder.

The accountant and the lawyer had no walk-in traffic. Two

women, one using a cane, entered the church arm in arm. The priest came back. Cal Tjader went into "Leyte," his vibes turning vaguely Latin and mysterious. The hairdresser lady emerged with a big puffy 'do.

At twelve forty-five, the priest reappeared. I didn't recognize him at first because he wore tennis shoes, shorts, and a Phoenix Suns T-shirt. He shot hoops with three neighborhood boys who had gathered on the church playground's half-court. The boys seemed to welcome him. They shouted an admiring bilingual "Whoa, *padre!*" whenever he made a good shot.

For three hours, that was the highlight.

At three-fifteen, a new Ford sedan pulled to the curb in front of the lawyer's office. A couple got out and walked to the office door. Bored, I turned the binoculars on them. They appeared to be in their mid-thirties. Anglos. Both were tan and fit, with brown muscular calves beneath their tourist shorts. The woman wore big, showy sunglasses with red frames. The man tugged the brim on a blue Yankees cap. Their expressions were stern, but not hostile. The man took the woman's hand as they walked up to the door. Making a will, I thought, or suing their landlord.

When I panned the glasses back to the car, I saw the little gold Hertz sticker on the rear window. Probably not local, then, so they weren't making a will with a local lawyer. Then I remembered that the office belonged to an immigration lawyer.

About fifteen minutes later, a woman with garishly dyed red hair emerged from the house that Sandra Crain had been watching. She wore tight white pants and a bright flowered blouse and precariously high heels. She carried a baby. I had no idea how old the infant was, but the small woman held her little bundle easily. She turned left at the sidewalk and started up the street. Afternoon prayers for Mom, I figured, or perhaps a blessing for baby.

Instead of going to the church, though, the woman turned up the lawyer's walk. She opened the door, keeping one arm under the baby, and disappeared inside.

I began to think that the lawyer lived in the house next door to his office, and this must be Mom and baby coming to brighten Daddy's workday for a few minutes. But Daddy had clients in the office.

The couple appeared at the front door. The man held it open for his companion, who was now carrying the baby. The woman from next door held a big package of Pampers under one arm and a brown paper bag under the other. At the rental car, the woman got in back with the baby. Everyone exchanged farewells, but nobody shook hands. The man took the driver's seat and started down the road.

I didn't have a clue what this meant, if anything. But it was the only potentially interesting event on that street all day, so something told me to follow it. From my vantage point on high ground, I could see the rental car turn onto the street that fed into the northbound I-19. I should be able to catch them, I thought. Sure enough, the man was driving ten miles under the limit when I eased behind them on the freeway to Tucson.

AS I EXPECTED, the rental car took the Valencia off-ramp and headed east toward the airport. I had no intention of following them aboard some flight, but I did want to know who they were and where they were going.

At Tucson Boulevard they turned south, but didn't go all the way to the airport. The car pulled into a chain motel. The woman got out, carrying the baby, and walked quickly inside.

The man pulled out and drove on to the airport. He entered the car rental return area, left the car and took a receipt from the Hertz attendant, then walked over to the ground transportation stop. In a few minutes, he boarded a shuttle to the motel where he had left the woman and baby.

By the time I parked and followed him inside, he was halfway down one of the long hallways of motel rooms. I fell in behind, looking at the door numbers as I passed them, hoping to seem like a newly arrived guest. At a door on the left, he stopped and knocked. The door opened quickly and he entered. I walked past the door of Room 131 and kept going to the exit.

Near the swimming pool, I bought a cold soda from the vending machine and sat down to think about the couple. They were in a motel in late afternoon, suggesting an overnight stay. The motel was at the airport, which almost certainly meant they were coming or going by air. They had turned in their rental car, which probably meant they were leaving town and not doing any local sightseeing in the meantime.

I walked back inside and asked the front desk clerk for one of the all-airline timetables that the Airport Authority publishes. He produced one and I looked for the first flights of the day. They started about six o'clock every morning.

"Got a single?" I asked.

I HUNG AROUND the lobby until midnight, watching CNN and browsing in the tiny gift shop. A pizza delivery man had come in at seven and asked the clerk for Room 131. The clerk called the room, then sent the pizza guy back there. The gift shop closed at nine. At eleven, satisfied that the couple were tucked in for the night, I went to my own room and slept fitfully.

I was up at five, sipping overcooked courtesy coffee near the front desk and eyeballing the hallway to Room 131. They came out at six-fifteen. The man carried two suitcases. A Delta ticket folder jutted from his sport jacket pocket. The woman carried the baby and one of those shoulder bags that parents fill with baby things. The man checked out. They boarded the shuttle. I got on behind them. We nodded our good mornings and the couple turned their attention to the child.

At the Delta ticket counter, I hung back until they checked their luggage. Before the conveyor belt carried their second bag into the bowels of the terminal, I saw the big computer-generated baggage tag. It read LGA and beneath that, CVG. My little family was going to New York City by way of Cincinnati.

I needed a ticket to pass through security. I bought full fare to Dallas, figuring to get a refund later. The clerk gave me a long look but accepted my credit card and handed over the boarding pass.

The family took the escalator upstairs and went through security. The boarding area served two flights, one to Cincinnati and one to Dallas.

I went to the espresso stand for a decent coffee. The server had just handed it over when a man's voice behind me said, "We seem to be following each other around."

I turned and saw him smiling.

"Guess so," I said, chuckling as amiably as I could manage. "You going to Dallas, too?"

"No," he said, and I thought he sounded relieved. "We're, um, on the Cincinnati flight."

"Well, have a nice trip," I said.

"You, too." He turned to order a coffee as I walked back to the waiting area.

I had a moment of panic that the Dallas flight would be called first, but the schedule board said it would depart twenty minutes after the Cincinnati plane. I took a seat across from the woman and the baby, trying to figure out how to learn their names. O'Mara and Al would be unwilling to make an official request of the airline without something more than my undefined suspicion.

The infant gave a little cranky cry. The woman reached down to the baby bag and withdrew a yellow pacifier. Baby was not interested, so the woman put the pacifier back in the bag. When she zipped the bag, she turned it a bit, and I saw a business card stuck in a slot on the front. It bore the logo of a great national bank, an address on Third Avenue in New York City, and the legend "Marla Joffe, Regional Manager, Corporate Relations."

I just had time to memorize it before the flight was called. Passengers needing a little extra time to board, and those with small children, went first.

THIRTY-TWO

THE ARIZONA-SONORA Desert Museum opens early on summer mornings. Tourists avoid Tucson in the hot months, so wise locals, slathered in sunscreen and wearing big hats, have the place to themselves. Dolores was back from New York. She and Al and the Avila girls walked ahead, looking for the mountain lions. Anna took my arm and tugged to slow me down.

She said, "Let's see, now. Dolores is smart, pretty, kind, great with kids."

"She comes from a wonderful family," I said.

"That, too," Anna said. "And now she's probably going to get rich with her big new job. I can understand your reluctance to go away with her, Brink. A perfect guy like you shouldn't have to give up your glittering lifestyle here, just to settle for a girl like that."

Our path wound south. A vast, untouched saguaro forest spread out before us. The tall cacti could live for two hundred years, if nature and man allowed. Many of these had already reached their second century. They raised their great green arms in triumph: another year without a lightning strike or a bulldozer.

"Dolores has always wanted to go places, Brink," Anna said. "She's earned it. And she'd love to have you along for the ride."

"She hasn't exactly said that."

"She knows how we all feel about home," Anna said. "Al and I wouldn't leave. We have our kids and our relatives and our Arizona pension credits. You have her. And she's going."

"Can't force it, Anna," I said. "And this is a bad time. Maybe, just maybe, I've got the first little break in this Crain murder case. I'm looking at a grand jury appearance on the Border Patrol stuff, for sure. Sanchez, or the FBI, or somebody is trailing me around town. This is the last kind of stuff that she needs right now."

"Bad time?" she said. "How long have I known you, *chico?* First grade?"

"You and Al and me," I said. "Mrs. Robards's class."

"Right," she said. "So maybe we can keep the baloney to a minimum, you and me. You don't like anything to change. You stayed on the Border Patrol too long. You wouldn't leave your hometown for college and now you won't follow a beautiful woman to a city where anything is possible, so they say."

"What do you want me to say, Anna?"

"You don't have to say anything to me," she said. "But you owe Dolores a chance."

"I know," I said, and tried to look contrite.

"Look," Anna said, "I'm not trying to beat up on you. Al and the girls, you and Dolores, you're the most important people in the world to me. I want you to be happy. I get a little mad when I don't think you're trying hard enough."

AL AND ANNA took the girls to the cold drink stand. Dolores and I stood at the railing of the white-tailed deer exhibit. The deer strolled by us, looking hopefully for snacks in our hands, then moved on.

"Have you been subpoenaed yet?" she asked.

"No, but it's coming."

"Tell me something," she said. "You never let on much about problems on the Patrol. If there were so many abuses, how come you didn't report them? Why not get rid of the bad apples?"

"You should help me rehearse for the U.S. attorneys," I said. "They'll ask that question."

"So why didn't you do something?"

I thought for a moment. I was also stalling, hoping that Anita and Alicia would come running and drag us to the hummingbird enclosure before I could answer. No such luck.

"Did you ever do one of those news stories about old soldiers?" I said. "Thirty, forty, fifty years after the war, they get together and remember everything they ever did?"

Dolores was nodding. Every reporter has covered a few of those.

"They cry for the guys who died," I said. "This may sound silly, Dolores, but we had that same kind of brotherhood on the Border Patrol. Cops have it, too. No matter how bad things get, you stick together. Even when you know that your friends, your comrades, are doing wrong, you stick together. It's the only way to survive under fire.

"That's how we all felt on the Patrol. Under fire. We did have guys killed and wounded down there. Not just me. The only other time we made the news was when an agent got in trouble. Charged with abusing an illegal, or taking a bribe, or smuggling dope. Some of the charges were true. Some were total bullshit. But you never heard about the vindication. So we all figured, there's nobody on our side but us."

Dolores said, "Yes, but at some point, you go over the line, don't you? That attitude changes from solidarity to criminality."

"Sure," I said. "But when you're living that life, it's hard to recognize the 'some point.' Later, it's easy. And it's really easy from the outside."

"Touché," she said.

"But now I won't have a choice. When the U.S. attorney asks, I have to answer."

"What about Sanchez?"

"I don't know what he'll do. He tries to sound menacing. Maybe he is. If he knew for sure that I would put the feds on to him, he might come after me."

"Good grief, Brink," Dolores said. "How can you just walk around, knowing that? How could you live with me, knowing that, and not say something?"

"I didn't want to frighten you anymore," I said, "especially after the shooting. But I've been looking over my shoulder for a long time. If somebody like Sanchez is going to come after me, maybe it's better just to get it over with."

She was incredulous. "Get it over with?" she said. "Get yourself killed?"

"I didn't say that," I said. "There are some better possibilities."

Dolores and I had come in my car, the Avilas in theirs. We parted at the parking lot. The girls gave me energetic hugs and ordered me to visit them soon.

Anna hugged me, too, and whispered, "Don't be a jerk, now."

Alicia heard. She tugged on Anna's jeans and said, "Mom, you told us we're not supposed to call our friends jerks."

Anna knelt down and smiled at her daughter. "That's right, honey," she said, deliberately loud enough for me to hear. "But sometimes it's okay if you're an adult, and you've thought very carefully about it, and decided that they really are jerks."

"Oh," said Alicia. "Okay, I'll wait until I'm an adult." She gave me a hard right jab to the knee and ran off, laughing. The kid could punch me in the nose or kick me in the groin, and she had done both playfully; as long as I saw her healthy and loved, I was happy.

As we walked to the car, Dolores said, "What was that all about? The jerk business?"

I smiled. "Anna's making plans again," I said. "When we don't do what she wants, on her timetable, she gets anxious."

We reached the car, climbed in, and rolled down the windows. We sat for a moment while the air conditioner blew out the hot, stuffy air.

"You have to give Anna a little latitude," she said. "Brink, Anna's a wonderful sister. And you're her family, just as much as I am. You know, we supposedly go there so much because she's my sis and you're practically Al's brother. But it's more. She's Mom now, for all of us."

"Mi casa es su casa," I said. "It's her motto."

"But she sees the world as it ought to be," Dolores said. "All happiness and doing things the way Mom and Dad did them. Why shouldn't she? Her life worked out that way. She married the one man she ever loved. He's been promoted above danger. She has a great job, too. They live in the town where they grew up. They have those adorable kids. Even the thing with Alicia worked right. Every day is a fun ride on a pretty merry-go-round. Naturally she thinks we should all want the same things."

She sat back and pulled on her safety belt.

I said, "You're letting me off the hook for not going."

"If you want to thank me, but you're not sure how," she said, "take me to a cool, dark bar and buy us a pitcher of margaritas."

THIRTY-THREE

"WANT TO PLAY DETECTIVE?" I asked Dolores.

"Right here?" she said. She was sitting in bed, reading the *New York Times*. She read it every day now.

"Call up a woman in New York. Tell her that you're a Tucson reporter doing a story on couples who adopt children out here, near the border. You heard about them and you'd like to interview them."

"In other words," she said, "I'd be posing as a reporter doing a real story, even though I'm not doing the story. And I'd really be helping you, and you're sort of working with the cops. Which means that I would be a reporter working in league with the cops."

"Well," I said, "I suppose that's one way of putting it."

"This would be a fairly huge ethics problem for me, Brink."

"Television news ethics?" I said.

"That's not fair," she said. She pushed the newspaper aside and sat up straighter. "Maybe the business is a little sleazy right now, but I try to be ethical. You know that."

"I do know that," I said. "How about if you *really* cover the story?"

"Oh, right," she said. "Unring the bell for me. Anyway, what's the story? Couple adopts baby from Mexico? You don't even know that was a Mexican baby. Whatever you saw happened on this side. What am I supposed to do? Ambush some poor woman on the street, badgering her with questions about adoption?"

"You could just call her."

"Sometimes," Dolores said, "I don't think you understand anything about what I do."

She was on her feet now, bare feet, walking around the bedroom and looking over her shoulder at me.

"There's something else," she said. "More important than any of this. Those people in New York have a life. You don't know whether they stole a baby, or bought it, or just left it with that bad-hair woman while they went shopping. She could be a licensed child care person, for all you know. But you're willing to go torpedo their life, or have me do it, with a bunch of questions."

"I'm not doing this for fun, Dolores. Sandra Crain was watching that place in the days before she died."

"According to a little boy," she said.

"I just have one of those gut feelings," I said. "Don't reporters get those, too?"

"Yes," she said. "But I had an old journalism prof who said we're not in the gut feeling business. We're in the facts business. We try to get some facts before we go barging into people's private lives. They should teach that in detective school, too."

THE NEXT MORNING, I cornered Rubén Allejandro in his office at Allejandro & Katz. His coffee cup was filled to the brim, double cream and sugar. I wondered how he kept the big drooping moustache dry.

"Can you tell me about adoptions in Nogales?" I said.

He sipped the coffee and leaned back in his desk chair. "What do you want to know for?" he asked.

"The Crain case may be pointing in that direction."

"Oh, Jesus," he said. "That's all I need."

"What do you mean?"

"That kind of business works best when it's done quietly," he said. "You make contacts. Figure out who on the other side will play straight with you. Keep it about ninety-five percent legit, so if some unusual need arises, like Alicia, say, you can deal with it smoothly."

He stressed Alicia's name, and his tone said be careful with this.

"So what happened?" he asked.

I told him about little Pedro's tip, my staking out the house, and the New York couple.

"Could all be totally on the up-and-up," Allejandro said.

"But Mrs. Crain must have thought something about it was strange."

"You base this on a seven-year-old witness and a couple who struck you as slightly furtive?"

"Help me out here, Rubén," I said.

He looked out the office window. A dove was perched on the big saguaro cactus in the office courtyard.

"This lawyer's office," he said, "it didn't happen to be close to the fence, down the street from an old Catholic church?"

"That's the one," I said.

He nodded. I think he smiled slightly, but it's hard to tell with the moustache.

"Ah," he said. "That would be Oswaldo White. Dual national, I think, and definitely licensed to practice law in both Arizona and Mexico. He does immigration work and an unusually large number of adoptions, I hear. The word is, he's crooked as an arthritic rattlesnake. And meaner sometimes."

The name seemed familiar to me, but I couldn't think why.

"Funny thing about a guy like that," Allejandro said. "Licensed on both sides, he could get rich just filling out NAFTA forms and checking boilerplate contracts for fruit and vegetable brokers and truckers."

"What does he do?"

"Look," Allejandro said. "That fence casts a long shadow. It covers a lot of sins, but it makes good things possible, too. I don't have to tell you that, and I don't have to tell Al and Anna that. *Entiendes?*"

"I get it," I said.

He was on his feet, standing in front of a big portrait of himself in western garb, packing twin revolvers, towering over a background map of Arizona and Sonora. One of his clients had made it for him after Allejandro successfully appealed the man's murder conviction. He turned to the picture and pointed at the top of his painted boot, right about where the border ran.

"Along here," he said, "there are ways of doing things. You act discreetly. You're selective. Even down there, if you go to the well too often, you get hurt. Too many people can talk. You have a government built entirely on corruption. It's like in *Traffic*. You see that movie? A guy says law enforcement in Mexico is an entrepreneurial job. The whole government is like that. That means your contracts are binding only until somebody pays more to break them than you paid to keep them. But there's more honor among some thieves than others. So you stick with them, don't tempt them often, make it worth their while when you do. You find out all you can about them, so if they try to hurt you, you can hurt back. And they know it."

Allejandro and I had come to trust each other, I thought. But even friends talking about deals in Mexico speak as though a tape recorder is running somewhere.

"So," he said, "that's the right way to do it. The Nordstrom or Neiman-Marcus approach, you might say. On the other hand, Oswaldo White takes the Wal-Mart approach. He deals in high volume. Lower cost. That's fine in U.S. retail, but in quiet border business, it means higher risk. People in Oswaldo's niche get careless. They're not as discriminating about their customers or their contacts."

I leaned across the edge of his desk. "Rubén, I need to find out exactly what this guy does," I said.

"I'm just telling you what I know," Allejandro said. "You want particulars, you'll have to watch him yourself."

I nodded and rose to leave.

"Here's what I'd look for," he said as I reached his door. "There's probably a woman working on this. Somebody who can pose as a mother and bring babies across. The babies could be bought or kidnapped or plucked out of orphanages. Once in a while, they might even get them legally. A woman would be good for talking the real mothers into signing over custody."

"This fits," I said.

He gave me a "where have you been?" smile.

"Here's another thing, I'll bet," he said. "Guys like Oswaldo White have agents out in the great American heartland. They're hooking up with couples who want a baby now. Couples who don't want to wait two years and don't want black babies or crippled babies and don't want to fly to Albania."

"But they'll take a Mexican child," I said.

"Sure. You've spent enough time down there. You know

that Mexicans don't all look alike. We're not all Cisco and Pancho. You know the Mexican saying? *'Tan blanca y tan linda.'* How fair and how pretty. Mexicans have lots of kids like that. Give an Oswaldo White or some other creep two hours in Nogales or Tijuana or Juarez and he'll come back with a baby who'll look right at home in an Iowa farmhouse."

"Thanks, Rubén," I said. "This gives me something to go on."

"Brinker," he said, "watch your ass. Some low-rent lawyer isn't going to shoot you at his own front door. But Oswaldo will have help. Plenty of people down there feed their families by helping guys like him. They keep the system well oiled, you know? They don't let the pipeline get clogged. They'll slit your throat and call it economic development."

THIRTY-FOUR

I PHONED MY HOUSE. Dolores answered a little out of breath, as if she had just rushed in.

"Shopping," she said. "I need a few things for when I go back to New York. Where are you?"

"At the office. I'll be home in a couple of hours."

"Well, I had an interesting phone conversation today," she said. "One of the station's lawyers in New York. I met her last week when I was back there. She does contracts and intellectual property now, but she used to work in the Manhattan District Attorney's Office, so she knows criminal law."

"Dolores," I said, "I hope you didn't tell her that you've been living with a guy who might be jammed up with a federal grand jury."

"Relax," she said, laughing. "I said I was covering some Border Patrol agents, and this source of mine might be involved in an investigation. She says her old bosses were always glad to have witnesses from the inside, you know? Getting them to roll for us, she called it. They would agree to testify, and sometimes she got them complete immunity."

"You think I need immunity?"

"Brink," she said, "I don't know what you need."

"I'm sorry," I said.

Dolores said, "I asked a smart lawyer what she thought. If you want, I'll tell you what she told me."

"Okay."

"Okay. She said that if a person saw things, and that person wasn't part of any really bad stuff, he'd have a good chance to come out clean. The thing is, this hypothetical person needs to get to the prosecutors and volunteer. That way, right from the start, they'll think of the person as their guy."

"First to get aboard."

"Exactly."

"Dolores," I said, "some ugly stories will come out of these grand jury hearings. I don't think I have anything serious to hide, but some people will have reason to make me look bad."

"I know," she said. "Look, Brink, I've been with you for a couple of years, and Al and Anna have been together forever. We know that some bad things happened on the border, but we know you guys, too. We're not going to lose faith in you."

"That means more than I can tell you, Dolores."

"Feel free to try," she said with a little laugh. "By the way, your pal David Katz is pretty famous. Even my new lawyer friend has heard of him."

"He's the best."

"Talk to him, then."

"You're right," I said. "I know he'll help me. He'll probably let me work off the bill. I'll talk to him, Dolores."

"Okay," she said. "Oh, there's a message on your machine from Mo Crain. He said call him right away. He sounds mad."

"Screw him," I said.

"He's a big sponsor," she said, laughing, "but I won't go that far."

The television was playing softly in the background. Insistent music, squealing tires, and gunfire.

"What are you watching?" I asked.

"Kojak rerun on cable," she said. "Hokey, but I liked old Telly Savalas."

"I did, too."

"Who loves ya, baby?" Dolores said.

I stared through the window at the gathering darkness, avoiding my reflection in the glass, wondering.

THIRTY-FIVE

THE FREEWAY INTO NOGALES makes a broad, sweeping curve to the east and runs parallel to the border fence. From the road, you can see *ambos Nogales,* both cities of Nogales. On the Mexican side, a few houses perch on hills rising from the downtown shopping district. The cardboard shacks and the places built on muddy lots from tin and duct tape are out of sight, off the tourist track. As I slowed for the exit, I spotted red and blue lights flashing on the American side, below me and to the south.

Nogales police cars jammed the block. Two uniformed officers stood on the sidewalk outside Oswaldo White's office. The usual crowd of gawkers had formed. Police were keeping them several houses away.

I recognized a Nogales cop, Carlos Rivera, who was on the Border Patrol with me. He had married a Nogales woman, I remembered, and quit when the Patrol wanted to transfer him to El Paso. Rivera was standing with a group of civilians in the street by the church.

"Sergeant's stripes," I said as we shook hands.

"Yeah, it's a good job," he said. "I'll never get rich, but it's nice to be settled down. Jennifer's happy with her family so close."

"You have kids?"

"A boy. And one due next week. We hope it's a girl this time. What brings you down here, Brinker?"

I hadn't known Rivera well on the Patrol. I hadn't seen him for at least three years.

"Going across to get some pain pills," I said, patting my hip. "I couldn't resist checking out the commotion."

Rivera would remember the shooting at Lovers Crossing. He would know that many Arizonans drove down to Mexico for cheap prescription medicines at the border *farmacias*.

I pointed to White's office and said, "What's up here?"

"Local lawyer got clipped," Rivera said. "We had an anonymous call from a pay phone in town. Said check out the office and you'll find a guy shot. Officers came out, found the front door open. Sure enough, there he was in the waiting room."

"He walked in on a burglary, maybe?"

"Doesn't look that way. He had some money in his desk and in his wallet. Nothing was messed up in there."

"Any witnesses?"

"Nothing yet. We're not too hopeful. This is a pretty quiet block. Lot of those houses are empty. Hardly anybody comes to church, especially so early on a weekday. We're figuring time of death was about six this morning."

"What about the house next door?" I asked.

"We knocked, but nobody's around. They could be working. We found the phone for that address, but nobody answers."

A citizen approached Rivera and asked him what was happening. He said a few words to the man and guided him back to the sidewalk, away from the scene.

"Hey, Brinker," he said. "You remember this lawyer? Oswaldo White?"

The name had seemed familiar when Rubén Allejandro mentioned it, but I still couldn't match it with a face or an event.

Rivera said, "Yeah, this guy was a snitch for us on the Patrol. He got caught driving a couple of illegals up to Tucson. He claimed they were just hitchhikers that he picked up, but the illegals said he helped them. They paid somebody in Mexico five hundred bucks, and they were told to contact White when they got here. Can you believe that? The guy's a lawyer and he's driving illegals around. Anyway, one of the agents leaned on him and he decided to save his sorry ass and his law license. He started giving information about illegals coming over. He even knew about some drug mules."

"I remember something about that now," I said. "But I don't think I ever met the guy or got in on those busts."

"Well, you probably wouldn't," Rivera said. "The agent who tripped him up and kept him on the string was Henry Sanchez. Your old pal Sanchez."

Too much coincidence, I thought. "You talk to Sanchez?"

"I didn't," Rivera said. "But detectives already pulled him off patrol and talked to him. He started at eight o'clock on the I-19 checkpoint. Before that, he was in the sack with his girlfriend at her apartment up on Western Avenue. She confirms it."

"Handy alibi," I said.

"Well, Sanchez isn't my favorite guy, either," Rivera said. "But that doesn't mean that he's responsible for any crime where his name comes up. He's got no reason to kill White. Sanchez said he didn't have much contact with the guy for the last year or so. White must have gone straight, at least by lawyer standards."

"Who's the girlfriend?" I asked.

"You're pretty interested in this one, Brinker. You know anything I should know?"

"Somebody who dealt with Sanchez gets shot," I said, "I kind of identify with him."

Rivera smiled slightly and looked across the street. A plain-clothes cop, wearing blue jeans and a white T-shirt with an embroidered police badge, had come out of the office and stopped to talk with the uniforms at the sidewalk. Rivera walked over to him. They spoke for a moment. The plain-clothesman looked across the street at me, then back to Rivera. He said a few words. Rivera walked back to me.

"Lucy Delgado," he said. "That big complex on Western, second floor, Apartment Number 207. Licensed practical nurse, presently unemployed. If you go over there, don't make trouble, Brinker. I vouched for you, but the detectives aren't thrilled about giving out a name like that."

"I owe you," I said. "And I hope it's a girl next week."

IT WAS ALMOST NOON when I got to Western Avenue. I tried to remember if I had ever met Lucy Delgado and if she would recognize me. I didn't think so, because Sanchez and I didn't drink in the same places or go to the same parties when I was on the Patrol. She might not even have been his girlfriend then.

I parked at the northwest end of the apartment complex parking lot. My spot afforded a clear view of the outside stairs leading to the second floor. A white Grand Cherokee, like the one Sanchez drove, was parked at the foot of the stairs. He probably took a Border Patrol vehicle on duty, leaving the Cherokee with Lucy.

Just the thought of another stakeout made me groggy, but this time, I got lucky. Not five minutes after I began watching, the door to Apartment 207 opened. A woman emerged and locked the door. She teetered on absurdly high heels, walking along the outer balcony toward the stairs. She had a small build, wore too-tight pants, and had badly dyed red hair, trending toward purple.

Lucy Delgado got into the Cherokee and started up Western. I followed her to the Safeway, waited for a half hour while she shopped, then followed her back to the apartment building. She made three trips to carry her sacks of groceries up to the second floor.

I checked my watch. What I wanted to do was get into the house where I had seen Lucy before, the *casita* between Oswaldo White's law office and the church. But there would be no getting near it today or even late tonight. The police would probably return tomorrow. Sanchez and Lucy would know this. They wouldn't go near the place until the scene had cooled. That gave me time to search for an answer elsewhere.

At the I-19 checkpoint, orange cones diverted traffic off the freeway into a single line. A Border Patrol agent looked into oncoming vehicles and waved most of them through. Drivers with brown faces got a harder look than the Anglos. A van with Sonora plates was ordered to the secondary inspection line. As I drew close, I realized that the agent was Sanchez. He saw my white face and waved me on, but then he recognized me as I passed him. He kept watching me, and I thought he laughed as I drove through the station and sped onto the freeway.

THIRTY-SIX

DAVID KATZ'S TRAVEL AGENT tried to explain that going across the country from Tucson at night was almost impossible. It took two plane changes, unless I wanted to go backward to Los Angeles and catch a coast-to-coast red-eye. I opted for that, figuring that I would have several uninterrupted hours to sleep between L.A. and New York. The overnight plane to JFK was about half full. With a row to myself, I slept until the landing gear clunked down. We pulled into the gate at seven-fifteen a.m.

My only carry-on baggage was the travel kit that I always keep handy in my car. In the terminal men's room, I brushed my teeth and shaved with an electric razor. Then I walked out to the gray New York morning. The cabbie was a thin man in a turban who seemed to slouch down at the wheel to avoid touching the roof liner of the cab. I gave him the address and he pulled away without a word.

Somewhere between the airport exit and the Long Island Expressway, I thought this might be a fool's errand. Marla Joffe could be on vacation or home with her new baby. She might refuse to see me. I was betting that she would be in town, at work, and afraid to dismiss me without at least learning why I followed her across the country.

We slogged along in morning rush-hour traffic. People in Tucson thought traffic was bad. I laughed silently. If all these cars were going to the island of Manhattan, where would they park?

The city's great buildings materialized through the morning scud. I looked for something familiar. The World Trade Center towers were gone, of course, but even the Empire State Building was nowhere to be seen in the haze. I realized that it was surrounded by other skyscrapers. We dove into a tunnel. In a few minutes, we emerged to the noise and bustle of the city streets. For the second time in a few days, I felt a million miles away from Tucson. Here, the densely compacted buildings blocked the sun. It was the polar opposite of Arizona. The people walked fast and the cars moved slowly.

At the bank building on Third Avenue, the lobby guard directed me to Corporate Relations on the twenty-fourth floor. The elevator door opened to a reception desk and a smiling young black woman who seemed genuinely glad to see me. I gave her my card.

"I wonder if Marla is in today," I said, hoping to sound like a friend. "Marla Joffe."

"Oh, I'm sorry, sir," the receptionist said, and my heart sank. I felt like an idiot for not calling, but I hadn't dared to risk spooking her.

"She's not here this week," the woman said. "She and Bill have a new baby at home, so she's taking leave. Ms. Rabinowitz is filling in. Would you like me to ring her office?"

"No, thank you," I said. "I'm an old friend, in town briefly. I'll call her."

"Very good, sir. Have a pleasant day."

New Yorkers are nicer than advertised, I thought. I took the elevator back to the lobby and went to a phone bank on the north wall. The Manhattan directory showed a W & M Joffe at a low number in the East Eighties. William and Marla, I hoped. I caught a cab and we pressed uptown through the heavy traffic.

The address was just east of Fifth Avenue. The apartment building had a nondescript brick façade, but a dark green awning over the entrance looked new. The doorway glass and brasswork gleamed. A doorman dressed like a general in the Duchy of Grand Fenwick army said good morning as I approached. I asked for Mrs. Joffe.

"Oh, you just missed her, sir," he said, and once again I felt the fool for this trip. Then the doorman pointed casually toward Fifth Avenue and said, "She took that new baby to the park. Should be home soon, I'd think, if you'd like to make yourself comfortable in the lobby."

"That's all right," I said. "I'll run some errands and catch her later." I started toward Central Park. At Fifth Avenue, I saw a woman pushing a stroller past the Metropolitan Museum of Art. She looked like the woman I had seen in Tucson and Nogales, so I started after her. I recognized the reservoir beyond the museum and guessed that she would walk around there. She was a couple of blocks ahead of me, but moving slowly. I closed the gap quickly. Almost everyone who passed her looked down at the stroller. When she turned into the reservoir track entrance, she quickly found a bench and began adjusting the baby's blanket.

I moved to sit at the opposite end of the bench. "May I?" I said.

She nodded absently and fussed over the child. I gazed across the reservoir to the west. Two towers of old buildings, stars of many a New York City movie, rose from the west side. I knew them well, but had no idea what they were. For a few moments, I was caught up in the place. The familiar yet foreign skyline, the feeling of a country lake even though I sat no more than fifty feet from Fifth Avenue.

She was watching me.

"Tucson," she said quietly. "You were at the hotel and the airport."

I smiled and tried to look nonthreatening as I met her gaze. Her large green eyes registered fear and confusion.

"Yes."

"What do you want?"

"I'm not here to make trouble for you, Ms. Joffe. This must be scary for you, but please believe me. I mean no harm to you. Or your child."

At the last words, an acknowledgment of her maternity, she seemed to ease back on the bench. Not relaxing, but hoping that my presence might not be some cruel twist, after all. She reached down and grasped the baby's hand in her fingertips.

She asked again, "What do you want?"

"I need to tell you some things that happened since you left Nogales," I said. "Then I'm going to ask you to trust me with information about what you did there."

"My husband should be here," she said.

I took my cell phone from my jacket pocket and held it out to her. "Call him if you like," I said. "I think you have to dial one and the area code here, because it's a Tucson phone."

She started to reach for the phone, but pulled back. "You're not going to ruin this?" she said, looking down to the baby.

"I am not," I said.

"Then tell me what you have to say."

"Yesterday," I said, "Oswaldo White, the attorney in Nogales, was murdered."

She was shocked, but she was cool. She had already decided to take command of this crisis, whatever it was.

"I'm sorry to hear that," she said. "I met him only twice."

"Tell me how the adoption worked," I said.

"We used an agency here. The owner said she could arrange expedited adoptions because there are so many orphans out there. She handled the arrangements with Mr. White. We flew out to Arizona and met Billy." She looked lovingly at the child. "It was love at first sight for Bill and me. We paid Mr. White the fee and signed the papers. We went back the next day to pick up our baby. Then we came home."

She sat a bit straighter and spoke with a new confidence. "Now, listen. This was entirely legal. We did nothing wrong. We have the adoption papers from Mr. White, all approved by the state. So I'm terribly sorry the man was killed, but I really don't see what this has to do with us."

"Did White say your baby was from Arizona or from Mexico?"

"Mexico," she said. "There were no secrets. I'm telling you, it's completely legal. We have his Mexican birth certificate, and the release of custody from his birth mother, and approval from INS."

Another woman pushed a stroller past us, headed for Fifth Avenue. Marla Joffe looked after her, perhaps envying any mother who could enjoy an uncomplicated walk in the park with her child.

"It must have been terrible for that girl," she said. "I've tried to imagine her. Some poor kid with no money and no father there for her baby. She must have felt so alone and helpless and failed."

"You didn't actually meet her, did you?"

"Oh, no. The lawyer was the intermediary. He handled everything. But I remember her name from the documents. It was Lucille Enrique. I made a little promise to myself that I would never forget it. Lucille Enrique. I'd always keep a special little place of gratitude to her in my heart."

The name seemed so obvious that I resisted belief. The little house in Nogales was rented to Mrs. Enrique. I had seen Lucy Delgado there. She must have felt clever, signing the phony adoption papers with her own first name, probably Lucille, and with Sanchez's. Enrique is Spanish for Henry.

"How long did the process take, Ms. Joffe?"

"It was about two weeks from the time we went to the agency here until we got Billy."

"Didn't that strike you as pretty fast?"

"Not really. We were just in Arizona for a little while, but you could see the poverty in that town, Nogales. I'm not surprised that people have to give up their babies."

"Who was the New York adoption agent?" I asked.

She watched the runners on the track that circled the reservoir. Finally she said, "No. I've told you enough."

"Ms. Joffe," I said, "it may not seem like it now, but I'm your best chance to keep your family safe from disruption. A man was murdered yesterday. Everything has changed now. Police will be looking at his files. If he did anything even slightly illegal, they'll check it. If anything about your adoption wasn't completely straightforward, you'll have cops back here, and child welfare people, and immigration. You'll have to answer their questions."

"Why are you my best chance?"

I thought of Al and me in the tunnel one Christmas Eve.

"Because I know exactly how you feel," I said. "I'll do everything I can to keep you out of it."

THE AGENCY ADDRESS turned out to be a modest Midtown apartment building off Second Avenue. There was no doorman. I buzzed 518, the number Marla Joffe had given me. No answer. I tried 517. A man hollered into the intercom as if he didn't really believe it could amplify his voice.

"Hello!"

"Yes, sir," I said. "I'm looking for Annette Smythe in 518. I had an appointment, but I got no answer when I buzzed."

"You probably won't," the crackly voice blared. "She went out yesterday with her suitcase. In a damn big hurry, too. I asked her where she was going, but she just said it was a business trip. It wasn't a pleasure trip, that's for damn sure. She looked white as a damn sheet."

Outside the building, a couple of guys sat in a dark blue Ford sedan. I was tired and hungry and couldn't think of any reason why feds would follow me to New York. I forgot about them and flagged a cab.

THIRTY-SEVEN

I DROVE THROUGH A FOG of bone-deep fatigue, headed again for Nogales. Coach seat naps on the westbound flights were no match for the strain of two cross-country journeys in twenty-four hours. Oncoming headlights penetrated my vision like lasers, but I kept rolling south through the night.

The crime scene tape still circled Oswaldo White's office. The street was deserted. I didn't care about the office. Police and evidence techs would have picked it clean the day before. I parked across the street, took a big flashlight from the trunk of my car, and ran into the shadows between White's office and the small house next door.

Some of the nearby buildings were dark, but I could see the glow of television through a few windows. The ten o'clock news would soon be sending people to sleep with dreams of carjackings and missing children.

There were no side or back doors on the house where Lucy Delgado had kept the baby. I would have to go in through the front door or a window. I remembered an old story about firefighters who broke down doors to enter buildings, only to find that the doors were unlocked. Maybe windows are, too, I thought. I heard no air conditioner running, so perhaps the windows were left slightly open for ventilation.

The second window I checked was open six inches. I pushed it the rest of the way, pulled myself up, and slid inside. The room was apparently a back bedroom, but even in the dark I could see that it had no furniture. Stacks of disposable diaper packages were placed against one wall.

The next door led to a bathroom. I shone my flashlight in the medicine cabinet and saw only a bottle of children's aspirin. There was a bar of soap on the sink and another in a dish beside the bathtub. A blue cotton towel hung on a rack. Inside the linen closet I found more towels and washcloths and another stack of diapers.

The second bedroom did have a bed, queen-sized, and a battered old bureau. The drawers were empty. The room emitted a musty smell that I had not noticed in the others. I checked the sheets and pillowcases, but they were fairly fresh. I aimed the flashlight under the bed. The floor there seemed slightly cracked and bulging.

I pulled back the bed. What looked like a trapdoor had been cut in the floor. It had no handle. I used my pocketknife to pry it slightly up and get a grip with my fingers. The door pulled free fairly easily. I looked down into a hole that dropped about five feet, then curved and headed toward the back of the house.

The back of the house was near the border fence. Mexico was less than fifty feet away.

I tried to get my bearings. Where would a tunnel from this house come out? What was on the other side of the fence? I pictured a map of *Ambos Nogales,* tracing the streets and buildings.

Then I realized that I needed no map. The musty smell had grown stronger since I opened the trapdoor. Sounds carried through the opening. Shouts, cries, the hollow rushing of a large open space. I recognized exactly where it was coming from.

The little tunnel from this house led to the huge one under

Grand Avenue. The tunnel that carried sewage and rainwater from Sonora to Arizona. The tunnel where homeless children slept and young thugs preyed on the weak. It was the same sewer tunnel where Al and I had found Alicia.

I heard a car drive along the street in front of the house. The tires crunched across the gritty asphalt very slowly, even for a residential neighborhood. The police, making a routine pass at the crime scene, I thought. I snapped off the flashlight and wondered if its glow could have been seen from a passing car. Through the bedroom window, I had a clear line of sight to the front room. But a thin white drape covered the window that faced the street, so I felt safe.

The tunnel seemed barely big enough for my six-foot frame. Going into it by myself was out of the question. I lay on the floor and leaned over the hole, extending my arm and shining the flashlight beam as close to the bottom as possible. The horizontal segment, running toward Mexico, looked no larger than the vertical portion leading up to the house. Drug dealers often used ropes and pulleys to shuttle contraband through tunnels under the border. But I saw no ropes below and no sign of any in the room.

I replaced the trapdoor and pushed the bed back over it. I returned to the window where I had entered, crawled through, and lowered myself to the ground. As I stood, something smashed into the window frame, spraying slivers of wood against my face. In the next instant, I heard the gunshot and hit the ground. Another slug tore into the side of the house, then a third churned up the dirt beside me. I rolled into the deepest shadows and crawled to the back of the house.

Headlights swung into the street. Not the shooter, because this car was coming from the block below. It glided by and turned into the church parking lot. The priest I had seen a few days ago got out and walked toward the church residence. Put a little something in the plate next time you're here, Brinker, I thought. The priest's car must have spooked the shooter. I looked to the hills above me and saw taillights racing toward the freeway on-ramp.

No house lights came on. No residents came to their doors. It was night along the border. Three gunshots were just background noise.

ADRENALINE OVERCAME FATIGUE as I drove back to Tucson. I let myself into the house and checked all the door locks and the alarm. Dolores was asleep in our bedroom, breathing deeply and surely dreaming something sweet and safe. I watched her for a while, thinking of Anna's lecture at the Desert Museum. Then I went to the kitchen, got a Dos Equis from the refrigerator, and thought about what just happened.

A tunnel ran from Mexico to the little house next to Oswaldo White's office.

Lucy Delgado brought a baby from that house to White and the Joffes.

Sanchez and Lucy Delgado were a team.

Sandra Crain had seen something at White's office and the house next door.

The phone rang. I grabbed it before it could wake Dolores.

"You enjoy your visit to Nogales tonight?" Henry Sanchez said.

"Yeah," I said. "An interesting trip."

"Dangerous place," Sanchez said. "You need to be careful down there."

I didn't respond.

"See the news?" he asked.

"No."

"The U.S. attorney plans to start subpoenaing people next week."

"About time," I said.

"What are you going to do?"

"If they subpoena me," I said, "I'll go."

"I know that, asshole. And I know they will subpoena you. What are you going to say?"

"I'll answer the questions."

I heard him breathing into his phone.

"So you're gonna roll over," he said.

"I'll answer the questions."

Another long pause.

"Word is, Marky Marques is rolling over, too. He got anything on you?"

"Ask him," I said. "Maybe you could put a tail on him. Take a shot at him."

"Hey, no offense, man. Just seeing what you're up to. I'm interested in your welfare."

"Sure," I said.

"How about your friend Hector Ortiz? You gonna tell the feds about him? How he's still doing favors for you?"

"What are you going to do, Sanchez?"

"What I'm going to do is give you some valuable advice, Brinker. Two words of advice, in fact. Number one, remember that the feds might like to hear some stories about you and your friends on the Patrol. Number two, back off the Oswaldo White thing right now. You know what can happen to people who snoop around in that. Somebody might take a shot at you."

"Sanchez," I said, "I've had enough of you for tonight."

"Yeah, get some sleep. Maybe tickle that nice little news honey first. How is that, anyway?"

"How's Lucy?" I said.

It was a stupid mistake, blurted out in frustration and fatigue. I knew it even as I spoke the words. Sanchez said nothing. There was a moment of silence, then the line went dead.

THIRTY-EIGHT

DOLORES STORMED around the kitchen, opening cupboard doors and slamming them shut.

"I'm a big girl," she said. "I have a gun here. I can use it. You know that."

She stopped the door-slamming and turned to face me, raising her fist. Her eyes were damp and red.

"I will not run for cover. I'm going to New York soon enough, but I will not be forced out of my home just because some crooked old crony of yours makes vague threats. You will not order me out of here."

"Dolores, I'm not ordering. I'm begging. Look, Sanchez has come after me already. Now he's using you to do it. If he hurt you, I couldn't live with myself."

"He won't live at all," she shouted. "I'll kill the son of a bitch before I'll run."

She stopped moving around and stood facing me defiantly. I walked to her and put my hands gently on her arms.

"Dolores, please. Go stay with Al and Anna. I don't think Sanchez knows where they live. If he did, even he wouldn't come into a cop's house. The girls are away at camp in Flagstaff. Al and Anna and I, we all think this would be smart."

"Al has a job," she said. "He's not going to stand in the driveway with a shotgun, protecting us. Give Anna a gun and she'd probably shoot the dog by mistake. I'm not putting her or anyone else in harm's way."

When Dolores felt passionately about something and cranked up her professional talking skills, resistance quickly became futile.

"And how long does this go on, Brink? Until I go to New York? Does Sanchez follow me there? What if the investigation runs for a year, maybe more? I'll be like Salman Rushdie or some poor frightened jerk in the Witness Protection Program, locked up in a safe house. To hell with that."

"It won't be long. I'll testify as soon as I can. David Katz can probably get me in there fast. Once that happens, Sanchez has no leverage on me. I'll have done whatever harm I can do."

"No," she said. "I'll be careful. I'll practice shooting. But I will not run."

She had her hands on her hips. She breathed hard and rapidly, the way she did when she was angry but didn't want to cry.

"This is terrible," I said. "Our worst quarrel."

"And you lose," she said.

I waited for her to crack. It didn't happen. I walked to the wall phone by the refrigerator.

"I'll call Al," I said. "He can get you some time on the police shooting range."

THE NEXT MORNING, Hector called the Allejandro & Katz office. He gave me a number, told me to call it from a pay phone in ten minutes, and hung up. His number was in Tucson; I wondered if he had sneaked into the States or if he used some elaborate phone cut-out system to make calls from Mexico.

I walked fast through El Presidio Park, breaking a sweat in the ninety-degree morning heat. The municipal building exterior walkways were deserted, as city and county workers took refuge in their air-conditioned offices. A security guard checked me through the courthouse metal detectors and pointed out the new bank of telephones. Hector answered on the first ring.

"Got a follow-up to that rumor I told you about when you were down here," he said. "Some people I know arrange international travel. You understand?"

"Yes," I said.

"They've been asked to stand by for somebody who wants to come this way without the usual formalities. Whoever it is must want to get lost down here. They've already taken care of some Sonora police and some *federales*."

"How come you're telling me, Hector?"

"Spirit of friendship. Last time we met, we talked about somebody moving money down here. Now somebody's gonna visit. Maybe they're connected, you know?"

"When's this happening?" I asked.

"I don't know yet. But 'stand by' means soon, right? Don't know who, when, or what."

"Whoever it is won't go through one of the Ports of Entry?"

"Could be done, but it sounds tricky. If he's carrying weapons, he'd better come off-road."

"Lovers Crossing?"

"Maybe," Hector said.

"Can't get a vehicle through there," I said.

"Anybody could take a four-wheel to the American side of the canyon, hike through, have somebody waiting on the Mexican side with another four-wheel to get back to the road."

"That could work."

"Yeah," Hector said. "He'll have to bring some good

money. Bank accounts or not, it takes cash. You know how it works here. He might need something for your guys, too, if he plans to go through Lovers Crossing."

"It could happen," I said.

"I'm shocked, shocked," Hector said, laughing. "Meter's running, my friend. I'll talk to you later if I hear anything."

THIRTY-NINE

DAVID KATZ disliked walking in hot weather. He had a young associate drive us a few blocks to the United States Attorney's Office on Church Street. Katz wore a suit, tailored in London, that transformed him from chubby nebbish to gentleman of substance. Although he often opposed the lawyers in this building, they greeted him deferentially. Everyone smiled and held doors for us. They watched with something like awe as Katz led us to the boss.

"Why are they so nice to you?" I asked. "You're the enemy."

"Only in their present positions," he said. "Hardly anyone stays here forever. These jobs are stepping-stones to a lucrative private practice. Like mine."

He smiled proudly as he said it. I thought, What a thing, to be at the top of your game and admired even by your adversaries.

Wilhelmina Schmidt worked in civil servant heaven, her own commodious corner office on the ninth floor. The carpet was new and the windows were clean. From her desk chair, beneath a great carved wooden emblem of the Justice Department, she could keep her eyes on the prize: the federal courthouse on Broadway. She was a lock for the next judgeship over there, as long as she didn't botch anything publicly between now and nomination day.

Schmidt was a tall woman with the broad shoulders of a

competitive swimmer. Her sun-streaked, short blond hair suggested that she still worked at it. She walked across her office in long, purposeful strides, greeting Katz with a hearty handshake and me with a polite one.

There is an ethical rule among lawyers that attorneys generally may not speak directly to a person known to be represented by counsel, unless counsel gives permission. So for a few moments, I sat silently, while the lawyers discussed me as if I were a lab specimen.

"To get to the heart of the matter, Willie," Katz said, "my client is prepared to give you everything he's got."

"And from us, he wants what?" Wilhelmina Schmidt asked.

"Everything you've got," Katz said.

I expected a poker face and an afternoon of hard bargaining. But Wilhelmina Schmidt laughed, a robust, friendly laugh, and said, "Okay, probably." She had a deep voice and a hint of accent that reminded me of Marlene Dietrich.

"We are talking about full immunity?" Katz asked.

"That's what we're talking," Schmidt said. "Let's be absolutely clear, David. It isn't offered yet. I need to ask your client what he can provide. After that, my deputy will have more specific questions."

Katz smiled and said, "Please proceed."

Schmidt looked at me, taking my measure. She was on a take-no-prisoners march to the United States District Court judge's chambers, and I did not want to be her enemy.

"Mr. Brinker, you know that we're investigating allegations of abuse by Border Patrol agents. What kind of abuses did you personally observe?"

Katz interrupted.

"Willie," he said, "I don't mean to be nitpicky at this early stage, especially with your being so helpful. But that question might require my client to admit a crime, if in fact he actually saw abuses and did not report them. I'd really like to deal with the immunity issue before we go into that area."

"I'll play the game, David," Schmidt said. "But I won't show you mine until you show me yours."

"Of course," Katz said. "How would it be if I simply specify areas of possible inquiry in which my client is prepared to be helpful?"

"That would be nice," she said.

"Mr. Brinker can be helpful in the matter of undocumented aliens being allowed entry into the United States in exchange for certain gifts and sexual favors provided by the aliens to Border Patrol agents. He can help in certain instances of unnecessarily violent treatment of persons by agents along the border area. He can provide information regarding the transportation of narcotics into the United States and along the corridor between Nogales and Phoenix. Is this good, so far?"

"Promising," Schmidt said.

"Willie, are you aware of an agent named Henry Sanchez?"

"Oh, yeah," she said, not bothering to suppress a smile.

"My client will provide information on Mr. Sanchez's misuse of Border Patrol authority, including an event in which Mr. Sanchez may have colluded in the serious wounding of a fellow agent."

Wilhelmina Schmidt looked in my direction, but did not meet my gaze. It took me a moment to realize that she was staring at my shoulder.

"I'm wondering," she said, "if Mr. Brinker has any useful information about Sanchez's actions in the border area recently."

Katz looked at me. I nodded to him.

"He would," Katz said. "There is potentially helpful information regarding the possibly illegal movement of certain persons across the border in the city of Nogales. My client has limited information on this matter. Some things came to his attention only recently. But perhaps what he knows would supplement your own investigations."

For a moment, Schmidt actually seemed to be grinning. "Yes," she said. "That might be helpful."

"Good," Katz said.

"How is that?" she asked, gesturing toward my shoulder.

"Better, thanks," I said. "We had a cold, wet day in March. It hurt then."

She gave us that pleasant, open laugh. "You should probably avoid Alcatraz, then," she said.

"That's closed," I said, hoping to sound genial.

"Well," Schmidt said, "prisons are like they said in those old corn chip commercials. We'll make more."

"Which brings us back to immunity," Katz said.

She stood up. "I'll turn you over to Jon Kravitz, my lead guy on this," she said. "It's Jon's call, but I'll tell him that I think this is the way to go. He'll get to you later today, David."

She shook hands with Katz and nodded to me. At the office door, I turned back to face her.

"Most of the Border Patrol," I said, "they're good people."

"I know," she said. "The good ones have nothing to fear from us." It was exactly what I told Sanchez. He didn't believe me. I feared that I couldn't believe Willie Schmidt.

"They're overworked and underpaid. They still show up every day and do the best they can. They're honest."

She nodded, but looked impatient.

David Katz said, "Let's be on our way, Brink."

"If you're not careful," I told her, "when you indict some, you'll take them all down. They'll all be smeared by front-page news about a few of them. When their kids go to school, the other kids will laugh at them. Even their wives and husbands will be suspicious."

"I understand," she said.

"Sure," I said. "Well, when you have your press conference, mention the good guys, too."

Schmidt walked around her desk and came to stand only a foot away from me. She spoke softly, but her eyes never left mine. Her voice was tempered steel.

"I understand your loyalty to former colleagues," she said. "I understand your cynicism about political appointees like me. I know some prosecutors would burn the Constitution on the courthouse steps to get a conviction or thirty seconds on the news. Not me."

She took a breath and said, "I was born in East Berlin. People now barely remember that the city was divided. Cut right in two, one free and one slave. I was born long before the Wall came down. I know something about borders. When I was seven years old, I ran away from home. I wandered around for an hour and found myself by the Wall. I was scared to death and feeling stupid. A guard gave me some apple juice in exchange for my telling him my name and where I lived. When his work ended, he took me home on the bus."

She paused and pursed her lips. "We called those men Vopos. That's short for Volkspolitzei, a perfectly good word that means a sort of people's police. But because the Vopos were among those who guarded the Wall, keeping us from freedom, they were hated."

One of her desk telephones chimed softly, but she ignored it.

"Here, we have *immigración,* perfectly good word, but some Mexicans, some Mexican-Americans, for that matter, talk about *la migra* with the same fear and hatred that we felt when we talked about the Vopos. Sometimes that's justified. Sometimes not.

"You didn't invent the wheel with your experience here, Mr. Brinker. I know that some border policemen are nice people who help little lost girls like me get home safely. Some are criminals. I truly hope that the Border Patrol will be helped, not damaged, by our investigation. That's over the long term. But in the short term, Mr. Brinker, the crooks are going down. Make no mistake about that. When you testify under oath to the federal grand jury, be very sure where your loyalties lie."

David Katz said, "I'll see that he does, Willie. Thank you." He took my arm and steered me toward the door.

"Mr. Brinker," Schmidt called out.

I stopped, my hand on the doorknob.

"You probably know something about little Mexican girls getting home safely, don't you?"

Don't flinch, I told myself. Don't avert your eyes.

"We've had a lot of people looking at the Border Patrol for a long time," Schmidt said.

David Katz, law partner of Rubén Allejandro, who arranged in some mysterious way for the Avilas' adoption of Alicia, was smart enough to stay out of this one.

Schmidt said, "It could have been the stork, I suppose."

"I'm sorry," I said. "I can't help you with that."

She let me wait awhile, then said, "No. Well, maybe I won't need your help with that. There are developments in that investigation that take it way beyond any need for you or the Avilas to be involved."

I nodded.

Schmidt said, "So there's good faith here, yes? We're on the same team?"

"Yes," I said.

Katz thanked her again and pushed me out the door. Several people shared our elevator, so we rode in silence to the ground floor.

On the street, I said, "Did I blow it?"

"Close," he said, "but she needs you. She has all victims so far. You're what she doesn't have yet, an agent with personal, eyewitness evidence to give."

"No indictment?"

"As I see it, not if you play the game. She wants you to think she would charge you. Maybe she would, just to keep the heat on. But she couldn't do much except make your life miserable. Much better for her if you just testify."

"What about Al?"

Katz shrugged. "She made it pretty clear that she's not interested. She just wanted you to know that she knows. It's her job to know things like that and to use them. When we get back to the office, I'll speak to Rubén."

"Thanks, David."

"Now," Katz said, "keep out of Sanchez's gun sights for a few more days. Immunity is a wonderful thing, but Willie can't immunize you against a bullet in the back."

FORTY

DAVID KATZ reached me by cell phone as I drove to the Avilas' house.

"You didn't tell me that you went to New York," he said.

I lost my concentration on the traffic and almost rear-ended a minivan at a red light. I pulled into a drugstore parking lot on Grant, put down the windows, and shut off the engine.

"How did you find out I was back there?"

"Jon Kravitz, Willie Schmidt's assistant, called me to talk about your coming grand jury testimony. Apparently, they're looking into Sanchez for more than drugs and civil rights violations. They're now interested in illegal border trade in babies."

I remembered what Gabriela Corona had told me. They have something special on Sanchez, she said, but they hesitated to move because it somehow involved me.

"They followed me to New York?"

"They already had agents watching the adoption agency. Not very well, apparently, since the woman who ran it gave them the slip. In any event, the watchers had been alerted that you might show up. Mr. Kravitz says his people knew that you had tumbled to something in Nogales, and they knew that you went to New York to follow up on it."

Two men, looking like FBI agents, sitting outside the adoption agent's apartment in Midtown Manhattan.

"Why is Kravitz telling you this stuff, David?"

"I imagine it's so that I'll let you know that he knows. He expects that this will encourage you to give him everything you have on the baby business. It's all new to me, but I bluffed him along with cooperative noises."

"I'm sorry I didn't keep you posted on this," I said. "I just hadn't put the baby thing together. I still don't know what's happening there. I stumbled into it because of the Crain murder case and I'm trying to piece the two together."

"The government has some ideas, apparently," Katz said. "This actually is excellent news. In my judgment, it means that Willie and Kravitz are ready to go after Sanchez with both barrels, and that he wants you completely aboard with him. I did not dissuade him from that approach."

The traffic sped by on Grant. Several teenagers walked past my car, headed for the fast-food place across the parking lot.

"David," I said, "I got a tip from a reporter friend days ago. This was before I stumbled into the baby business, whatever it is. So I don't understand why the feds would have held back on Sanchez because something involved me."

"It's Alicia," he said. "Willie Schmidt all but told us as much today."

The air in my car felt heavier. I got out and leaned against the door.

Katz said, "They know that if you're a witness, Sanchez's attorneys can chew up your credibility because you and Al brought a Mexican child into this country with, shall we say, expedited legal procedures. They would ask, what's the difference? They were afraid that you would be compromised. And I must say, I think these prosecutors are decent people. I believe they want to avoid hurting the Avila family."

"So what's different now?" I asked.

"Oswaldo White is what's different," Katz said. "That's murder, so the stakes are much higher now. It also increases the chance that Sanchez will realize how deep he's in. He may run. He better do it quickly, because Willie is sending her troops after him tonight."

"They'll want my testimony fast, then."

"Tomorrow morning," Katz said. "Ten o'clock. Be in my office at eight. We'll talk, then walk over to meet Kravitz at nine. I'll work out the immunity and try to set some parameters on the questioning."

"All right."

"You didn't hear this from me," he said, "but you should talk to Al and Anna."

I said, "I'm on my way."

"Good."

"David, this is what got Mrs. Crain killed. Mo didn't have anything to do with it. He may be a phony who screwed around, but he didn't kill his wife."

"In my experience," Katz said, "that's usually how it works."

ANNA GAVE ME COFFEE. Al poured a little glass of Kahlúa to go with it. The girls were gone to camp in the cool mountains, but Arf still lay on guard outside their bedroom door.

My cell phone rang.

I heard loud American rock music and a cacophony of laughter and Spanish chatter. The voice on the line, incongruously serious, said, "Amigo."

"Something new, Hector?"

"Tonight's the night, my friend," he said. He sounded as

though he had downed a few of those *conmemorativos,* but he could handle them. "Little while ago, somebody called some guys, and they know some guys that I know. It's set up to help three Americans come over at Lovers Crossing, just like we thought. They drive to the American side of the canyon. Then they ditch their car, walk through the canyon, and the guys I heard about pick 'em up on the other end."

"Hector, I can't go down there tonight."

"Maybe you better."

"What do you mean?"

"The guys I know say it's one man, bringing two women. One woman might be trouble. These guys were promised they could have all the fun they want with a girl on TV, then just finish her off."

The dread rose in my chest, the same fear I felt before the bullets hit me at Lovers Crossing.

"Hector, when are they going over?"

"Next couple of hours. Maybe right now. Sorry, man. I tried all your numbers. Your home phone and cell phones were busy just now."

I had been talking to Katz. Dolores, at home, could have been talking to anyone, or even left the phone off the hook while she rested.

"Thanks, Hector."

I hung up and turned to Al.

"Can you go over to my house? If Dolores is there, great. Stick with her. If not, it means someone grabbed her. Sanchez or somebody he's hired. They'll use her as a hostage to go into Mexico. And they won't leave a witness."

I gestured to Al with my cell phone. "Call me when you get to my place."

Without a word, Al reached for his keys. Anna stood there, looking horrified. I remember how Dolores said Anna was happy because Al had been promoted out of danger. And how I promised her to give up the case if it turned ugly.

I ran for my car.

FORTY-ONE

HURTLING THROUGH THE NIGHT, ninety miles an hour down I-19. I hoped that I was wrong about Dolores. She had a gun. She could use it. But I had expected Sanchez or some goon knocking at the door. She would never open up for him. Even if she did, he would be the one in danger.

What if Lucy Delgado knocked? Dolores had no reason to know her, let alone suspect her of anything. A friendly female face, the mention of familiar names that Sanchez could give to Lucy…

South of Tucson, speeding past the Mission San Xavier del Bac, its white façade and unfinished tower lit up through the night.

When the phone rang, I prayed that it would be Dolores.

Al said, "She's not here."

"They're going over," I said. "Hector told me it's Lovers Crossing."

"I remember the spot," Al said. "I'll be twenty minutes behind you."

"Call the Patrol," I said. "Maybe we can get somebody out there to intercept them."

"Okay," he said, barely finishing the word before breaking off to dial the Border Patrol station. I could still remember the emergency agents-only number. I hoped he could, too, and that it still worked.

Racing past the retirement community of Green Valley. Exit 63, but the markers on this highway were in kilometers, not miles. That meant I was thirty-seven or thirty-eight miles from the border. Twenty-five minutes, if I could keep up the speed. Please, let all the state troopers be having coffee or car trouble, I prayed.

Green Valley's lights flickering in the rearview mirror now. The old folks were bedding down after a hard day of golf and canasta. Darkness looming ahead on the lightly traveled interstate.

It seemed like an hour, but only eight or ten minutes had passed when Al called back.

"No help," he said. "Half the Nogales agents were deployed to Douglas today because of illegals roaming residential areas, robbing houses. And another big crew rolled on a multiple fatal find in the desert around Sasabe. I talked to a guy I know, Brink, and he said forget it."

"We're on our own, then," I said. "Step on it, Al."

I cursed myself for not stressing the danger that Sanchez would come for Dolores. She still would have made up her own mind, but had I done enough? Would he let her go after they made it into Mexico? Could he? He killed Sandra Crain, or had her killed, to protect himself. There was an Arizona death penalty for murder. In Mexico, there was only prison, and perhaps not even that, if he could work the flexible Mexican justice system.

Tubac. Another old presidio, remade as an artists' village and tourist shopping mecca. Dolores loved it. She dragged me down there a couple of times a year to prowl the galleries and buy presents for the Avila girls.

Just a little more than twenty miles from the border.

Bright headlights bearing down from behind, coming fast. Cops, I thought. I had only a few seconds to decide. Stop or try to outrun them. I slowed down to the legal limit, seventy-five there, hoping that the police might only now be aware of me.

My gun was on the seat beside me. I shoved it into the glove compartment and hoped the cops would not dream up a reason to search the vehicle.

The headlights drew closer.

Nothing red or blue yet. No siren.

I was already in the right-hand lane. It was crazy to get into a chase with state police. Even if I pulled away, they could just radio ahead to officers in Nogales. I prepared to ease over and stop. Get the ticket and hope the cops were quick about it.

But that would be the end of it. Sanchez would be free to drag Dolores through Lovers Crossing into Mexico.

The lights were almost on me now.

Suddenly the pursuing car swung into the left lane and raced past. It was a Corvette. It must have been going 110, 120. My own headlights caught the two people in the car as it lurched back into the right lane. Both young men, wearing baseball caps backward, laughing as their car roared by. One held a Coors can.

Good luck, locos, I thought. Even better luck to anyone in your path.

The Corvette slid around the next bend in the interstate. A beer can flew out the passenger-side window and bounced along the roadside.

Once again, I was alone on the dark road to Nogales. I took the gun out of the glove compartment and bore down harder on the gas.

I left the freeway and bumped over the hilly, potholed streets east of town. Even on a dark night, I could see the serpentine shadow of the steel fence, marking the international border. A few miles from Nogales, the solid barrier gave way to chain link, much of it broken down and cut through.

The paved road swung north. The county's dirt road went south. I followed it into the darkness. Amazingly, I remembered the terrain from nights on patrol at Lovers Crossing. The little canyon would be only another four miles or so. On the moonlit horizon, I could already see the distant speck that agents were taught to recognize as a vehicle, running dark. No lights. I gunned my own car over the mesa, toward the border.

Sanchez had pulled the white Cherokee four-wheeler right up to the edge of the canyon. The SUV's engine still hissed and the hood felt hot to the touch as I ran past it to the edge of Lovers Crossing.

I stopped and held my breath, listening.

Sound came from down in the canyon. It was distant, barely within my hearing. Running. Feet pounding the brush and rocks. I had almost caught them. Sanchez must have driven slowly to be safe from cops, just as I had slowed when I thought the state police were on my tail.

I jumped down into the canyon, dropping six or seven feet to the narrow, worn footpath. For immigrants and smugglers coming the other way, this spot was the last hard pull up to the mesa and into the United States. For me, it was a quick plunge. Pain from my hip jarred my whole body as I hit the ground. Up ahead, I thought I heard someone fall. A female voice said something unintelligible, but angry. A woman's voice cried out. Dolores or Lucy?

The path snaked left, then right in one S-turn after another.

It had been worn down by thousands, maybe millions of footsteps, but it was still narrow, cutting closely between clumps of brush and sparse cacti. They must be moving single file. Sanchez probably was pushing Dolores at gunpoint from behind. That would slow them down.

How long was this damn canyon? I realized that I had never stepped into it before. The actual border was somewhere in the canyon, but I didn't know exactly where. On patrol, we agents simply waited on the American side for the illegal entrants to pull themselves up that last ridge and start walking across the mesa, where we took them easily.

Then I was moving upward again, the path leading me to another mesa on the Mexican side. It was rockier here. I stumbled twice on the loose stones along the path. Keep moving fast, I told myself, but carefully. Don't twist an ankle here or it's over.

I heard engines running. A man tried to shout over them. When I hauled myself up the last few steps and stood on the flat ground, they were only forty feet away.

Two old Jeeps stood idling, with two Mexican men standing by each. All four carried weapons. Automatic pistols, if I was seeing clearly in the darkness. Sanchez and Dolores stood next to the Jeeps. Lucy Delgado sat in the back of one Jeep, trembling. Sanchez wore a backpack. He held a small handgun to Dolores's side.

I took a step in their direction, but Sanchez shouted, "No closer, asshole!"

Gun in hand, I took another step.

"I'll kill her right now if you come closer," Sanchez said. "You got any doubt about that?"

That stopped me. He kept his eyes on me and lifted the gun close to Dolores's head.

"How stupid do you feel now, *pendejo?*" Sanchez said. "All that time, you playing Mr. Superior on the Patrol. And now here we are. I'm off to happy days at the beach, and you and your girlfriend are dead meat, if I want you to be."

I took a step forward. Sanchez moved the gun barrel up to Dolores's ear.

"Ah-ah!" he shouted. "This could go either way, Brinker."

"What do you want?"

"I'm thinking. I didn't expect you down here tonight. I thought maybe I'd get this far, leave the TV sweetie with my pals here, and take off. But I could pop you both. You'd be freebies because there's no death penalty down here. Even if Mexico extradites me for the Crain woman, Arizona'd have to promise no death penalty."

I watched Dolores, trying to think of some way to get her free. But she was fifty feet away, in the grip of a man with little to lose.

"If they do send you back," I said, "it might go harder if you've killed us."

"Maybe," Sanchez said.

Keep him talking. Dolores's old interview trick seem cruelly out of place, but it was all I could think of.

"Why did you have to kill Mrs. Crain?" I shouted.

"She might have figured it out," Sanchez said. "We had a perfect setup until she showed up. She actually staked out the house, the stupid broad. Never did know how she found us."

"A little boy at the children's center told her," I said. "You were tripped up by a seven-year-old boy, Sanchez."

He laughed. "Who's tripped up here? I'm going to retire at the beach and you're half dead. You're the one over your head, just like she was. She saw Lucy with three baby seats in the Cherokee one time, and she saw Lucy with me. Then we spotted her and decided she had to go."

"Sanchez, she might have told her husband already. He would have called the police. You would have committed a murder for nothing."

"He was next," Sanchez said. "But as soon as he got back from Canada, the cops put guards on him. Then enough time went by with nobody sniffing around me. I figured that she never told him. I was right, wasn't I?"

He was enjoying this, I realized. It was a chance to tell someone how brilliant he was.

"Should have done it anyway," he said. "If I had put him out of business a few weeks earlier, he wouldn't have hired you. And I missed my best shot at you when you were coming out of the house the other night."

"What was the tunnel for?"

"We brought some of the babies through there. Pushed them along in a little wagon. That was our way out, too, until you screwed that up. A straight line into Mexico. But I couldn't take a chance even going onto that street with cops cruising by White's office. Then you went into the house and found the tunnel. So here we are at Lovers Crossing. You and me again."

One of the gunmen said, *"Bastante. Vámonos."* Enough. Let's go. He got behind the wheel of the front Jeep. His partner came around to the passenger side. Sanchez turned and pushed Dolores up and into the Jeep, then lowered his gun.

"Think I'll give sweetie pie here a quick tour of northern Mexico," he said.

He took a rifle that was resting against the Jeep's fender and raised it to aim at me. He was laughing.

"Just like shooting a stray dog, Brinker," he said, "only this will be even more fun."

The man on the passenger side lifted his weapon and said, "*Señor.*"

As Sanchez turned toward him, the man shot him in the face. The rounds came so quickly that they sounded like one. Sanchez fell heavily to the ground. He landed on his back, with no face to stare up at the Sonoran sky. The gunman put two more shots into his body.

Lucy Delgado was screaming. Dolores stayed silent. I watched her and realized that she was doing what she did at news scenes, glancing around quickly, trying to anticipate. This time, she was looking for the way out. Her gaze settled on the man who shot Sanchez. She had to be wondering if the killer of her enemy was her friend.

She was way ahead of me on that. I was waiting for the next shot to take me down. It never came. The shooter held up his free hand, palm outward. The gesture said, Be cool, stay put, you'll stay alive. There was no reason to believe him, though. I had just seen him commit murder. His comrades covered me with their guns.

The gunman watched me for a moment, making sure that I got his message, then walked to Sanchez's body. He pulled the bloody backpack off and slung it over his own shoulder. Without a word, he grabbed Dolores and jerked her out of the Jeep.

Right then, I came within an instant of making a fatal mistake.

I wanted to raise my gun and shoot the man. It was a western movie moment of craziness, with three other men there to return my fire, yet it seemed like the only way to save Dolores. But fear paralyzed me for a moment, and in that second, the gunman pushed Dolores toward me. She fell. She looked back, then started crawling away from the killer.

Something is wrong here, I thought. Dolores and I should both be dead.

The gunman stepped into the Jeep and both vehicles raced away.

Dolores crawled and I ran across the short distance between us. She pulled herself up onto her knees and I dropped to mine. We knelt there, our arms around each other. She seemed to be sobbing a prayer of thanks, something in Spanish that I could not follow. Dolores never looked back at the body, but I could not take my eyes away from the fallen shape that was Sanchez.

I helped Dolores to her feet. We started back through Lovers Crossing. She didn't cry again or say a word. When I offered my hand to help her climb a steep stretch of the path, she grabbed a clump of brush and pulled herself up.

FORTY-TWO

WHEN HE HEARD THE SHOTS, Al had called the Border Patrol on his car phone. "Shots fired" got their attention. By the time Dolores and I came out of the canyon, a couple of Patrol vehicles were there, and an ambulance. The agents seemed bewildered when we crawled up onto the mesa, a big Anglo guy and a Hispanic woman. A female paramedic from Nogales took Dolores aside. Al and I stood with an INS big shot named Sandy Rosen, recently brought in from Washington to clean up the Arizona sector.

"What a night," he said. "I'm watching baseball, Cubbies doing pretty well, nice evening. Then the phone rings. Between the Sasabe bodies and this shit, it hasn't stopped ringing."

Just visible in the ambulance's faint interior light, the paramedic appeared to be speaking softly. She leaned forward, her arms reaching out to hold Dolores's hands. It was a comforting gesture, probably practiced on victims of domestic violence and auto accidents and street crime. I caught Al's eye and inclined my head toward the ambulance.

"Sandy," Al said, "is there anything we can do to help Dolores through this without a lot of hassle?"

"Dolores is the woman they grabbed?"

"Yes."

"She the one on TV?"

"Right."

"Great," Rosen said. "Just what we need."

"I don't think she'll be reporting this one," I told him.

"Well, I'm for that," Rosen said. He watched the ambulance for a moment, then turned to stare across the dark canyon. He drew a slow, deep breath of night air, held it, and let it out wearily.

"What did you say when you radioed?" he asked Al.

"Shots fired. Agent needs help, Lovers Crossing."

Rosen said, "What agent would that be, Al?"

"Brinker's a former agent," Al said. "Close enough."

"You didn't say anything about a kidnap, or fugitives going into Mexico?"

"No," Al said.

Rosen rocked on his heels and looked down at the pointed tips of his new Tony Lamas. He ground his teeth and pursed his lips. After a moment, he faced Al.

"This is going to be a lousy month," he said. "Prosecutors screwed this up. They had Sanchez cold. Couple of his friends, too. I'm surprised Willie Schmidt even bothered with the grand jury. Bribery, drug smuggling, two murders that I know about. He'd been in bed with some truly nasty people on both sides of the border. They should have reeled him in days ago."

Al nodded.

"The Patrol is going to look like shit," Rosen said. "Can't be helped. It'll be worth it to have a bad apple like Sanchez out of here."

"I agree completely," Al said.

Rosen turned to me. "Well, my boy," he said, "you're about to get the deal of the century. I talked with the United States attorney on the way over here, and she's feeling like a Grade A government idiot for waiting too long on Sanchez. I don't think they're going to be asking you at the grand jury about this little incident. Christ, a Border Patrol agent dragging Americans across the border into Mexico. It's goddam surreal. The grand jury doesn't need that. Too confusing. It might obscure the important issues. Wouldn't you say that's right, Brinker?"

"Absolutely," I said.

"Which means," Rosen said, "that Willie Schmidt is going to owe you a big one."

He turned to Al. "If Brinker gets a free pass, that'll be a good thing for anybody who has a history with him. Wouldn't you say, Lieutenant?"

Al just nodded.

Rosen played the gruff anti-bureaucrat, but his craftiness was already the talk of the sector. His hard look seemed to bore through my skull, like an MRI scanning for hidden dangers.

He said, "Wait here," and walked to the ambulance. He leaned in the open side door and spoke to the female paramedic. She called to her male partner, who was standing with two Border Patrol agents a few yards away. Rosen and the paramedics talked for less than a minute, then he shook their hands and came back to Al and me.

"They'll write up their run as a false alarm," Rosen said. "Al, you identify yourself to them and tell them the lady will go with you. If this hits the fan, they'll say they blew it off at a Tucson police lieutenant's request. That's their out. I never talked to them. The Patrol agents, I'll handle. There'll be some field promotions here tonight. That work for you?"

"It's good for everyone," Al said. "I won't forget it, Sandy."

"Forget it, please," Rosen said. "Brinker, get the hell out of here. We never met."

"Okay," I said. "What about Sanchez?"

Rosen pursed his lips again, twisted his boot heel in the dirt, and stared through the night over Lovers Crossing. It was too far and too dark to see one broken body.

"Who shot him, do you think?"

"Coyotes, most likely," I said. "Bandits pretending to be guides. The poor Mexican *pollos,* trying to come into the States, get double-crossed like that all the time. Now it happens to him, going the other way. He just picked the wrong crooks to help him."

"Coyotes?" Rosen asked. He said "kai-oaties," with an eastern accent that I couldn't quite place.

Al and Dolores were coming toward us. She held his arm and walked as if she were in a trance. They stopped and Dolores looked at me. Her eyes didn't quite focus.

"I brought this down on you," I said.

"Yes, you did," she said. Simple words, just agreeing with me, but she might as well have driven a knife into my heart.

"I'm so sorry, Dolores." I reached to take her hands. She leaned back, out of reach, moving close to Al for support.

Al said, "She should stay with Anna and me tonight." I nodded. He put his arm around her shoulders and led her toward his car. Rosen and I watched them go. Dolores slumped against Al and they trudged away. They looked like a pair of captured illegals, resignedly bearing their broken dreams back into Mexico.

Rosen said, "Whatever you get out of this, you'd probably have been better off with her."

"Don't I know it," I said.

"So," Rosen said. "Coyotes, right?"

"That's what it looked like. Sanchez had a backpack. You

need dollars to lose yourself in Mexico. I'll bet he brought some serious cash. The guy who shot him took the pack off his body."

"Coyotes with automatic weapons? Coyotes who knew what was in the backpack? Pretty sophisticated for coyotes."

He was faster than he let on.

I stuck with the story.

"Wouldn't be the first time. They probably knew that big money was coming across. They wouldn't try to take it without firepower."

"Yeah, I suppose," Rosen said. "Where's Miss Delgado?"

"You know about her?"

"I've become a much better informed citizen in the last couple of hours," he said. "A fellow can learn a lot, talking to a nervous U.S. attorney who needs a favor."

"Lucy was in the Jeep when they drove away," I said. "I guess it all depends on what they decide to do with her. They might help her. They might let her out on the side of the road. They might kill her."

Al's car drove past. Dolores, in the front passenger seat, huddled against the door. Despite the warm night, she had put on a jacket that Al kept in the trunk.

"So," I said, "what are you going to do about the body?"

He shook his head. "Hell," he said, "leave it for the *federales* or the buzzards. Let the Tijuana cartel come claim him, for all I care."

He turned away from the border and walked toward his car. "That place over there, it might as well be Mars," he said. "Other planets are out of my jurisdiction. Go home, Brinker."

I drove toward Tucson on I-19. Halfway to Green Valley, the Spanish-language billboards began advertising Tucson merchants to moneyed Mexicans who enter freely with their visitor permits and Visa cards. There was a sign for the mall where Sandra Crain died. BIENVENIDOS AMIGOS MEXICANOS, it read.

My cell phone rang. When I answered, a familiar voice with just a trace of Spanish accent said, "Now we'll call it even. Okay, my friend?"

I couldn't manage an answer. The man on the phone laughed and said, "I never did like that guy."

The line went dead before I could answer.

Minutes later, a famous face smiled down at me from the biggest billboard on the highway. The warm and friendly car dealer, as seen on TV. His slogan stood out in brightly lit letters: THERE'S NO PAIN WITH MO CRAIN!

I lowered the window. Fresh air lashed my face. Even hitting me at seventy-five miles an hour, it felt softer, less dry than it had a few hours earlier on the mesa above Lovers Crossing. In the rearview mirror, I saw the distant glow of lightning somewhere deep in Sonora. The great monsoon clouds were forming.

I sped toward home through the lonely desert night.

FORTY-THREE

AFTER TWO DAYS with Anna, Dolores came to the house. The monsoon season had begun in earnest. A severe thunderstorm warning was out for most of southern Arizona. The sky was oddly dark for midday. Dolores stood on the patio, her arms folded across her chest, not getting close to me. She looked out to the saguaros and up toward the Catalinas.

"I will miss this," she said. "The sunset, especially."

"It'll be here for you," I said.

She turned to face me. "Will you?" she asked.

"I'm not going anywhere," I said.

"Did you know that Sanchez had hired that lawyer, Logan, to buy property for him in Mexico?" she said. "He had no idea that Logan was Mo's attorney. He just heard that Logan did legal work on international real estate. Talk about weird connections."

"Hector told me about Logan," I said. "It was good information, but I didn't know what to make of it. I don't think Logan had any idea that Sanchez killed Mrs. Crain. He certainly didn't say anything to me."

We had an orange tree in the backyard. Dolores walked close to the tree, testing the air for a scent of blossoms that were long gone.

"The job in New York is a couple of years, at least," she said. "That's a long time for both of us, you know." She spoke softly, in a kind voice, as if trying to spare me some pain of my own making.

I felt the heat in my face and struggled to keep my eyes on hers.

"That woman in Canada," she said. I had told Al and Anna about Catharine. Maybe one of them told Dolores. "Did you sleep with her?"

"No," I said.

"Did you want to?"

"Not enough to act on it when the moment came."

"You thought I had abandoned you," she said.

I didn't answer.

"I hadn't," she said.

She was walking around the edge of the backyard, past the four cedar trees that some unknown Mormon pioneer had planted to alert others to a friendly resting place for travelers. She ran her fingers over the little clay statue of Saint Francis that she bought in Tubac.

"I'm going to New York this afternoon," she said. "I start next week. I have everything I need for now. When I get an apartment, Anna will come over and pack the rest of my things. Is that okay?"

"Sure," I said.

Staring off to the south, she said, "I'll miss the Fourth of July here. Think the fireworks will set 'A' Mountain on fire again?"

"They always do," I said.

"Well, I'll cover some big East Coast celebration. The Statue of Liberty, maybe. I'll work every day until I drop, and keep my mind on the job. Maybe I'll sweat out some of this poison. Maybe some time will help."

Then, moving closer to me, but still out of reach, she said,

"Should I even care about this? You won't come, but I want to think that you care."

"More than you know," I said. "More than I knew."

"That's what Anna tells me," she said.

I smiled. "My guardian angel. She never gives up on me."

"She comes from a determined family," Dolores said. She held my arms to my sides and leaned in to kiss my lips too briefly, then quickly stood back.

She said, "I've been prepping for work, reading famous New York quotes. You ever hear of Fiorello LaGuardia?"

"Just the airport. Wasn't he the guy who read the comics on the radio?"

"I'll have to look that up," she said. "But once, when he appointed some jerk to a city job and it came back to haunt him, he said, 'When I make a mistake, it's a beaut.'" She held my gaze when she said it.

"All the real New Yorkers probably know that stuff already," I said.

Dolores smiled. "Not necessarily. I never went to the Desert Museum until I was seventeen. Sometimes good things are right before your eyes, and you miss them."

"Fiorello was right," I said. "I know how he felt."

"Hold that thought," Dolores said. "*Nos vemos,* Brink."

I started to speak, but she held up her hand, then turned and walked through the house. I heard her steps on the tile floor in the entry and the front door closing and her car starting and the crunch of tires moving over the gravel driveway. The first drops of a light rain dampened the ground, stirring up the smells of wet sand and desert brush.

But she had said "*Nos vemos.*" I felt the beginning of a hopeful smile even as she left our house.

SIX WEEKS AFTER the carnage at Lovers Crossing, an envelope with a Mexican stamp arrived in the mail.

The handwritten letter was in Spanish. It came from La Casita de Ayuda, the Little House of Help, a charity home for abandoned kids in Nogales, Sonora. The director thanked me for my $50,000 donation, which she assured me would be treated as Anonymous, in accordance with the wish expressed by the nice young Mexican gentleman who delivered the cash for me. What a glorious surprise, she wrote, to see all those American bills. They would be so valuable in these sad days of the beleaguered peso. She pledged to employ this gift for the Lord's work to help His children. God, she believed, would bless me doubly for my generosity and modesty.

I'm for that. The whole thing was news to me, but I will take any blessings I can get.

Wilhelmina Schmidt announced that the current federal grand jury term would be extended by ninety days. Her statement gave no reason, but David Katz described the courthouse buzz as "authoritative." Schmidt wanted just a few more facts to slam-dunk a couple of Sanchez's brother turncoats. I would still be subpoenaed, but not charged with anything.

Tucson police declared the Sandra Crain murder case closed and cleared. They blamed Sanchez and said he was "later found dead" in Mexico. The newspapers took the official statements at face value and did no more reporting on the story, to the puzzlement of some staff members.

Mo Crain, in one of the American automobile industry's largest deals, bought seventeen dealerships in Phoenix. Building on his hometown success formula, Crain's expanded operation would soon have the largest advertising budget of any business in Arizona. He has not remarried, but one Catharine

Richard of Vancouver, British Columbia, is often seen with him lately.

Mo never thanked me. Maybe it was the business card under that hotel room door. He never asked for a bill, but he sent me an inflated check for my work. I thought about sending it back. It felt like dirty money, since he and Catharine had snookered me with their charm and self-righteous lies. In the end, though, I endorsed it over to Elena Grijalva's children's center in Nogales. She called me with tearful gratitude and invited me to come make peanut butter and jelly sandwiches anytime. The kids sent me a homemade thank-you card, with Pedro's signature in big red Crayola. I had the card framed and hung it on the wall of my office. It's the first thing I see when I walk in the door.

I hope that Pedro meets Alicia and Anita someday. The girls get prettier every time I see them, but I'm prejudiced. They're developing their mother's quick intelligence and their father's equanimity, and they love me.

Anna gave me Dolores's new address and telephone number, saying, "Give her a while." I did, then I phoned. Dolores has not called back.

Friends ask about her. I tell them that she wanted to be safe, so she moved to New York. Everyone laughs politely and lets it go at that.

Dolores calls Anna almost every day, I hear. But what they say remains *entre hermanas,* between sisters.